THE SWORDSMAN OF MARS

Otis Adelbert Kline

THE SWORDSMAN OF MARS

OTIS ADELBERT KLINE

COVER BY

ROBERT A. GRAEF

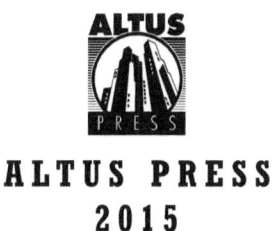

ALTUS PRESS
2015

EDITED AND DESIGNED BY
Matthew Moring

PUBLISHING HISTORY
"The Swordsman of Mars" originally appeared in the January 7, 14, 21, and 28, and February 4 and 11, 1933 issues of *Argosy* magazine (Vol. 235 No. 3–Vol. 236 No. 2). Copyright © 1933 by The Frank A. Munsey Company. Copyright renewed © 1960 and assigned to Steeger Properties, LLC. All rights reserved.
"About the Author" originally appeared in the January 1930 issue of *The Writer* magazine.

THANKS TO
Joel Frieman, Chris Kalb, Everard P. Digges LaTouche, Gerd Pircher, and Jonathan Sweet

ISBN
978-1-61827-191-4

Visit *altuspress.com* for more books like this.
Printed in the United States of America.

TABLE OF CONTENTS

The Swordsman of Mars 1

About the Author   219

CHAPTER I

A VERY STRANGE VISITOR

"**IS MR. MCGINNIS** in?"

The girl who presided at the information desk and switch-board of the McGinnis Physical Culture Institute suspended her gum chewing long enough to reply: "I'll see. What's the name?"

"Thorne. Harry Thorne."

As she connected the office phone of her employer, the girl surveyed the young man before her with a look of approval. He was tall and slender, with wavy hair of a chestnut brown shade, and there was a pantherish suppleness about his movements which hinted of powerful muscles, perfectly controlled. His faultless attire and aristocratic air told her that he was likely to prove a wealthy prospect for the services which Mr. McGinnis had to offer, so she rang three times, a signal which her employer would understand.

"Mr. Harry Thorne to see you, sir."

She nodded and smiled at the young man. "You may go in, Mr. Thorne. The first office at your right."

"Thank you." Thorne followed her directions, and was welcomed at the door of the office by the beaming proprietor of the institution, a middle-aged gentleman with bulging chest and biceps, a broken nose, and cauliflower ears.

"Come right in, Mr. Thorne. Take a chair. A wonderful frame you have to put muscle on. Now with our system of training

The Martian tried to throw and dodge at the same time.

we guarantee to add an inch to the circumference of your biceps in less than—"

"One moment, Mr. McGinnis. I came here to be built up, not physically, but financially. In short, I am after that job you advertised in this morning's paper."

McGinnis settled back, a look of disappointment on his face.

"Oh, so you want a job as my assistant fencing master. Can you handle a foil?"

"Fencing has been a hobby of mine."

"A hobby, eh? You'll have to make it a profession if you work here. But come. I'll try you out."

McGinnis led him down the hallway, and through a large room where a group of perspiring financiers dressed in shorts and jerseys were going through various contortions under the direction of a husky looking young man wearing a striped sweater. A conspicuous majority of these striving athletes looked as if their chests had slipped down beneath their belts, and the calves and biceps were undeveloped.

They passed through another room, where a number of cor-

pulent gentlemen were being mauled, poked, pinched, prodded and steam-cooked, and thence into a small empty gymnasium.

McGinnis removed his coat and invited Thorne to do likewise. Then he handed him plastron, mask, glove and foil, and both men armed themselves.

"Now, my lad," said McGinnis, when Thorne was ready, "we'll see what we'll see. On guard!"

They saluted and engaged. Before he had got fairly warmed up, McGinnis, much to his surprise, was hit. "Accidents will happen," he said. "We'll try again."

They did, and this time McGinnis was disarmed. The sudden realization of this made him quite red in the face—he, a fencing master, disarmed by this amateur.

"That was a coincidence," he said, as Thorne politely handed him his foil. "We'll try it once more."

Much to his astonishment and chagrin, the master was hit in the fifth disengage. He threw down his foil and tore off his mask. "Enough's enough," he growled.

"Do I get the job?" asked Thorne.

"Not in a thousand years, my boy. Do you think I'd be fool enough to hire an assistant who can beat me? Don't slam the door as you go out."

OUT ON the street once more, Thorne fished his last fifty cent piece from his pocket and bought an early edition of an afternoon paper. Pocketing his change, he retired to a doorway to scan the "Help Wanted" column.

Evening found him still tramping, after having followed five more fruitless leads. He fingered the change in his pocket reflectively. Not enough for a decent meal, but if husbanded carefully it would keep body and soul together for the next two or three days. He expended five cents on coffee and doughnuts, his first meal of the day. Then he returned to the cheap hotel where he had taken lodging and where his room rent, which had been paid in advance, would expire on the morrow.

As the clerk handed him his key, he said: "A gentleman called to see you, Mr. Thorne. Said he'd be back later."

"A gentleman to see me! That's strange. Did he leave any message?"

"Only that he'd be back later."

"Thanks."

Thorne climbed the creaky stairs with their covering of dusty, moth-eaten carpet, and entered his room. Shortly thereafter, in dressing gown and slippers and with his pipe going, he sat down in his creaky rocker, vintage of 1880, to think out the situation in which he found himself. He had already pawned his watch and ring, and the money was all but gone. The dressing gown would be next, he decided. Then his reverie was interrupted by a knock at the door.

"Come in," he said, wearily.

He looked up curiously as the door opened, then suppressed a gasp of amazement at sight of the striking individual who entered. His visitor, almost a giant in stature, was obviously a tremendously powerful man. But the impression of great physical strength which the stranger's physique induced was overshadowed by the promise of inconceivably greater mental force which shone from his face. His forehead was high and bulged outward over shaggy eyebrows that met above his aquiline nose. His piercing black eyes seemed to look through Thorne's own, and into his very brain. He wore a pointed, closely-cropped Vandyke, black with a slight sprinkling of gray hairs, and was dressed in faultlessly tailored evening clothes.

Thorne got to his feet as his singular visitor closed the door behind him. Then, in a booming bass voice, the big man said: "At last, Mr. Thorne, I have caught up with you. I am Dr. Morgan."

Surprised, Thorne took the proffered hand and muttered an acknowledgment. "Take the chair, doctor," he invited. "I'll sit here on the bed." As his visitor complied, he continued: "You say you have caught up with me. Am I to understand from this that you have been following me?"

"Halfway across the world and back again," was the reply. "I first saw your photograph in a local paper, accompanying an article which told of your hunting expedition in British East Africa. I followed you there, only to learn that you had sailed three days before my arrival."

"You saw my picture and followed me there? Why?"

"I'll come to that presently. When I reached New York, I called your father's home in Long Island. I was advised that you had left, and that no one knew of your whereabouts. After that, it was not easy to trace you. I learned that you had sailed for home sooner than you planned, because of a wire from your father. I also discovered that on your return, you and your father had quarreled, and that as a result you were disowned and disinherited."

"You seem to have taken a remarkably keen interest in my affairs," said Thorne, amazed at the intimate details of his private business with which this strange individual was familiar.

"Exactly. And I presume you have seen the evening paper."

"Only the 'Help Wanted' columns."

"In that case," said the doctor, "you missed some news which will be of interest to you." He took a clipping from his pocket and passed it to Thorne.

With a shock that turned him suddenly pale beneath his coat of tan, he read:

FIANCÉE OF HARRY THORNE
ELOPES WITH OTHER MAN

Sylvia Thompson, daughter of Dr. and Mrs. Horatio Thompson, of Newport, whose engagement to Harry Thorne, scion of the wealthy Long Island family, was recently announced, has eloped with Herbert Lloyd Vandevetter.

THERE were details, but Thorne did not read these. Instead, he looked at the pictures of his lovely fiancee, his best friend, and himself, conspicuously displayed beside the article. Then the page blurred and he turned away. A great sorrow gripped his heart. Sylvia Thompson was the one person in whom he had not lost faith. Before leaving for Chicago he had confided in her, had told her that he was penniless, and must seek out a new means of livelihood before they could be married. She had promised to wait. And now—this!

"She was false—a cheat, a fraud!" he said, bitterly. "I'll never believe any woman again. I'll never believe anybody."

"Steady boy," admonished the doctor. "You're taking in a lot of territory."

"I mean it," said Thorne. "I—I don't care to live any longer."

"Suppose you were offered a new interest in life. Excitement and adventures beyond your wildest dreams. A chance to view new scenes that no earthly being save one has ever glimpsed. To meet new and strange peoples."

"All that is old stuff to me," replied Thorne. "I've traveled until I'm sick of it. I've hunted big game in Asia, Africa and the Americas. I've been in every important country on the globe. The only adventure I have not tried is death, and just now it is the one adventure that intrigues me."

He got up suddenly, and stepping to where his suitcase lay open on the grip-rack, drew therefrom a .38 caliber pistol. "I don't know why you've come here, doctor," he said, "and I don't much care. But I'll appreciate the favor if you will notify my fond relatives of my demise. I don't like being messy, and I haven't the slightest desire to be dramatic, so I'll go into the bathroom for the last act."

"One moment, before you go," said the doctor. "Do you realize that if you do this deed while I am present you will implicate me as a murderer?"

"Right. I hadn't thought of that. Sorry. I'll say good-by then, and give you time to get away."

The doctor rose. "That's considerate of you, my boy, and I'll be glad to notify your relatives for you. Good-by." He held out his hand.

Thorne listlessly grasped the extended hand. As he did so, he felt a sharp pricking sensation in his palm, followed by a numbness which shot up his arm and traveled rapidly through the rest of his body. The gun, which he had been holding in his left hand, clattered to the floor. A moment later things went black before his eyes. His knees buckled under him, and the doctor, catching him beneath the arms, eased him back upon the bed. Then consciousness left him.

CHAPTER II

A PLUNGE THROUGH SPACE

WHEN THORNE'S SENSES returned he gazed about him with a startled expression. This was not the tawdry hotel bedroom in which he had fainted, but looked more like a prison cell. It was a small room with bare, concrete walls, a door of hardwood planking studded with bolts, and a window that was securely barred. The only articles of furniture were the cot on which he was lying, a chair, and a small table.

Thorne sat up, and for some time fought off a feeling of giddiness that followed the effort. Then he got unsteadily to his feet and staggered to the window. Supporting himself by gripping the thick iron bars he peered out. It was broad daylight and the sun was high in the heavens. Below him stretched a deep valley, through which a narrow stream meandered. And as far as he could see in all directions there were mountains, though the highest peaks were all below the level of his own eyes.

To Thorne, it all seemed incredible. He had lost consciousness in a Chicago hotel room, and now regained his senses in a tiny cell at the peak of a high mountain. What could it mean?

He turned from the window at the sound of a key grating in a lock. Then the heavy door swung inward, and a giant Negro entered the cell, bearing a tray of food and a steaming pot of coffee. Behind the Negro he recognized the striking figure of Dr. Morgan.

"That will be all, Plato," said the doctor, when the huge black had placed the tray on the table.

As the Negro silently passed out the door, the doctor waved his hand invitingly toward the tray. "I ordered breakfast served in your room," he said, in his booming bass voice. "I especially urge you to try the coffee. It will counteract the effect of the narcotic I was compelled to use on you last evening, in order to save your life."

"Really, doctor, you've gone to a lot of trouble to save my worthless skin," said Thorne. "May I ask why you are interfering in my affairs?"

"Not for any altruistic reason, I assure you," the big man replied crisply. "Suppose you tackle this breakfast. It will put you in a better frame of mind for what I am going to tell you."

Thorne walked unsteadily to the wooden chair which the doctor held for him at the table, and sat down. Then the latter seated himself on the cot.

A cup of steaming coffee, taken neat, cleared Thorne's head considerably, and he became conscious of a sharp appetite. He ate his breakfast with a relish, then settled back in his chair, poured more coffee, and lighted a cigarette from a package of his own brand which had been brought in with his breakfast.

"**NOW,** doctor," he said. "Where am I, and why?"

"You are in a room in my mountain observatory, where I watch the movements of the planets, and where you were brought in my airplane after you fainted. Last night you were ready to take a blind plunge into that unknown region from which no man returns, the state of existence or nonexistence called death. Had you succeeded, you would have thwarted forever the plans which I have been at considerable trouble and expense to perfect for you ever since I saw your picture. Needless to say, I am glad that I arrived in time."

"Since you saw my picture? I don't get you."

"I do not expect you to, yet. Let me explain. You have heard of telepathy?"

"Of course. Who hasn't? A name invented by fake mind readers to cover their tricks."

"Hardly that. I'll admit that there are stage charlatans who, by trickery, simulate telepathy. There are, however, many genuine mind readers—thousands of them. All of us are potential mind readers, every man, woman and child on this planet. In most, the power of telepathy is latent, seldom coming to the surface of the conscious mind except in some extreme emergency, such as the deadly peril or death of a loved one.

"Telepathy, the communication of thoughts or ideas from one mind to another without the use of any physical medium whatever, is not influenced or hampered either by time or space. It has been definitely proved, time and again, that telepathic messages can travel half way around the world instantly. Radio messages move with the speed of light, 186,000 miles per second, which makes them almost instantaneous. But that 'almost' places a limitation on them—the limitation of time and space. Telepathy takes no cognizance of either time or space, hence it is a far more potent means of communication between two worlds, separated by millions of miles of space, than radio can ever be, even though our sending and receiving instruments are made a thousand times as powerful as they are to-day.

"I will not go into details, except to say that it was by exercise of this power, which I have been able to develop to an unusual degree, that I was able to get in touch with a being on Mars, the Martian scientist and psychologist, Lal Vak. From the simple exchange of visual and auditory impressions which marked our first communications, we progressed until each had learned the language of the other to a degree that enabled us to exchange abstract as well as concrete ideas.

"It was Lal Vak who suggested to me that if we could find a man on Mars and one on Earth whose bodies were identical, we could, by astral projection, cause the two individuals to exchange bodies. Thus Earth could be viewed through Martian eyes, while Mars could be seen at first hand by a man from Earth. Lal Vak projected to me many images of Martians willing to make this exchange, and at last I located the double of one of them in an Alaskan mining camp, an adventurer named Frank Boyd, whose reputation was none too savory. He scoffed at the idea when I took it up with him, and he refused to make the attempt. But I was desperate. The thing meant so much for me that I kidnaped him and brought him here. He was offered the alternative of death or the Martian adventure, and he naturally chose the latter."

A FROWN came over the doctor's face. "Lal Vak and I had hoped, by this exchange, to make it possible for each of us to view the other's planet through the eyes of a man from his own world, by means of telepathy. In this, Lal Vak was successful, for Sel Han, who has now become Frank Boyd, had cooperated with him from the start. Not so, Frank Boyd. Shortly after he arrived on Mars I lost *rapport* with him. It is impossible to maintain such communication with any one against his will. I have learned through Lal Vak that Boyd has allied himself with a small group of Martians who are working on an invention with which they hope to conquer all Mars, and eventually Earth and Venus as well.

"Naturally, I looked around for another representative, and when I saw your picture I recognized you for a perfect double of Borgen Takkor of Mars, a young friend of Lal Vak's, who had volunteered to make the trip to Earth. I take it that you, who have exhausted all possibilities of adventure in this world, who deliberately chose death in preference to an existence on a planet which had become unbearable, will be willing to exchange bodies with him."

"Assuming that you can send me on this strange trip, as you say, what would you want me to do?" asked Thorne.

"Only two things. Refrain from willing to break *rapport* with me, and if you can, slay Frank Boyd, the Martian Sel Han. He is a deadly menace which I have unwittingly released on Mars, and through you I would rectify my mistake if possible. Otherwise, your life on Mars will be your own, to live as you choose, or as the Martians choose to let you. If you are able to rise above your environment you will find opportunities for success there which you could never hope for here. You will find a world of romance and undreamed-of adventure. And if you are not equally quick with sword and wits, you will find death."

"The prospect intrigues me," said Thorne. "Of course I refuse to promise to murder a man I have never seen—"

"If you oppose his designs, I assure you that you'll have to kill him or be killed… Then you will go?"

"I'll at least make the attempt, with your assistance."

"Good. If Lal Vak is ready we will try now. One moment."

The doctor passed his hand over his eyes, and sat for some minutes in silence. Presently he looked up and said: "Lal Vak is ready, and will be on hand to meet you. Come and lie here on the cot."

Thorne did as directed.

The doctor laid his hand on his forehead.

"Now sleep," he commanded. "Sleep, and think of that distant planet—beckoning."

Thorne felt drowsy. A pleasant lassitude claimed him. Suddenly it seemed that he was sinking, sinking into a cool, swirling flood. The doctor's voice faded, trailed away into nothingness.

CHAPTER III

A STRANGE WORLD

IT SEEMED TO Thorne that not more than a second had elapsed after the doctor's voice faded from his consciousness, when he began to feel uncomfortably warm. He opened his eyes and looked up into a cloudless blue-gray sky that was like a vault of burnished steel. A diminutive sun blazed down upon him—a blue-white sun shrunk to a diameter much smaller than when viewed from Earth, but oddly enough, with its heat and light seemingly unimpaired.

The heat, in fact, was so great that it caused him instinctively to draw back into the relatively cold shade of the scaly-trunked conifer that towered above him, its crown of needle-like foliage gathered into a bellshaped tuft. For a moment Thorne stared dazedly up into that alien sky, with its strangely shrunken sun. Then conviction came to him. He was really on Mars! Wide awake, now, he sat bolt upright and looked about him. The tree that sheltered him stood alone in a small depression, surrounded by a billowing sea of ochre-yellow sand.

He scrambled to his feet, and as he did so, something clanked at his side. Two straight-bladed weapons hung there, both sheathed in a gray metal that resembled aluminum. It was the sound of these sheaths striking together as he arose that had attracted his attention. One, he judged, was a Martian dagger, and the other a sword. The hilt of the larger weapon was fashioned of a metal of the color of brass, the pommel representing a serpent's head, the grip, its body, and the guard, the continuation of the body and tail coiled in the form of a figure eight. The hilt of the dagger was like that of the sword, but smaller.

Thorne drew the sword from its sheath. The steel blade was slender and two-edged, and tapered to a needlelike point. Both edges were armed with tiny, razor-sharp teeth which he instantly saw would add greatly to its effectiveness as a cutting weapon. He tested its balance and found he could wield it as easily as any dueling sword he had ever had in his hand.

Replacing the sword in the sheath, he examined the dagger, and found it also edged with tiny teeth. The blade of this weapon was about ten inches in length: "Long enough for the death," he reflected, recalling a favorite inscription which the ancient Romans were wont to engrave on their short swords.

Depending from the belt on the other side, and heavy enough to balance the weight of the sword and dagger, was a mace with a short brazen handle and a disk-shaped head of steel which was fastened fanwise on the haft, thick at the middle and tapering out at the edges to sawlike teeth, much coarser and longer than those on sword or dagger. Here was a weapon that was built for heavy work, such as shearing through bone or armor.

Having finished his examination of his strange weapons, Thorne turned his attention to his apparel. He was wearing a breechclout of soft leather. Beneath this, and down to the center of his shins, his limbs were bare and considerably sunburned. Below this point were the rolled tops of a pair of long boots, made from fur and fitted with clasps which were obviously for the purpose of attaching them to the bottom of the breechclout when they were drawn up to protect the legs from the weather.

Above the waist his sun-tanned body was bare of clothing, but he wore a pair of broad metal armlets, a pair of bracelets with long bars attached, evidently to protect the forearm from sword cuts, and a jeweled medallion, suspended on his chest from a chain around his neck and inscribed with strange characters.

On his head was a bundle of silky material with a short, soft nap, rolled much like a turban and held in place by one brass-studded strap that passed around his forehead, and another, depending from it, that went beneath his chin.

BEYOND a large sand dune, and not more than a quarter of a mile distant, he saw the waving bell-shaped crowns of a small grove of trees similar to the one that sheltered him. As no other landmark presented itself, he started toward the clump of conifers.

As soon as he stepped out into the blaze of the midday sun, Thorne began to feel uncomfortably warm. Though the apparent disk of the solar orb was considerably reduced by distance as compared to its seeming size on Earth, the cloudless atmosphere of this planet was so tenuous that it offered but slight resistance to the passage of its rays. The contrast, too, between the heat and light in the shade and in direct sunlight, was much greater than on Earth, due to the fact that the thin atmosphere did not retain as much heat or diffuse as much light as the more dense air of the Earth.

Soon he noted other signs of Martian life. Immense, gaudily tinted butterflies, some with wing spreads of more than six feet, flew up from the flower patches at his approach. A huge dragon fly zoomed past, looking much like a miniature airplane.

Suddenly he heard an angry hum beside him, and felt a searing pain in his left side. Seemingly out of nowhere a blood-sucking fly, yellow and red in color and about two feet in length, had darted down upon him and plunged its many-pointed proboscis into his flesh. Taken wholly by surprise, Thorne did not even have time to grasp his weapons. His first thought was to relieve that burning agony. Seizing the sharp bill of his assailant, he wrenched it from his side, cruelly tearing his own flesh and pricking his hands on the sharp barbs with which it was armed.

The insect buzzed violently in an effort to escape, but Thorne, still clinging to its bill with one lacerated hand, reached for his dagger with the other and cut off its head. Flinging the hideous thing at the body, which was flopping erratically on the ground, he caught up a handful of sand to stanch the bleeding of his wound. Presently, when the flow of blood had subsided, he started forward once more, this time keeping a wary eye on the air around him, as well as on the near-by terrain.

He was nearing the top of the dune behind which was the clump of trees he had chosen for his objective when he suddenly met, coming over the ridge from the other side, a most singular figure. At first glance it looked much like a walking umbrella. Then it resolved itself into a man wearing a long loose-sleeved cloak, which covered him from the crown of his head to his knees. Below the cloak the end of a scabbard was visible, as were a pair of rolled fur boots like those worn by Thorne. The face was covered with a mask of flexible transparent material.

Not knowing whether this newcomer was a friend or foe, Thorne stopped, and instinctively his hand went to his sword hilt.

THE OTHER halted, also, at a distance of about ten paces, and swept off his mask, revealing the kindly features of a man in the autumn of life. His face was smooth shaven and his hair and eyebrows were white.

"I have the honor of being the first man to welcome you to Mars, Harry Thorne," he said in English, and smilingly added: "I am Lal Vak."

Thorne returned his smile. "Thank you, Lal Vak. You speak excellent English."

"I learned your language from Dr. Morgan, just as he learned mine from me," replied Lal Vak. "Aural impressions are as readily transmitted by telepathy as visual impressions, you know."

"So the doctor informed me," said Thorne. "But where do we go from here? I'm beginning to feel uncomfortable with the sun beating down on my bare skin."

"I've been inexcusably thoughtless," apologized Lal Vak.

"Here, let me show you how to adjust your head-cloak." Reaching up to Thorne's turbanlike headpiece, he loosened a strap. The silky material instantly fell down about the Earth-man, reaching to his knees. A flexible, transparent mask also unrolled, and Lal Vak showed him how to draw it across his face.

"This material," he said, "is made from the skin of a large moth. The people of Xancibar, the nation of which you are now a citizen, use these cloaks much for summer wear, particularly when traveling in the desert. They keep out the sun's rays by day, and keep in considerable warmth at night. As you will learn, even our summer nights are quite cold, and warm garments are a necessity. The mask is made from the same material, but is treated with oil and has the nap scraped off to make it transparent."

"I feel better already," said Thorne. "Now what?"

"Now we will go to the oasis, get our mounts, and fly back to the military training school, which you, as Borgen Takkor, have attended and must continue to attend. At the school I am an instructor in tactics."

As they approached the small clump of trees which Thorne had previously noticed, he saw that they surrounded a small pool of water. Splashing about in this pool were two immense winged creatures, and Thorne noted with astonishment that they were covered with brown fur instead of feathers. They had long, sturdy legs, covered with yellow scales. Their wings were membranous, and their bills were flat, much like those of ducks, except that they had sharp, down-curved hooks at the end. And when one opened its mouth, Thorne saw that it was furnished with sharp, triangular teeth, tilted backward. These immense beast-birds, whose backs were about seven feet above the ground, and whose heads reached to a height of about twelve feet, were saddled with seats of gray metal.

The tips of each creature's wings were perforated, and tethered to the saddle by means of snap-hooks and short chains, evidently to prevent their taking to the air without their riders.

LAL VAK made a peculiar sound, a low quavering call. Instantly both of the grotesque mounts answered with hoarse honking sounds and came floundering up out of the water toward them. One of them, on coming up to Thorne, arched its neck, then lowered its head and nuzzled him so violently with its broad bill that he was nearly knocked over.

"Scratch his head," said Lal Vak, with an amused smile at the Earth-man's discomfiture. "Borgen Takkor made quite a pet of him, and you are now Borgen Takkor to him."

After a second prod from the huge beak, Thorne hastily scratched the creature's head, whereupon it held still, blinking contentedly, and making little guttural noises in its throat. He noticed that there was a light strand of twisted leather around its neck, fastened to the end of a flexible rod, which in turn was fastened to the ring-shaped pommel of the saddle.

"Is that the steering gear?" he asked, indicating the rod and leather with his free hand.

"You have guessed right, my friend," replied Lal Vak. "Pull up on the rod, and the gawr, for such is the name of these creatures, will fly upward. Push down and he will descend. A pull to the right or left and he will fly, walk or swim in the direction indicated, according to whether he is in the air, on the ground, or in the water. Pull straight backward, and he will stop or hover."

"Sounds easy."

"It is quite simple, I assure you. But before we go, let me warn you to speak to no one, whether you are spoken to or not. Salute those who greet you, thus." He raised his left hand to the level of his forehead, with the palm backward. "I must get you to your room as quickly as possible. There you will feign illness, and I will teach you our language before you venture out."

"But how can I remember all the friends and acquaintances of Borg—Borgen Takkor. What a name! Suppose something should come up—"

"I've provided against all that. Your illness will be blamed for your temporary loss of memory. This will give you time to find out things, and the right to ask questions rather than answer them. But, come, it grows late. Watch me carefully, and do as I do."

Lal Vak tugged at a folded wing, and his mount knelt. Then he climbed into the saddle and unfastened the snap-hooks which tethered the wings, hooking them through two rings in his own belt. Thorne watched and imitated his every movement, and was soon in the saddle.

"Now," said Lal Vak, "slap your gawr on the neck and pull up on the rod. He'll do the rest."

Thorne did as directed, and his mount responded with alacrity. It ran swiftly forward for about fifty feet, then with a tremendous flapping of its huge, membranous wings, it took off, lurching violently at first, so that the Earth-man was compelled to seize the saddle pommel in order to keep from falling off.

After he had reached a height of about two thousand feet, Lal Vak, who was leading, relaxed the lift on his guiding rod and settled down to a straightaway flight. Thorne kept close behind him.

When they had flown for what Thorne judged was a distance of about twenty-five miles, he noticed ahead of them what he took to be a small town or village. It consisted of a number of cylindrical buildings of various sizes, with perfectly flat roofs, built around a small lake, or lagoon. The oasis on which it was situated had a man-made look, as both it and the lagoon it encircled were perfectly square. The cylindrical buildings and the high wall surrounding the square inclosure shone in the sunlight like burnished metal.

RISING from and descending to the shores of the lagoon were a number of riders mounted on gawrs. And as they drew near, there flew up from the inclosure, not a gawr but a mighty airship that flapped its wings like a bird. It was over a hundred feet in length and made of metal in the semblance of a gawr even to the landing gear, which was formed and colored like a pair of the creature's yellow legs, and like them projected backward as it flew. No passengers were visible, but a number of small round windows in the sides of the body indicated their positions.

Lal Vak's mount now circled and then volplaned straight toward the margin of the lagoon. Thorne's gawr followed. As it alighted with a scarcely perceptible jar, an attendant whose sole article of apparel was a leather breechclout came running up, saluted Thorne by raising his hand, palm-inward, to the level of his forehead, and took charge of his mount, causing it to kneel by tugging at one wing.

Thorne returned the salute and seeing that Lal Vak had dismounted, followed his example, As he stood on his feet a sudden dizziness assailed him and he came near to falling. He noticed also that a numbness was spreading outward from the wound in his side, which had pained him considerably during the ride.

Both numbness and dizziness, however, he attributed to the effect of his flight, and braced himself to walk away with Lal Vak as if there were nothing the matter.

The scientist led him toward one of the smaller buildings, which Thorne now saw were made of blocks of a translucent material like clouded amber, cemented together with some transparent product.

As they were about to enter the circular door of the building, two young men came hurrying out, and one lunged heavily against Thorne. Harry suppressed a groan of anguish with difficulty, for the fellow's elbow had come in violent contact with his wound. The force of the blow broke it open, and he felt the warm blood trickling down his side.

Instantly the man who had jostled him, a huge fellow with a flat nose, beetling brows and a prognathous jaw, turned and spoke rapidly to him, a ferocious expression on his ruddy face and his hand on his sword hilt.

Lal Vak whispered in Thorne's ear. "This is regrettable," he said. "The fellow claims you purposely jostled him, and challenges you to a duel. You must fight, or be forever branded a coward."

Thorne felt the dizziness which had attacked him when he dismounted coming back worse than ever. "Must I fight him here and now?"

"Here and now," the scientist replied. "Doctor Morgan told me you were a good swordsman. That is fortunate, for this fellow is an instructor in swordsmanship and a notorious killer."

With his head reeling, and his wound smarting worse than ever, Thorne faced his opponent. He was dimly conscious that a ring of watchers was forming around them.

Both men drew their swords simultaneously. Thorne endeavored to raise his blade to engage that of his adversary, but found he was without strength. The circle of onlookers seemed whirling around him—the earth rocking precariously beneath his feet. His sword dropped from nerveless fingers and clattered to the pavement.

A sardonic grin came to the face of his opponent. Then he contemptuously raised his weapon and slashed the Earth-man's cheek with the keen, saw-edged blade, cutting it to the bone.

For an instant Thorne felt that searing pain. Then he pitched forward on his face and all went black.

CHAPTER IV

ATTACKED IN THE SKY

THORNE WOKE TO a weirdly beautiful sight. Two full moons were shining down on him from a black sky in which the stars sparkled like brilliant jewels. He was lying on a bed which was suspended by four chains on a single large flexible cable which depended from the ceiling, and had his view of the sky through a large circular window which occupied almost all of one side of the room in which he lay.

He turned on his side, the better to look around him, and as he did so, saw Lal Vak muffled in a large fur and seated on a legless chair suspended, like his bed, on a single cable which was fastened to the ceiling.

"Hello, Lal Vak," he said. "What happened? Went out like a light, didn't I?"

"I regret to inform you that you are technically in disgrace," said the white-haired scientist. "If you had told me, before the duel, that you were wounded and weak from loss of blood, I could have delayed the meeting. It was only after I had brought you here that I discovered your body-wound, and by that time the news had gone about that you were afraid to fight—that you had dropped your sword when faced by Sel Han."

"Sel Han! Why, that's the man Doctor Morgan wanted me to kill—the man he said was a deadly menace to Mars, and might prove a later menace to Earth as well."

"The same. On Earth he was Frank Boyd, a desperate and despicable character—a robber of miners and a jumper of claims, so the doctor informed me. We had hoped to make a man of him by this Martian adventure, but I fear he is wholly bad; a trickster, a cheat, a vicious criminal, so clever that despite our suspicions of his secret and sinister activities, we are unable to gather any evidence that will convict him."

"It seems I have been a miserable failure, right at the start," said Thorne.

"Your mistake was in not telling me of your wound."

"I'll challenge Sel Han as soon as I'm up and around again," said Thorne. "That ought to square everything, and if I win, why, the first part of my mission will have been accomplished."

"Unfortunately," replied the scientist, "that will be impossible. According to our Martian code, it would be unethical for you, under any circumstances, to provoke another duel with Sel Han. He, on the other hand, may insult or humiliate you all he likes, so long as he uses no physical violence, and does not have to stand challenge from you, for he is technically the victor. Of course, if he should prove magnanimous enough to offer to meet you again, this would be permissible. But it is unlikely that you will find Sel Han so generous."

"Then what am I to do?" Thorne asked.

"That will rest with Sheb Takkor. As Borgen Takkor, you are, of course, son of Sheb, the Rad of Takkor. If he were to die, your name would become Sheb. As it is, you are the Zorad of Takkor. Zorad, in your language, might be translated viscount, and Rad, earl. The titles, of course, no longer have meaning, except that they denote noble blood, as the Swarm has changed all that."

"The Swarm?"

LAL VAK nodded.

"I can think of no other English equivalent for our word Kamud, unless it might be the Hive. The Kamud is the new order of government which took control of Xancibar about ten Martian years, or nearly nineteen Earth years ago. At that time, like other Martian vilets, or empires, of the present day, we had a Vil, or emperor. Although his office was hereditary, he could be deposed at any time by the will of the people, and a new Vil elected.

"For the most part, our people were satisfied with the government. But there suddenly rose into power a man named Irintz Tel, who had strange new social theories. He taught that an ideal community could be attained by imitating the communal life of the black bees, and inculcating into the breasts of every man, woman and child, the feeling of Kamud—the spirit of the hive. Under his system the individuals exist for the benefit of the community, not the community for the benefit of the individuals.

"Irintz Tel did not gather many followers, but those who flocked to his banner were vociferous and vindictive. At length, they decided to resort to arms—to endeavor to establish their form of government by force. Hearing this, Miradon, our magnanimous Vil, abdicated rather than see his people involved in a bloody civil war. He could have crushed the upstart, of course, but many lives would have been lost, and he preferred the more peaceful way.

"As soon as Miradon Vil was gone, Irintz Tel and his henchmen seized the reins of government in Dukor, the capital of Xancibar. After considerable fighting, for our people did not all submit tamely to the new order, he established the Kamud, which now owns all land, buildings, waterways, mines and commercial enterprises within our borders. He promised us annual elections, but once he was firmly established as Dixtar of Xancibar, this promise was repudiated. Theoretically, like all other citizens, Irintz Tel owns nothing except his personal belongings. But actually, with the authority which he has seized, he owns and controls all of Xancibar in the name of the Kamud, and has the absolute power of life and death over every citizen."

"What do people think of this arrangement?" asked Thorne. "Do they submit tamely to such perfidy and tyranny?"

"They have no choice," replied Lal Vak. "Irintz Tel rules with an iron hand. His spies are everywhere. And those detected speaking against his regime are quickly done away with."

"What! Are people executed for expressing their thoughts? Is there no freedom of speech?"

"Some are executed, charged with some trumped up offense, usually treason to the Kamud. Men in high places are often challenged and slain by Irintz Tel's hired swordsmen. Others are sent to the mines, which means that they will not live long. I will leave you, now. You are a wounded man, and must sleep."

"My wounds—I had forgotten them," said Thorne. He raised his hand to his face where the sword of Sel Han had slashed him. He felt no soreness, only a porous pumicelike protrusion traveling the length of the gash. The wound in his side, also, had ceased to pain, and was covered with a similar substance.

"I had them dressed as soon as you were brought here," said the scientist. "They should not pain you, now."

"They don't. That's what amazes me. And what a strange kind of dressing."

"It is rjembal, a flexible aromatic gum which is antiseptic, protects the wound from infection, and is porous enough to absorb seepage. Wounds closed with this gum usually heal quickly, painlessly, and without leaving scars. We simply heat the gum until it flows easily, draw the wound together, and apply it.

"I go now. Sleep well, and to-morrow I will come to give you your first lesson in our language." Lal Vak raised his hand in the Martian salute and left the room.

Shortly thereafter, Thorne slept.

EARLY the next morning Thorne was awakened by a touch on his forehead. He saw the white-haired Lal Vak smiling down at him. Behind him stood an orderly, who carried a large bowl which he placed on a tripod beside the bed. The orderly saluted and withdrew.

The bowl was divided into sections like a scooped-out grapefruit. In one section reposed several slices of grilled food. In another was a whole raw fruit, purple in color, and cubical in shape. In the third was a hollow cube containing an aromatic pink beverage.

Thorne sampled one of the grilled slices. The flavor baffled him, as it did not appear to be either flesh or vegetable, though it resembled both. Having finished the strange grilled food, he tasted the pink beverage. It was slightly bitter and about as acid as a ripe orange. A sip sent an instant glow through his veins.

"What's this stuff?" he asked.

"Pulcho," replied Lal Vak. "A single cup is stimulating, but many are intoxicating."

Thorne finished the beverage, and Lal Vak instantly set about the serious business of teaching him the things he must know in order to establish himself as Borgen Takkor.

Although Thorne's wounds healed in a few days, Lal Vak used them as a pretense to keep him in his room for about twenty. During that time he taught him many things including the language of Xancibar, which he said was the tongue spoken by all white Martians of the old race. The Earth-man learned the language with exceeding rapidity, for stored in the brain-cells of the Martian body which had become his were the recollections of all the sounds and their meanings. It was therefore more like reviewing a once learned and partly forgotten lesson than acquiring a new language.

One day, as Thorne and Lal Vak were talking, an orderly came to announce that there was a man below calling himself Yirl Du, who asked to see Sheb Takkor.

"Let him come up," said Lal Vak. When the orderly had gone out he said to Thorne: "You heard what he said? He asked for Sheb Takkor."

"Yes. What does it mean?"

"It means," replied the scientist, "that Sheb Takkor, father of Borgen Takkor, is dead. Hence, you are Sheb Takkor. No doubt this is one of the Takkor retainers who knows you, so call him by name when he appears before us."

A moment later, a short, stocky man entered the room. His head-cloak was thrown back, revealing huge bulging muscles beneath his bare, sun-browned skin, and a tremendous breadth of shoulders and depth of chest. His arms dangled, apelike, almost to his knees, and his legs, though well muscled, were abnormally short. His features were coarse, but kindly.

HE RAISED one huge hand in salute, saying:

"I shield my eyes, my lord Sheb, Rad of Takkor."

Thorne smiled and returned his salute. "Greetings, Yirl Du," he responded. "This is my instructor, Lal Vak."

Yirl Du saluted the scientist with: "I shield my eyes, excellency."

"You forget that under the Kamud all men are equal," said Lal Vak, returning his salute, "and one man no longer says to another: 'I shield my eyes,' 'my lord,' or 'excellency.'"

"I do not forget that I am hereditary Jen of the Takkor Free Swordsmen, nor that Sheb Takkor is my liege," responded Yirl Du, with dignity. "From our isolated position, we of Takkor know little of the Kamud. We have submitted to it because our Rad, emulating Miradon Vil, saw fit to do so to prevent bloodshed. So long as a Takkor Rad continues to rule us, though he is only the agent of the Kamud, we are content, and life goes on much as usual."

"You have come to escort your new Rad back to Takkor, I presume."

"That is my purpose, excellency."

"Then suppose you go and see about the gawrs while we make ready for the journey. I will accompany your Rad, and spend a few days with him."

"I go, excellency." Yirl Du saluted and withdrew.

"Strange," said Thorne, when he had gone. "He said nothing about the death of Sheb Takkor, the elder."

"His words conveyed the tidings," said Lal Vak. "For him to have mentioned the matter further, or for you to have questioned him, would have been highly improper. A dead man's friends or relatives must not speak of him nor of his death until his ashes have been ceremonially scattered."

"When will that take place?"

"Upon your arrival. As his son and successor, you should be present at the ceremony. When it is completed, you may talk as freely as you like."

"I suppose there is a reason for this custom?"

"There is, a reason grounded on superstition. Our ancestors believed, and the majority of the people still believe, that those who speak of the dead before their ashes have been ceremonially scattered are sure to be haunted for the rest of their days."

While they were talking both men had belted on their weapons and adjusted their head-cloaks. They descended to the courtyard and crossed to the lagoon, where Yirl Du waited with three gawrs attended by orderlies. Thorne noticed that as he passed various groups of the soldier-students, not one spoke to him or saluted, though all were most polite in their greetings of Lal Vak.

Lal Vak edged close to him. "Watch Yirl Du and me, and set your course as we do," he whispered. "You will be supposed to lead, but as you don't know the way you will have to depend on one or the other of us for guidance."

In a few moments all was in readiness. The three ungainly mounts trotted forward, spread their membranous wings and took to the air.

BY GLANCING right and left at his two companions, Thorne was easily able to gauge their course, and steer his bird-beast accordingly. They set out in a direction which he judged was due west, by his observation of the sun.

Then, far ahead, Thorne saw a straight, high wall which stretched as far as he could see to the north and south. It was constructed of black stone, and at intervals of about a half mile towers built from the same material projected above it. The aqueduct which they were following led straight up to and entered this wall. As they drew near it, armed men became visible, evidently sentries patrolling the battlements.

Soon Thorne was able to catch a glimpse of what lay beyond the wall. First there was the glint of water in a broad canal, then the rich green of luxuriant vegetation, dotted here and there with the gleam of cylindrical crystal dwellings, and sloping in a series of terraces to a much wider canal than the first. Beyond this in the dim distance another series of terraces ascended to another elevated canal as high as the first, flanked by a wall like the one over which they were flying.

Thorne judged that it took them about thirty minutes to fly completely across this tremendous man-made valley. This, he realized, must be one of the gigantic irrigation trenches which look like a network of narrow lines on the face of the planet to earthly astronomers, who designate them as the channels or canals of Mars.

Beyond the second wall they encountered desert once more, and for several hours continued their flight toward the west. Then the contour of the ground beneath them changed abruptly. It was as if they were on the shore of a vast ocean from which the water had suddenly evaporated. First they passed over rugged cliffs, then a gently sloping beach strewn with sand and bowlders. This presently dipped sharply to what had evidently once been me bottom of an ocean. It was now a marshy lowland, a vast expanse of shallow water dotted and streaked with patches of green vegetation.

So absorbed was Thorne in gazing at this totally different section of the Martian landscape that he did not notice the menace that had crept silently up behind him. A shout from Lal Vak and a backward gesture caused him to turn in time to see a cloaked and masked warrior mounted on a swiftly flying gawr in the act of hurling a javelin at him. Behind his assailant he caught a fleeting glimpse of four more riders flying in V formation. He dodged just in time to avoid the barbed weapon. As it whizzed past him he whirled his gawr, then seized one of his own javelins and hurled it at his attacker.

The rider avoided Thorne's shaft with ease, and in a moment more was above him with drawn sword. Thorne whipped out his own weapon, parried a vicious head-cut, and countered with a swift slash at the neck of his assailant. The blow fell true, nearly severing the fellow's head from his body. Then the blood-spattered corpse pitched from the saddle and hung dangling at the ends of the two safety chains which were snapped to the belt.

In the meantime, Lal Vak and Yirl Du were engaged in a lively conflict. Thorne saw the powerful Jen of the Free Swordsman hurl a javelin with such force that it passed completely through the body of his nearest enemy. Lal Vak was fighting a sword duel with another of the attackers. The two who remained each sought a single encounter, one with Yirl Du and the other with Thorne.

The Earth-man's new assailant hurled a javelin which fell short. He reached for another, and drew it back for a throw just as Thorne hurled his weapon mightily. The fellow tried to throw and dodge at the same time, and as a result made a bad job of both efforts. He ducked low, but not low enough. Thorne's javelin struck him in the eye, and passing through, pierced his brain. His own weapon flew wide of the mark, but struck a wing-joint of the Earth-man's mount.

A moment later Thorne found himself out of the saddle dangling by his safety chains, while his crippled gawr, fluttering futilely with its uninjured wing, turned over and over in the air as they hurtled swiftly toward the marsh, two thousand feet below.

CHAPTER V

THE MARSH GIRL

AS HIS BIRD-BEAST turned over and over with him in the air, Thorne, swinging at the ends of his safety chains, saw that they were falling toward a small lake in the midst of the marsh with fearful velocity. In that dizzying revolution of earth and sky he was unable to make out his embattled comrades above him, or to even surmise what their fate had been. As they neared the water the crippled gawr made valiant efforts to right itself, and partly succeeded, to the extent of changing the last few hundred feet to a glide and a dive.

They struck the water with an impact that almost robbed Thorne of consciousness. Dimly aware that he was being dragged down far below the surface of the lake, he held his breath and, unhooking his safety chains, struck out for the surface. Finding the weight of his weapons a serious encumbrance, and knowing that if he could not get his head above water soon all would be over with him, he unfastened his belt and let the weapons sink. Then, controlling his desire to inhale with a mighty effort of will, he fought his way swiftly to the top.

For some time the Earth-man was too busy getting his breath to take note of his surroundings. Then he looked around for his mount, and saw it swimming directly away from him at a distance of about three hundred yards. Although the gawr was moving at a speed which he could not possibly hope to equal, he was about to set out in futile pursuit when a huge and terrible reptilian head suddenly reared itself between them, a scaly, silver gray head balanced on a thin, spiny neck. The monster looked first at the retreating gawr, then at the man, and evidently deciding that the latter would be the easier prey, began gliding swiftly toward him.

Thorne glanced around him. Although it seemed utterly futile for him even to attempt to make the shore, about a quarter of a mile distant, where a dense fringe of trees nodded over the water, no other avenue of escape was open to him, and he struck out desperately.

It was manifest from the start that he could not hope to outstrip his fearful aquatic enemy. As he forged ahead with long, powerful overhand strokes, he glanced back from time to time, and saw that the monster was swiftly gaining on him. Soon the terrific pace began to tell on him. His arms grew numb, and it seemed that they moved automatically, while breathing momentarily became more difficult. But the thought of those dreadful jaws, now gaping close behind him, spurred him on.

With the shore but two hundred feet distant, he felt his last ounce of strength ebbing. A backward glance showed his monstrous pursuer so near that it was arching its neck for the kill. Then just ahead of him he noticed a tiny ripple in the water, and there emerged a pair of jaws like those of a crocodile, but larger than those of any crocodile he had ever seen or heard of. There followed a broad, flat head, and thick neck, both covered with glossy fur, the head black, the neck ringed with a bright yellow band.

Hemmed thus between the two aquatic monsters, he did the only thing left for him to do. Filling his lungs, he plunged beneath the surface and dived under the oncoming beast. For a moment he heard the rush and swirl of the swimming thing above him, and felt the eddying currents which it kicked downward and backward. These passed, he forged onward, remaining under water until compelled to return to the surface for air.

WHEN he had shaken the water out of his eyes, Thorne saw a fearsome sight. The two monsters had met, and were engaged in a terrific struggle. The silver-gray scales of the one which had been following him flashed in the sun as it endeavored to shake off its smaller adversary which had seized it by the lower lip.

Suddenly it reared its head until the black-furred creature was drawn completely out of the water, and he saw that the latter was a web-footed animal about as large as a full-grown terrestrial lion, with short legs and a leathery, paddle-shaped tail which was edged with sharp spines. With the exception of the tail and claws, the body was covered with fur. The scaly monster shook its head, dislodging its smaller enemy and losing most of its lower lip in the process. Then, as the furry creature splashed into the water, it arched its neck and struck.

Thorne expected to see the smaller creature instantly slain. Instead, he saw a startling demonstration of its superior cunning and quickness. With a speed his eye could scarcely follow, it avoided the lunge of that terrible head, and turning, seized the slender, stalklike neck of its adversary in its own relatively large jaws. One powerful crunch, and the battle was over. The severed head sank from sight, and the huge body, floundering about with reptilian tenacity to life, churned the water to a foam and sent huge waves scurrying in all directions.

So absorbed had he been in this strange battle that Thorne had momentarily forgotten his own exhaustion and the peril that menaced him. Now, as the victor turned from the carcass of its vanquished enemy and swam straight toward him, the realization of his danger redoubled. He struck out for the shore, essaying the fast overhand stroke he had previously used on the surface, but his weary muscles had reached the limit of their endurance. A few feeble efforts, and a backward glance at the swiftly moving beast, convinced him that he was doomed. Better death by drowning than in those horrible jaws. He filled his lungs and dived. At a depth of about fifteen feet he found a large water plant to which he clung with his last remaining strength.

But it seemed he was not even to be given his choice of deaths. Suddenly he became aware of a dark object in the green water above him. Then a huge pair of jaws closed around his waist, and with a deft twist, broke his hold on the water plant. A moment later he was lifted clear of the water, choking and strangling, his lungs paining violently.

The creature was carrying him swiftly toward the shore, much more swiftly than he could have traveled unaided even with his full strength, and this despite the fact that his feet and hands trailing in the water must have impeded it considerably. Before they reached the fringe of trees he coughed up most of the water remaining in his lungs. He guessed that the monster was taking him to its lair, but on looking up, saw that it was heading directly toward the mouth of a narrow bayou. There, to his astonishment, he saw a small, flat boat, and standing in the boat a slender, nearly naked girl, who cried:

"Good old Tezzu. Careful! Hold him gently."

Thorne's astonishment increased, for it was obvious that the girl was talking to the creature that carried him. Moreover, he assumed from her speech that she had sent this monster out to save his life, and that it had performed its task with the skill and fidelity of an intelligent dog.

The stern of the little craft sloped toward the water, and it was to this that the animal brought him. The girl seized a leg and an arm, and her efficient beast, releasing its hold on him, placed its snout beneath his body and rolled him into the boat.

THORNE essayed to sit up, but fell back weakly. A gray mist swam before his eyes. Dimly, as through a haze, he saw the girl toss a rope to the beast, then felt the tug as the boat was towed ahead. The girl sat down, raised his head from the bottom of the boat and propped it in her lap. She smoothed back the wet hair from his forehead. Her gentle touch soothed him.

He wished that he might see her face more clearly.

"Who—who are you?" he asked, his voice so faint he scarcely recognized it for his own.

She seemed surprised. "You do not know me?"

He stared hard. "I can scarcely see you. That haze—"

"Don't try. You are exhausted. Close your eyes and try to sleep. Later we will talk."

It was easy for Thorne to obey her. Soon a pleasant lassitude crept over him. It was good to lie there and relax with that gentle hand on his forehead. Despite his exhaustion, he could not sleep. But he could rest—and think. Obviously, this girl had been an acquaintance of Borgen Takkor. She expected him to recognize her as soon as his vision cleared. What should he do?

Somehow, he wanted to make a clean breast of everything with her—to tell who he really was. Yet he felt that he owed it to Dr. Morgan and Lal Vak not to reveal his impersonation of the man whose place he had taken on Mars.

Presently, opening his eyes, he found that his vision had cleared, and saw that they were gliding through a narrow channel in the marsh. Trees hung over the water, their branches so interlaced and festooned with moss and lianas that only occasional shafts of sunlight penetrated to the rippling surface.

Thorne glanced up at the girl. She was looking out across the marsh and did not notice that he had opened his eyes. By any standard she was unquestionably beautiful, with her slightly tip-tilted nose, her glossy black hair, and her dark brown eyes shaded by long curling lashes. Though she was small and slender she was undoubtedly, athletic. The sun and wind had put a healthy glow in her cheeks, and coated her velvety skin with a wholesome tan. Her sole articles of apparel were a narrow band of soft leather which incased her small, firm breasts, a cincture of the same material about her smooth, tanned thighs, and the belt from which her sword, dagger and mace were suspended.

It was when he caught a glimpse of the clear sky through a rift in the branches that Thorne suddenly thought of Lal Vak and Yirl Da, whom he had left battling in the air. He sat up abruptly, thereby startling a little scream from his fair rescuer.

"What's wrong?" she asked.

"I must go back," he said, "at once."

The girl looked puzzled. "Back? How? Where? What do you mean?"

"Back to the lake where I left my friends fighting. If they survived they will be searching for me."

She shook her head. "It is too late to go back now. As it is we will barely make shelter before sundown. Tomorrow, if you like, I will take you back."

"But to-morrow will be too late. They will think me dead."

"Then, Borgen, they will be the more pleasantly surprised when you return to Castle Takkor."

"Not Borgen," he corrected her. "Sheb."

For a moment she regarded him with a look of shocked surprise. Then sudden tears welled in her eyes as she asked: "Has the ceremony been performed?"

"No. I was on my way to attend it with Lal Vak and Yirl Du when we were attacked, and you so kindly rescued me."

"Oh."

Thorne now realized that she must have been very well acquainted with Sheb Takkor the elder, and that she undoubtedly knew far more about the man whose place he had taken than he did himself. Due to the restraint imposed by custom, however, she could make no mention of the deceased so long as his ashes had not been ceremonially scattered. He wondered what her relationship had been with Borgen Takkor. Had they been playmates? Friends? Not lovers, he felt sure, for what man would consent to give up the love of this ravishing creature, even for the magnificent adventure of traveling to another world?

SUDDENLY the girl seized a long, barbed spear which lay in the bottom of the boat, and lunged at something she saw in the rushes that lined the bank. Then, before Thorne could rise to help her, she drew a huge iridescent beetle about three feet long into the boat. Plunging the point of the spear into the planking to keep it from escaping, she then put an end to the impaled insect's struggles by splitting its armored head with her mace. This done, she turned to the Earth-man with a smile.

"We will fare well this evening," she said. "Now I can prepare your favorite dish."

Thorne looked askance at the beetle and began to have strong misgivings I as to what his favorite dish would be like. But he resolved to eat it and act I as if he enjoyed it, no matter what she should set before him.

At this moment the beast towing the boat ran up on a small island, dragging it after him onto a sloping beach that bore the marks of many landings.

"Enough, Tezzu," called the girl, whereupon the creature dropped the tow-rope and came cavorting down to the boat like an affectionate dog, to be petted.

"You may bring the anuba, Sheb," said the girl. "Tezzu will carry the javelins."

As he saw nothing else portable, Thorne judged that the anuba was the beetle. He withdrew the point of the spear from the planking while the girl handed the sheaf of javelins to her beast, then shouldered the heavy insect and followed her up a narrow path that wound through the undergrowth.

After walking about two hundred feet they came to a small cylindrical hut, made from stout posts driven into the ground in a compact circle and chinked with clay. The flat roof was made from the same crude materials, and the circular door was a thick cross section of an immense log.

"Don't you remember this camp, Sheb?" asked the girl, reaching for the door fastener.

"I—"Thorne was trying to frame a reply when, to his astonishment, the door flew open. A slender, spidery arm shot out and seized the girl by the wrist, jerking her through the opening. Then the door slammed shut.

Almost at the same instant a net dropped over the Earth-man, jerking him backward. As he struggled in its enveloping meshes, he saw the girl's faithful beast drop the sheaf of javelins and with a roar of rage dash straight at the door where she had disappeared.

CHAPTER VI

THE MA GONGI

AS THORNE WAS jerked backward by the net which had been dropped over his head, his first thought was of the girl who had been dragged into the hut. But in order to go to her assistance he must first free himself. He was still carrying the beetle over his shoulder, hanging on the long spear on which it had been impaled. He thrust upward with the spear. The beetle prevented it from slipping through the meshes, and with the long handle he was able to raise the net and pitch it back over his head.

Scarcely had he freed himself when he saw descending from the branches of the surrounding trees six grotesque specimens of humanity. Not one of them was more than five feet tall. Their skins were bright yellow in color, and their spindly arms and legs branched out from bodies that were almost globular. Their Mongoloid features were surmounted by queer pagoda-shaped helmets of yellow metal, and their bodies were protected by armor.

As they converged on him, shouting wildly, they brandished long, slightly curved swords with blunt ends, small oval guards and hilts long enough to be grasped in both hands.

Thorne ran his nearest foe through the belly with the long spear which still held the carcass of the anuba beetle. The barbed point stuck, leaving him weaponless for the instant. Then he leaped forward, seized the sword dropped by his fallen enemy, and came on guard in time to meet the attack of the next.

39

Swiftly parrying a lightning cut at his legs which would instantly have laid him at the mercy of his attackers, he countered with a sudden moulinet which sheared down through the left shoulder of his second adversary, inflicting a mortal wound that instantly put him out of the fight.

The four that remained seemed taken aback by this display of the Earth-man's brilliant and deadly swordplay, and now approached him more warily. They were closing in on him from all sides when the girl's fierce beast gave up its futile attempts to tear down the door of the hut and suddenly rushed to his assistance. Thorne was in need of help.

A leap, a crunch of those powerful jaws, and one foeman fell with his head crushed to a shapeless pulp. At the same time Thorne's sword disemboweled another of his antagonists. With shrieks of terror, the two survivors turned and fled. But the beast, despite its short legs, pursued them with incredible swiftness. One went down with his head between those relentless jaws, to rise no more, and the last, catching a liana, scampered up for a little way only to be pulled down and as swiftly dispatched.

Thorne now rushed to the door of the hut and flung himself against it, but it remained immovable. Inside he heard the sound of clashing blades and the moaning of some one as if in mortal agony. A moment later the sounds of conflict ceased. Then he heard the inner bolt slide back and the door was flung open.

His sword ready for action, he was about to spring through the opening when to his amazement he saw the girl framed in the doorway, dagger in one hand and sword in the other, both dripping blood. Behind her, barely visible in the dim light of the interior, lay one dead and one dying foeman.

"Why—why, I thought—" stammered Thorne, lowering his point.

The girl smiled amusedly at his obvious bewilderment and stepped out of the hut.

"So you believed these clumsy Ma Gongi had cut me down,"

*Thorne whipped
the assassin's sword
from his hand.*

she said, carefully cleaning her weapons on the broad leaf of a shrub. "Really, Sheb, I gave you credit for a better memory. Have you forgotten the many times this blade of mine has bested yours? Or must I read you another lesson to convince you that Thaíne's wrist has not weakened nor her eye grown less sure?"

"So her name is Thaíne," mused Thorne. Aloud he said: "Your demonstration has been most convincing; yet I have not lost my ambition to improve my swordsmanship, and when the time is propitious I should be grateful for further instruction."

"No better time than now, as we have but had an opportunity to limber our sword arms. Still, I have you at a disadvantage, since you hold an inferior weapon."

"It is a handicap which a man should accord a girl," Thorne replied.

"Not one *this* girl requires," she answered. "Yet if you will have it so, then take the consequences."

She sheathed her dagger and extended her blade. Thorne engaged it with his captured weapon which, though more heavy and clumsy, was somewhat similar to a saber, a weapon with which he had once been on terms of close familiarity.

He instantly found that he had to deal with the swiftest and most dexterous fencer he had ever encountered, and time after time he barely saved himself from being touched, by his own uncanny quickness and intuitive perception of tricks which were wholly new to him.

"It seems your stay at the military school has improved your swordsmanship," smiled the girl, cutting, thrusting and parrying easily—almost effortlessly. "In the old days I would have touched you long ere this; yet you but prolong the inevitable."

"The inevitable," replied Thorne, "is sometimes perceptible only by deity. For instance, this"—beating sharply on her blade, then catching it on his with a rotary motion—"has often been known to end a conflict."

Wrenched from her grasp by his impetuous attack, her sword went spinning into the undergrowth.

Instead of taking her unexpected defeat badly, Thaíne actually beamed. "You have developed into a real swordsman, old comrade!" she exclaimed. "I am so glad I could almost kiss you."

"That," Thorne answered, recovering her weapon for her, "is a reward which should fire any man to supreme endeavor."

"It is evident that you have mastered courtly speech as well as fencing," she smiled. "And now, while Tezzu clears the camp of carrion, I will prepare your favorite dish for you." She called the brute. "Here, Tezzu," indicating the bodies. "Take these away."

THORNE marveled at its intelligence, when it instantly took up one of the corpses.

"A smart beast, that," he said.

"He is the most intelligent of all my father's dalfs," she replied. "That's why I always take him with me when I hunt."

While Tezzu methodically carried the bodies away and dropped them into the stream, Thaíne took her mace and chopped off the two thick hind legs of the beetle. From these, she lopped the thighs, and splitting the shells open, extracted two cylinders of white meat. With her dagger she sliced these into small, round steaks, piling them neatly on a broad leaf, then she gathered up the edges of the leaf and carried it into the hut.

Thorne followed her in. "May I help?" he asked.

"I'd like some water," she replied. "Fill the big jar, please." She indicated a large square jar artistically wrought from a metal that looked like gold, which stood beside the mud fireplace over which she now bent, placing faggots on a small heap of charcoal.

Thorne picked up the jar, and from its great weight was convinced that it really was gold. He also noticed that the figures on the sides were of exquisite workmanship. A golden jar in a hut of mud and logs was unusual. But then, he reflected, gold might be one of the baser metals on Mars.

When he returned with water from the stream, the interior of the hut had grown quite dark, but a shaft of moonlight lit up the lithe figure of the girl, kneeling before the fireplace. He went in and placed the jar beside her.

Having arranged the faggots to her satisfaction, she took a small bottle of sparkling powder from a pouch attached to her belt, and emptied a few grains on the wood. Then, dipping a cup into the jar, she poured part of its contents on the powder. Thorne was amazed to see the powder and the surrounding wood wherever the water had touched it burst into instant flame.

With the fire blazing merrily, the girl now dipped several cupfuls of water from the jar into a smaller container, dropped into it a handful of red berries taken from another jar, and set the mixture against the blaze. Then she arranged the small white steaks she had cut on a grill made from crossed metal rods.

With the point of her dagger Thaíne deftly turned the sputtering anuba steaks. Tezzu came in, his immense mouth full of faggots, which he dropped beside her. Then he touched her elbow with his nose. She turned and patted his head.

"Good boy," she said. "Bring more."

Obediently the beast turned and trotted out into the moonlight.

By the time the steaks were broiled, Tezzu had brought in a considerable quantity of wood. After removing her broiler, Thaíne threw more fuel on the coals. From the vessel into which she had put the red berries she now filled two cubical golden cups with a steaming pink liquid. Then, using a wide leaf for a platter, she piled it high with the grilled steaks, set two other bits of leaf on the floor for plates, and called:

"Come, Sheb. The banquet is ready for the victors."

Thorne sat opposite her and took the steaming cup from her hand. He had guessed that the beverage it contained was pulcho, and a sip confirmed this. Then came the realization that the time had arrived for him to simulate a liking for his "favorite dish."

"It is a banquet fit for a mighty conqueror," he said, reaching for one of the grilled steaks. He bit out a portion and instantly recognized the flavor. It was the same as that of the broiled food which had been served him for his first breakfast on Mars—the food which he had not been able to identify as either flesh or vegetable.

He had noted a swift, curious glance on the part of Thaíne, when she had seen him take up his steak in his hand. Now he saw that she used her dagger as a fork to convey a slice to her leaf-plate, and that she cut off a small piece which she raised to her mouth with her fingers.

Obviously he had made a *faux pas*, a Martian social error, which he sought to rectify by clumsily slicing a tidbit from his steak with the curved sword he had captured. But, in his confusion, he had no idea to what extent he had betrayed himself.

Suddenly the girl leaned forward, and looking him straight in the eyes, said: "Just who are you, masquerading as Sheb Takkor?"

For a moment Thorne was speechless with surprise. Then he replied:

"Ever since I met you I have been wanting to tell you, but the consideration of a duty restrained me."

"A duty?"

"Yes. To friends who have helped me."

For some time she was silent. Then: "And now, am I not—another friend who has helped you?"

"Decidedly!" he agreed. "Yet if I were to tell you, you would not believe me. I can scarcely believe, myself, that I am here."

"Don't be too sure that I would not believe. I *know*. You are—let me think—it is such an unusual name. You are Hahr Ree Thorne, and you were born on the planet, Dhu Gong, which you call Earth."

"How did you know that?" he gasped.

"Borgen told me what he was going to do," she replied. "I did not believe it possible, but I have been observing you closely, and now I know. You are so different. And you do not understand some of our Martian customs."

"For instance, my manner of eating?" he inquired. "Pray tell me where I erred."

"Having a dagger, you would have waited for me to take the first morsel," she said. "Lacking it, you would wait for me to hand you mine, then use it as I used it."

"I have been an inexcusable boor," he said contritely.

"Not at all," she replied. "One cannot be expected to know the customs of a new world without some instruction."

"It is generous of you to say that," he told her, taking the dagger which she now proffered him, "and I'm sure that I could not have found, on all this planet, a more charming and capable teacher."

Under the mellowing influence of the pulcho, and the sparkling beauty and pleasing personality of his young hostess, Thorne swiftly forgot his repugnance at the idea of eating beetle steaks, and actually enjoyed the well cooked flesh.

When both had eaten all they wanted, the remainder was tossed to the waiting dalf. Then the girl rose, closed and bolted the door, and selecting two large furs from a pile against the wall, gave one to the Earth-man and spread the other on the floor before the fire.

"It is time for sleep," she said, stretching her lithe young body and yawning. Then, without another word, she lay down on the fur and drawing its folds about her so that only her pretty, tousled head was visible, closed her eyes.

As he spread his fur and rolled himself therein, he again mentally compared the Newport beauty and the girl who slept calmly there beside him, and the comparison was overwhelmingly favorable to Thaíne.

Shortly thereafter, profound sleep came to him.

CHAPTER VII

CAPTURED BY SEL HAN

THORNE WAS AWAKENED by a gentle touch on his brow. He looked up into the smiling eyes of Thaíne.

"We must begin our journey if you would make Castle Takkor by midday," she said.

He threw off his fur and stood up. "I'm ready," he announced.

"First we will eat," she told him.

When they had finished their simple but satisfying meal, the girl began packing the utensils and furs together. Thorne helped her to make two large bundles of them, which Tezzu carried down to the boat.

"The Ma Gongi have discovered this camp," she told him, "and though we slew all the attacking party, others may know of it. So it must be abandoned forever."

"But where will you go?" asked Thorne.

"I have many better places hidden in the marsh," she replied. "This was merely an outpost."

They gathered up the weapons and went outside. Then the girl poured a small quantity of the sparkling fire-powder against the door jamb and dashed a cup of water over it. The logs instantly burst into flame, and when they reached the boat, Thorne, looking back, saw that a thick column of smoke was mounting skyward.

The morning sun was, by this time, halfway to the zenith. Most of the ice had melted in the stream, though there were a few sheets of it here and there in the more shady places. He noted, also, that many of the leaves where the sun had not yet penetrated were coated with hoar-frost that was rapidly melting into glistening beads of dew, and marveled at the hardiness of this vegetation, none of which seemed affected in the slightest degree by the extreme changes of heat and cold to which it was subjected.

When they had their cargo stowed, and had taken their places, the girl tossed the tow-rope to Tezzu and indicated with a wave of her hand the direction she wished to go. He plunged into the stream and set off rapidly, apparently not the least discommoded by the icy chill of the water.

They had only gone a short distance when Thaíne cried: "Look there! The boat of the Ma Gongi!"

THORNE looked in the direction she was pointing, and saw a flat boat, quite similar to the one they were in, drawn up on the bank.

"Stop, Tezzu," ordered the girl. Then: "Bring us that boat."

The beast obediently dropped the tow-rope, and swimming in to shore, dragged the boat into the water. Then, seizing its rope he towed it out to where they drifted. Save for a single bundle, wrapped in a silky covering, and a half dozen spade-shaped paddles, the boat was empty. Thorne was about to reach for the bundle when the girl checked him. "That is a bundle of their food," she said, "but it will do us no good, for it is prov-ender that we would not eat." Then she called to the dalf. "Sink it, Tezzu."

Instantly, the beast seized the side of the boat in his huge and powerful jaws. A single crunch crushed the heavy planking as if it had been an egg shell. Tezzu backed away, spitting out the slivers, and the boat filled and sank. Then he took up the tow-rope once more and proceeded on his way.

"I'm curious to know more about these Ma Gongi," Thorne said, "and this strange, forbidden food they eat. It seems odd to me that this round-bodied yellow race should inhabit the same planet as people like yours."

"They did not originate on this planet," replied the girl, "but, as their name indicates, on Ma Gong, the planet which now circles your world, but which once revolved in an orbit of its own, between your world and mine, around the great lord sun."

"That's interesting," said Thorne. "But I was never aware that our moon, as we call it, had ever been anything but a satellite. And how in the world were its inhabitants able to reach this planet?"

"It is a strange story, and a long one," she replied, "so I will only relate the main facts as told to me by my father, who taught me much of the history and traditions of our people. Long ages ago there existed on this world of Lu Gong, a mighty and ancient civilization. Although there were a number of racial groups, the Old Race, the white-skinned group to which I belong, was in control. War was abolished. Tremendous feats of scientific and engineering skill were accomplished. Mighty irrigation trenches were dug, many of them connecting the northern and the southern snow-caps, watering innumerable terraced gardens and forming water highways which connected the immense cities.

"In those days water was more plentiful than it is to-day, and there were seas which have since disappeared. We are now traversing the ancient bottom of one of the largest of them. Also, the atmosphere was more dense, and there were many plants and animals living under those conditions which have now vanished.

"Machines which flew in our atmosphere were even more common than they are to-day. But for thousands of years our scientists had been endeavoring to construct vehicles which could fly outside the atmosphere and travel from planet to planet in the system which is dominated by the great lord sun. At last they were successful.

"Their nearest planetary neighbor was Ma Gong, now your moon. Finally, after a number of disastrous attempts, they reached it. They found it inhabited principally by the round-bodied yellow race, members of which attacked us last night. This race, also, was a very ancient one, and well advanced in science. For years, its inventors had been working on interplanetary vehicles, and it seemed they were on the verge of success when our people came.

"A friendship sprang up between the two races, and they exchanged their scientific knowledge to their mutual advantage. Before another thousand years had elapsed, interplanetary travel was common, and there were regular commercial passenger and freight carriers between Ma Gong and Lu Gong. The entire solar system was explored. On your world, at that time, there were a few primitive savage men, who struggled for existence against terrible monsters of the land, sea and air. But there was no civilization, and there were no cities.

"For five thousand years this friendly intercourse endured between this planet and the one that is now your moon. Then war broke out. It seems that during that interval, many members of our white race had colonized the moon, and a number of the round-bodied yellow people had settled on Mars. For many generations there had been threats of trouble, principally because of the friction between these colonies and the native races, and the scientists of both planets had secretly developed terrible weapons of destruction.

"Our scientists had perfected a hot, energy-increasing red ray which, rotating in receding spirals, tore atoms of matter apart on contact, instantly making the heaviest metals less dense than air. Opposed to this was the cold, energy-decreasing, inter-rotating green ray of the Ma Gongi. Any substance touched by this ray would contract to less than one-hundredth of its normal size, with a corresponding increase in density.

"The toughest metals, under this ray, would become as brittle as glass and more dense than lead. But there is a limit to the contractile endurance of all matter, and once that limit is reached the atoms, which have been pushed in upon, themselves, explode and disintegrate. So you see the ultimate effect of their ray was much the same as that of ours—to destroy matter, that is, reduce it merely to a form of force.

"Tremendous interplanetary battles were fought with these rays, but they were not conclusive. And in the meantime new and even more destructive weapons were perfected. Our people built immensely powerful matter-condensing and projecting apparatus which could send lines of force clear across the solar system. With these they gathered great quantities of the meteoric matter of space into synthetic nebulae, condensed them into planetoids, and hurled them at Ma Gong, making great craters in the face of that planet, and doing incalculable damage.

"The Ma Gongi retaliated by building gigantic ray projectors, sending rays across the ether so powerful that they began to disintegrate our atmosphere. Our purpose was to batter them into submission; theirs to suffocate us.

"Our spies determined by making tests that for every ten cubic parsads of our atmosphere they sent out into space they were losing one parsad of their own, for the reason that the rays must pass through their atmosphere to reach ours, no interplanetary vehicles being large enough to carry this apparatus. Our scientists also found by checking the rate at which we were losing our atmosphere that we would be able with our meteoric projectiles to destroy their entire civilization before they could suffocate us.

"Their scientists must have realized this for some time, for one day Ma Gong began moving erratically in her orbit, making it difficult for us to aim our projectiles accurately. Our people, however, soon learned to allow for these perturbations, and began registering hits once more. Then it was learned that they were controlling the orbital motions of their planet with some new and powerful device and were endeavoring to hide behind your world, to use it as a shield against our projectiles. Evidently something went wrong with their apparatus or their plans, for Ma Gong, seized in the powerful grip of your planet's gravity pull, was dragged into her present orbit and became a satellite of your world.

"In the meantime, though we have been registering continuous hits on the enemy planet, our people found that their atmosphere was disintegrating so rapidly that they could no longer breathe without using special apparatus. They began dying by millions. Our leaders then resorted to the desperate expedient of concentrating one tremendous mass of matter, which they hoped would rend Ma Gong asunder. But after they had it condensed they were unable to project it. It was so heavy, in fact, that only by the employment of all the power stations on one side of the planet were they able to keep it from falling and crushing them. Presently, however, they were able to tear it apart and send the two fragments off at oblique angles. Still affected by the pull of our planet, they began circling it in orbits of their own where they quickly condensed into spheres. Thus were born our two moons.

"Despite the tremendous mortality among them, our fighting men and scientists stuck to their posts, hurling projectiles at the enemy to the last and eventually giving up their lives in the struggle. The interplanetary fleets were so evenly matched it is assumed that they destroyed each other. At any rate, they were never heard of more. Here and there, a few women and children survived suffocation by entering deep caves where the air was still dense enough to breathe, taking with them supplies of concentrated food, and food plants which could be grown underground.

"Because of the change in Ma Gong's orbit and the consequent disturbance in the solar system, the face of our planet was devastated by terrific electro-magnetic phenomena, earthquakes and volcanic eruptions. Meteoric matter easily penetrated our thin atmosphere, battering the face of our planet all out of semblance to its former contours—destroying and burying the ancient cities.

"But gradually the forces of nature found a new balance. The planet, little by little, released the gases which formed our new atmosphere, making life possible on the surface once more after many years had passed. The few animals and humans who managed to survive these terrors by living out their lives, generation after generation, deep in the bowels of the planet, formed the nucleus for our present fauna and the new civilization.

"All of our men of science together with their apparatus and their writings were lost. Their descendants were, at first, little better than savages. But gradually they endeavored to rebuild that which had been destroyed. Some of the old canals were cleaned of the debris of centuries, repaired, and put into use. New cities were built, some over the buried ruins of the old. And one by one the old inventions are being rediscovered.

"Our scientists have recently been able to determine that the surface atmosphere of Ma Gong is still insufficient to support human life. And to this day tremendous craters which dot the surface of that barren world bear witness to the devastation wrought by the projectiles of our ancestors. It is generally believed that she left her atmosphere disintegrators turned on until her own atmosphere had been dissipated, and all life destroyed."

"A remarkable chronicle," said Thorne, astounded at the scientific knowledge of this girl he had at first thought a savage. "It is borne out, in every respect, by the astronomical observations of my own people. And your father taught you all this?"

"Every bit," she replied. "Other than my father, the Takkors and Yirl Du, I have seen no one except a few Ma Gongi and the Little People."

"The Little People?"

"They are the friends and allies of my father and me. But the Ma Gongi eat them. That is why I told you the food you saw in their boat would be useless to us. It was the body of one of the Little People, cut up and wrapped in his skin."

"But who is your father, and why do you two live here in the marsh, instead of among your own kind?"

"My father's name is Miradon. Once he was Vil of Xancibar with a magnificent palace in Dukor and two hundred million

subjects to do his bidding. There was a revolt, led by a man
named Irintz Tel, who wished to establish a new order of government, abolish all property rights and make all men servants
of the state. In order to avoid the calamity of a civil war, my
father abdicated, and fled here with my mother, aided by Sheb
Takkor and the stout Jen of his Free Swordsmen, Yirl Du. These
two, alone, knew where we had gone. Here I was born, and here,
in giving me to the world, my brave little mother lost her life."

SHE PAUSED, tears glistening on her long lashes.

"And so," she continued, "the ashes of the mother I never
knew were scattered in this wild marsh, and here where I first
saw the light of day, my father reared me. We have been constantly hunted, constantly harassed by the minions of Irintz
Tel, and lately by the Ma Gongi as well. For three days, now,
my father has been absent, and the fear grows on me that he
has either been slain or captured."

"Then let me help you search for him."

"No, you must return to the castle for the ceremony, or if it
has been performed, to assume your rightful place. After that,
come if you will, and bring Yirl Du, but no other. He will know
how to find me."

For some time now they had been gliding tortuously through
a chain of shallow pools connected by narrow, half-hidden
channels which the beast that was towing them found so readily
that Thorne concluded he must be familiar with this route. Now
there suddenly came into view a broad lake which mirrored at
its far side an immense castle of odd and beautiful architectural design, the yellow, translucent masonry of which gleamed
like burnished gold in the sunshine. A short distance from it,
and also bordering the lake, rose the cylindrical, flat-roofed
buildings of a teeming city. A large number of gawrs were
swimming on the lake and many boats were moored at the
docks.

"This is as far as I dare take you," said Thaíne, after calling
to the beast to halt. "Yonder, beside Takkor City, lies Castle

Takkor. You can reach it by following the lake shore to the right."

Thorne rose and stretched his limbs, cramped from long sitting. Then he bent, took her hand and pressed it to his lips. She seemed startled. Evidently the gesture was unknown on Mars, for she asked:

"Why did you do that?"

"On my world it is a custom, a homage one pays to a lady at greeting or parting," he explained.

"What a queer custom," she exclaimed, touching her hand where his lips had pressed. "But I rather like it."

Thorne smiled. "Farewell, little comrade," he said. "Again I thank you for my life, for my entertainment, and most of all for the pleasure of having been with you. As soon as I have attended to my duties at Castle Takkor I will return with Yirl Du, and together we will search for your father."

"Deza go with you," she replied, "and keep you safe from harm. I will be waiting for you and be expecting you."

Resolutely he turned away from those glorious eyes, wistful now with parting, and stepped over the side of the boat. He stood there in the shallows watching until the little craft and its lovely passenger vanished around a bend in the narrow channel.

Keeping to the margin of the lake, sometimes in the water and sometimes on the shore, he eventually reached the docks without mishap. Most of its occupants were fishermen, and those whose duty it was to tend the gawrs. But he saw a number of warriors standing about, and was surprised to note that they wore the insigne of the Kamud. As he made his way toward the gate which led to the castle, two of them stopped him.

"**WHERE** are you going, fellow?" asked one. "And whom do you seek?"

"I go to Castle Takkor," replied. Thorne, "and whom I seek is my own affair."

"None of your insolence," growled the other soldier. "When you speak to us, you address the Kamud."

"When you speak to me, you address the Rad of Takkor," Thorne retorted. "Out of my way!"

"Sharp words call for sharper weapons," said one soldier. "Throw down your sword, or you die."

For answer, Thorne came on guard. Then both men attacked him simultaneously. While he could easily have bested either of them alone, he was sorely put to it to keep their two blades from reaching him, and fought desperately for his life. Presently, however, one soldier left his head unguarded. Instantly Thorne's sword sheared down through his brain.

For a moment Thorne's blade was held by that cloven skull, and he only escaped a deadly thrust from the other warrior by a swift leap to one side. Then, with a desperate jerk, he freed his weapon and easily disarmed his remaining foe, who instantly turned and fled, bawling lustily for help.

At this juncture a big man, resplendent in the purple head-cloak and gold trappings of a high officer of the Kamud, came down the steps that led from the castle gate, followed by a group of lesser officers and a file of soldiers.

"What's all this howling and bloodletting?" he roared. "Must I have brawling on the steps of my castle the first day of my arrival?"

Thorne looked up and recognized the beetling brows, flat nose and prognathous jaw of Sel Han, the man who had shamed him before his fellows at the military school, the man whom Dr. Morgan had requested him to kill, and against whom the Martian code of honor now forbade him to raise his weapon. Instantly he was surrounded by warriors.

"This impostor who murdered Tir Hanus claims to be the Rad of Takkor," cried the disarmed soldier, "yet we scattered his ashes this morning." Sel Han looked at Thorne, pretending not to recognize him.

"You have heard the words of this soldier," he said. "Do you still cling to your preposterous claim?"

"You scattered the ashes of Sheb Takkor the elder," said Thorne. "Not mine."

"We also scattered the ashes of Sheb Takkor the younger," replied Sel Han with a broad grin. "His two comrades, Lal Vak and Yirl Du, reported his death yesterday. He fell from his gawr, a distance that would crush him to pulp, therefore it is impossible that he could be alive to-day. Word was sent to Irintz Tel, and the Dixtar appointed me to come and administer the estates in the name of the Kamud. As we could not obtain the body of the unfortunate Rad, who fell in the marsh, we performed the ceremony by proxy, using ashes of the aromatic sebolis tree, as is the custom."

"Am I to understand from this that I am officially dead?" asked Thorne.

"You are to understand from this that the Rad of Takkor is dead. Also, the title has been abolished. Hereafter the estates will be strictly administered in accordance with the rules of the Kamud. As to who *you* are, that has not been established. You came to us wearing the stolen medal of the Takkor Zorad on your chest, armed with a sword of the Ma Gongi, and impersonating the dead Rad. When questioned, you slew a soldier of the Kamud. Under the circumstances, it is my duty to arrest you and send you to Dukor for trial."

"You make yourself absurd by claiming that I am dead," protested Thorne.

"Yield your sword, or you soon will be," promised Sel Han. "Seize him, men. If he resists, cut him down."

Seeing that resistance against such odds would be foolhardy, Thorne handed his sword to the nearest soldier. Another removed the medal that hung around his neck. Then he was led away by two warriors. They took him into the castle courtyard, where one of the large, bird-like flying machines he had previously seen stood ready to take off. He was hustled up a set of metal steps and into the body of the craft, where a score of prisoners, guarded by two armed warriors, were chained by metal collars to rings in the wall. A collar was snapped around his neck, and his captors went out.

A short time after, the ship, operated by a pilot he could not see, ran forward on its two metal legs, then took to the air with much lurching and a tremendous flapping of its huge wings.

With a sudden pang, Thorne remembered his promise to Thaíne, and wondered if he would be able to fulfill it.

CHAPTER VIII

IMPRISONED

THORNE'S JOURNEY, CHAINED in the hot, stuffy interior of the great metal bird-beast, was not a pleasant one. There were only two windows in the prisoners' compartment. These were closed, and too high to permit a view of the scenery below, though the passenger compartment ahead, where the soldiers rode, was well lighted and ventilated.

Like the other prisoners, the Earth-man was compelled by the lurching of the ship to keep a tight hold on his chain with both hands, and thus ease the sudden jerks on his metal collar that would otherwise have cut and choked him. Consequently he was thankful when, after more than an hour of riding, he sensed that the ship was settling, then felt the shock of its landing on its springy metal legs.

A moment later the door was flung open by one of the guards and the folding metal steps were dropped. The other guard opened the prisoners' collars, one by one, with a key he carried, and ordered them out the door. Thorne, the third to step out, saw that they were in a large walled inclosure in which were several hundred men, some lying on the ground or lolling against the walls, others pacing up and down, or conversing in small groups.

At the bottom of the ladder an officer waited, attended by two soldiers, one of whom carried a bundle of metal rings. The officer was scanning a paper which the first guard had handed him, evidently a list of the prisoners. As each man descended, he asked his name and checked the list. Then the soldier with the rings fastened one about the prisoner's neck and called the number engraved on the ring.

When it came Thorne's turn, the officer asked:

"Your name?"

"Sheb Takkor."

"What is your *real* name?" asked the officer.

"I have told you," Thorne replied.

The officer shrugged.

"It will be so entered," he said, "though the report on the list says you are an impostor. But that will be a matter for the judges."

He signed to the soldier with the rings, who clamped one about Thorne's neck and called the number. The soldier gave him a violent push that sent him stumbling into the yard, and the officer began questioning the next prisoner.

Recovering his balance, the Earth-man walked morosely to the center of the inclosure. A glance about him at the high walls patrolled by heavily armed warriors convinced him that escape from this place would be next to impossible. Beyond the walls on all sides he saw the upper stories of many cylindrical, flat-topped buildings. He concluded, from this, that he must be in the midst of a large and populous city.

Having completed his inspection of his surroundings, he found a place where he could sit and lean against the wall, and think. His case, it seemed, was well nigh hopeless. From what Lal Vak had told him of the ruthlessness of the Kamud, he could not expect any sentence short of death. And while, only a short time before, he had been ready to take his life with his own hand, he now wanted to live—wanted it most intensely.

The reason for this radical change in his outlook on life he found in the memory of a wistful little figure as last he had seen her, seated in a boat drawn by a hideous but faithful monster, bidding him farewell as he stood in the shallows. And with this clear picture came the recollection of Thaine's parting words:

"Deza go with you and keep you safe from harm. I will be waiting." He *must* contrive to live, somehow—to make his escape for her sake.

As he sat there, cudgeling his brain for some plan of action, Thorne noticed coming toward him a man with a huge chest and shoulders, long, ape-like arms, and abnormally short legs. With a start of surprise, he recognized the Jen of the Takkor Free Swordsmen.

"Yirl Du!" he exclaimed.

"I shield my eyes, my lord Sheb," said the Jen, raising his hand in salute, "and thank Deza that you still live. Lal Vak and I both thought you dead, and so reported at the castle."

"What evil twist of fortune brought you here?" Thorne asked.

"My arrest came so suddenly," replied Yirl Du, "that I am still bewildered by it. Perhaps it was because I am a poor dissembler, unable to conceal my dislike for the Kamud and its officers, particularly that overbearing Deputy Dixtar, Sel Han, whom Irintz Tel instantly thrust upon us once he was advised of your supposed death. Perhaps, also, spies have been at work. At any rate, I was sent here this morning charged with inciting the Free Swordsmen to revolt against the Kamud."

"And should they be able to prove such an absurd charge, what will be the penalty?"

"Death. In what form, I know not. The seven dread judges of the Kamud deal out death in many fiendish forms. They have tortures that will make a man beg for death over and over, day after day, and greet it as a precious boon when at last it is vouchsafed him. Their most merciful sentence is sudden death— the stroke of the sword, the thrust of a lance or the blow of a mace. Then there are the mines. A sentence to the mines is really a death sentence, for few men survive their rigors for many days, and all succumb in the end."

"And what sentence do you think they will pass on me?"

"Of what is my lord accused?"

"I slew a soldier of the Kamud who attacked me. Also I am

to be charged with impersonating myself, because I am officially dead. Furthermore, there is some suspicion attached to
me, which I cannot fathom, because I was wearing a sword of
the Ma Gongi."

Yirl Du groaned. "I can readily understand how the first two
charges came about," he said, "but there is damning evidence
in a sword of the Ma Gongi. You might have obtained an ac-
quittal on the first two counts, but I fear this latter spells your
doom." His kindly eyes suddenly grew moist, and there was a
strange, husky note in his voice as he continued "Deza grant
that I, Yirl Du, Jen of the Takkor Free Swordsmen, may never
live to see my Rad die in such dishonor."

"But why should a sword of the Ma Gongi constitute such
damning evidence?"

"It is believed," the Jen told him, "that the Ma Gongi are
plotting to overthrow the Old Race—to conquer all Mars. There
have been persistent rumors that one of their archaeologists
has unearthed the secret of the deadly green-ray used in warfare
by their ancestors, that he has turned the plans over to their
scientists, and that they are even now endeavoring to manufacture the projectors in some secret hiding place.

"Although we would not dare to publicly voice our suspicions,
there are also those among us who suspect Sel Han of plotting
with the Ma Gongi. He has so wormed himself into the good
graces of Irintz Tel that a word breathed against him would
bring instant disaster to almost any man. We have seen how
quickly he was granted the Raddek of Takkor, and this only
confirms the popular belief that Irintz Tel will give him almost
anything for which he asks.

"It is said, also, that the Dixtar intends to wed his daughter
Neva to this arch-plotter, and that through marriage with her
he will eventually succeed to the dictatorship of Xancibar. To
most, Irintz Tel is a man of iron, but under the influence of the
blandishments of his fair daughter and the uncanny persuasive-
ness of Sel Han, he appears to be fashioned of the softest clay."

"It is obvious that this Sel Han is indeed a menace to all mankind," said Thorne. "If I had only had the strength to use my sword that day I faced him! It was my one big chance to do something really worth while."

"I have a further suspicion," went on Yirl Du, "born when you told me of the disappearance of Thaíne's father. Miradon Vil, a prisoner, would be of inestimable value to Sel Han in his plans for conquest. With the Vil in his power, he could hold the royalists as well as the Kamud in the hollow of his hand. A colony of the Ma Gongi inhabits a part of the marsh not far from Miradon's hiding place. And it may well be that they, at the instigation of their ally, Sel Han, have captured the Vil and are holding him in some secret hiding place until the arch-traitor shall have use for him."

Thorne was about to reply when a shrill whistle sounded.

"**COME**," said Yirl Du. "That was the food signal, and the last ten men in line always go hungry."

They both sprang forward to where a long line of prisoners was forming before a table containing some small cakes and cubical cups of pulcho, presided over by four orderlies who had already begun to hand a cup and cake to each man, under the watchful eyes of a half dozen soldiers with drawn swords. Swift as they were in taking their places, Thorne saw, on looking back, that there were exactly ten men behind him. He was not particularly hungry, but the long ride had made him very thirsty, and he thought of that cup of pulcho with pleasant anticipation.

Shuffling forward with the others, and thirstily watching the food and drink being passed out to the men ahead, he was surprised to feel a powerful hand clapped on his shoulder. Before he could offer the slightest resistance, he was spun around, and found himself walking behind the man who had previously been just behind him. The guards evidently had not noticed the trick, for they gave no sign. And Yirl Du, walking ahead, was totally unaware of it.

For a moment Thorne was too astounded to do anything at

all. Then, in a sudden flare of anger, he seized the brawny arm of the man who had supplanted him and swung him around. He had a swift glimpse of a glaring, bestial face, crisscrossed by a frightful pattern of livid scars. Then he drove a smashing right hook to the point of the jaw that sent the bully reeling backward to the ground.

In a moment the fellow began to recover from the effect of the blow, and sat up looking about him and holding his jaw, a dazed expression on his ugly face, as if he could not quite remember what had happened. Suddenly spying Thorne, recollection came to him. He shook his bullet head, then lurched to his feet, and with a bellow like that of an enraged bull, charged.

Thorne turned at the sound, and prepared to meet the shock of the attack. With both arms outstretched, the bully attempted to seize him, but a blow in the solar plexus followed by a swift uppercut felled him to the ground once more, where he lay writhing and gasping out lurid curses.

Instantly, Yirl Du, who had drained his pulcho cup and was munching his cake, tossed the food aside and sprang forward.

"Let me handle this beast, my lord," he said. "He is Sur Det, the most dreaded duelist and assassin in all Xancibar. And the guards may bring out swords."

By this time most of the prisoners who, attracted by the roar of Sur Det, had seen the encounter, were crowding around, talking excitedly while they munched and drank.

"Swords!" some one shouted. "Bring swords!" And the cry was taken up by the entire multitude.

A group of guards came shouldering through the crowd, making way for a handsome, blond haired young fellow who wore the purple cloak of an officer of the Kamud.

"What's this, Sur Det?" he asked. "Fighting again?"

The bully scrambled to his feet and saluted.

"That fellow," he said, glaring at Thorne, "has twice assaulted me. I ask settlement by swords, which is my right according to the prison rules."

The officer turned to Thorne. "What say you?" he asked. "Do you, also, desire settlement by swords?"

"I do," the Earth-man replied, in spite of Yirl Du's frantic signals to him to answer in the negative.

"Obviously you are a stranger in Dukor, and have not heard of the prowess of Sur Det," said the officer. "But on your own head be your decision. Give them swords, soldiers, and let a circle be formed."

CHAPTER IX

A MARTIAN CITY

AS HE STOOD, sword in hand, before his scar-faced opponent, Thorne was hooted by the multitude. A few who had heard of his supposed cowardice in his duel with Sel Han, quickly spread the word by taunting him with it. An overwhelming majority of both guards and prisoners seemed convinced that this would be an easy victory for Sur Det, and were shouting encouragement to their favorite.

"Don't puncture him too quickly, Sur Det," called one. "Give us a good exhibition."

"Slice him neatly," shouted another. "Let us see how good a meat-cutter you are."

They saluted. Then Sur Det, instead of engaging Thorne's extended blade as was the custom, avoided it and attacked with a swift, vicious lunge. So unexpected was this cowardly thrust that the Earth-man had no opportunity to parry, and was barely able to save his life by side-stepping the point.

But Sur Det, by making this desperate, unethical try for an easy victory, had left himself completely uncovered with his antagonist's blade in line with his breast. Thorne now had but to extend his point, and the duel would be over. He started the lunge, but checked the impulse just as his point touched that hairy chest, and instead of sending the blade home, with a deft motion of his wrist cut the Martian symbol for the digraph "sh," a perpendicular line with a short hook to the right at the bottom.

A murmur of surprise went up from the crowd at this. For they knew he had his enemy at his mercy, and for some unknown reason had spared him. Both men recovered, and for some time the spectators were unable to understand what the Earth-man was about. But when, after a bewildering swirl of blades so swift that the eye could scarcely follow, Thorne found a second opening, and instead of piercing the heart of his antagonist, slashed two horizontal lines beside the first character, the Martian symbol for "e," some of them began to understand what he was about, and to shout uproariously.

"He's writing his name on the killer!" cried one in amazement.

"Write him a love letter!" yelled another.

"Draw us a picture!" howled a third.

When Thorne marked his chest for the second time without inflicting death, Sur Det began to realize that this strange young swordsman from Takkor, whom he had expected to slay so easily, was only playing with him—that it lay in his power to take his life at any time. With that realization, a sickly pallor overspread his scarred features, and he went berserk with fear.

Cool, suave, smiling, Thorne met the desperate attack that followed, contenting himself with merely parrying and sidestepping until he felt his opponent's wrist began to weaken. Then with a graceful, easy lunge, he carved the last symbol of his Martian name on that barrel chest, the "b."

At this, the crowd roared its applause, but Thorne had not yet finished. For now, with a complete change of tactics, he suddenly beat down his opponent's blade with a sharp blow close to the guard—then, before the confused Sur Det could recover his grip, caught it, bound it with his own blade, and with a sudden twirling wrench, sent it flashing away over the heads of the spectators.

For a moment the bewildered killer stood looking in blank amazement at the blade, which now menaced his defenseless chest. Then, with a shriek of terror, he turned and fled. Thorne, to complete his chastisement, followed closely at his heels, spanking him soundly with the flat of his sword while the multitude laughed and hooted, until the creature fell down and begged for mercy.

But now, not a voice in that fickle crowd was raised in sympathy for the fallen champion.

"Puncture the boastful bladder and let out the wind," a spectator shouted.

"Carve your name on his craven heart," cried another.

Satisfied that the killer had been sufficiently humbled, Thorne left him groveling and whining in the dust, and returning to where the young officer stood, saluted.

"I am obliged to you for this interesting diversion," he said, tendering the sword.

"The obligation is entirely ours," replied the officer, taking the weapon. "By the great name of Deza, I have never seen such marvelous sword-work, nor, I am convinced, has any one in all Xancibar. We have all been royally entertained. And now, to the victor goes the reward. Ho, orderly!"

At this a man came up, bearing a steaming jar of pulcho, a cup and a great platter heaped with cakes.

"What's this?" asked Thorne in surprise.

"The prize," smiled the officer, taking the jar from the orderly and filling a cup which he handed to the Earth-man. "I regret that so distinguished a swordsman and so gallant a gentleman may not be more suitably rewarded. But this, after all, is a prison, and only the judges, or the Dixtar himself, and not Kov Lutas, Jen of the Prison Guard, may say what shall be done with the prisoners."

"I drink to your long life, Kov Lutas," smiled Thorne, draining his cup. Then he turned to the orderly. "Distribute the cakes and the rest of the pulcho to the ten who were not served," he said, "including my defeated opponent."

AT THIS added evidence of the generosity of their new champion, the multitude shouted its approbation, while prisoners and guards alike began crowding around him.

More than a half hour elapsed before Thorne was able to get away from his numerous admirers and sit alone once more with Yirl Du.

"That was a marvelous fight, my lord," said the Jen, when they had seated themselves in the shadow of the wall. "It will surely remove the stigma attached to your name by that unfortunate incident at the military school. The great pity of it is that it comes inside prison walls, and at a time when death by order of the Kamud is almost certain to be your lot."

"It will be certain enough if Sel Han has his way," said Thorne.

"We have many good reasons to kill that flat-nosed traitor," replied Yirl Du, "and there are two which I have not related to you. One is, that among the men who attacked us in the air as we flew to Castle Takkor, I recognized one of his henchmen. So it was he who sent those assassins to slay us."

"What is the other?" asked Thorne.

"I have hesitated to tell you that one, as I would not give you needless pain on what may well be your last day of life, yet duty bids me reveal it. Know, then, that Sheb Takkor the elder did not die a natural death, but was murdered. I was making my last round of the castle before retiring, to see if all was well, when I noticed him seated before the fireplace in his great swinging chair, hunched over in a most unnatural position. Alarmed, I called to him, but he made no response. I ran to his side, and saw that he was dead. A dagger had been driven into his back up to the hilt."

"And you think it was Sel Han who struck the blow?"

"More likely one of his hired assassins. Yet he may have had the hardihood to risk his own neck in the venture. He, and no one else, had much to gain by the death of our beloved Rad. And he alone profited by it."

"Perhaps there was an enemy with a grudge."

"That is not likely. The Rad never left Takkor except to hunt in the marshes or the desert, or to secretly do what he could for our deposed sovereign and his daughter. So he had no opportunity to make enemies in other than his own raddek. And I'll swear that there was not a man, woman or child among his people who did not love and revere him. Moreover, the dagger was of foreign make and delicate workmanship, not the plain sturdy kind our Takkor folk are wont to carry. So impressed was I with this fact that I hid it in a secret place in the castle, hoping that it might some day afford us proof of the identity of the assassin."

At this juncture two guards with drawn swords in their hands who had been walking through the inclosure as if searching for some one, stopped before Thorne.

"Are you he who calls himself Sheb Takkor?" asked one.

"I am," Thorne replied.

"The Dixtar has sent for you. Come with us."

Thorne stood up, but as he did so Yirl Du flung himself between the Earth-man and the guards.

"Wait! Don't take him! Take me! I am Sheb Takkor!"

One of the guards laughed contemptuously. "Out of the way, O great oaf," he said, raising his sword threateningly, "ere I cut you down. My comrade and I sat on the wall and saw this man defeat Sur Det, the killer. Do you think you could pass for him? Moreover, have we not eyes to read the numbers on your collars?"

Yirl Du bowed his great shaggy head, then turned to Thorne. "I fear it is the end, my lord," he groaned. "Few prisoners who face Irintz Tel live afterward." He saluted. "Farewell, my lord. Deza grant you life, yet if that be not His will, a brave death."

Thorne returned the salute. "Farewell, my faithful friend," he answered. Then, to the guards: "I am ready."

As he was marched across the inclosure Thorne saw that all eyes were upon him. The glances of all the prisoners were friendly and sympathetic, with one exception. That exception was Sur Det, the killer, who, abandoned by his former admirers, sulked by himself in a corner. As he passed, Thorne saw on his scarred, bestial face a look of intense, malignant hatred.

The Earth-man was led through a gate into what was obviously one of the streets of a large city. It was paved with a tough, resilient material of a reddish-brown color, and was thronged with people and strange vehicles of many descriptions. There was one thing, however, which the vehicles all had in common. They did not travel on wheels, but ran about on multiple sets of jointed metal legs shod with balls of the resilient reddish-brown substance. The smallest of these odd vehicles had only two pairs of legs, but some of the larger ones had so many that they reminded him of gigantic caterpillars, moving smoothly and swiftly along the thoroughfare.

In a moment an open vehicle with twelve pairs of legs drew up before the gate and stopped. There were three saddle-shaped seats with high backs, one in front and two side by side in the rear. A canopy overhead shaded the passengers. The front seat was occupied by a driver in military uniform. In one of the rear seats sat Kov Lutas, Jen of the Prison Guards. He smiled down at Thorne.

"The Dixtar has commanded that I bring you before him," he said. "Give me your word that you will not attempt to escape while in my custody, and I will spare you the ignominy of chains."

The Earth-man thought for a moment. If he were to go in chains there would certainly be no opportunity for escape. If he gave his word, once out of the custody of Kov Lutas, he could, with honor, make the attempt.

"I give my word that I will not try to escape while in your custody," he promised.

The Jen ordered the guards to remove Thorne's prison collar, and when this was done, dismissed them with a wave of his hand.

"Get in," he invited.

Thorne climbed aboard and into the vacant saddle. The driver, who sat holding two levers that projected up through the floor at either side of his saddle, now slowly moved these forward. At this, the vehicle started smoothly and silently, save for the soft thudding of its padded feet on the resilient pavement, and was soon moving through the traffic at a considerable speed.

Thorne saw that when the driver wished to turn to the right he advanced the left lever and drew back the right, and that he reversed the process when he desired to turn to the left. To increase the speed, he pushed both levers forward, and to decrease it drew them backward. When they were drawn back to a certain point, the vehicle came to a full stop.

HAVING satisfied his curiosity regarding the vehicle, Thorne turned his attention to the strange sights about him.

Noting the Earth-man's keen interest in his surroundings, Kov Eutas said: "Apparently this is your first visit to Dukor. Perhaps you would like to have me explain some of the sights of the city."

"I should be grateful," Thorne replied.

"Dukor," said Kov Lutas, "is divided into four equal quarters by the intersecting triple canals, Zeelan and Corvid. We are now in the northwest quarter of the city, and about to cross the Zeelan Canal into the northeast quarter, where the palace which formerly belonged to the Vil, but is now occupied by the Dixtar, is located."

"It must be a tremendous city," said Thorne, impressed by the considerable distance they had already traveled.

"There are approximately five million people residing in each quarter," replied Kov Lutas, "or twenty million in all. Also, we have each day about ten million transients who come on commercial or state business, or simply to visit and to see the sights. Dukor is a fair-sized city as cities go. Of course it does not seem large in comparison with Raliad, capital city of Kalsivar, which commands the intersections of four great triple canals, for Raliad is said to have a population of a hundred million."

While he was speaking they came to the approach of a tremendous arched bridge, so long they could not see the farther end of it. In a moment they were out upon it, and Thorne was looking down upon the surface of the first of the three canals which collectively bore the name of Zeelan because they occupied the same huge trench. This canal swarmed with craft of many sizes and shapes, a large number of which were discharging freight into the dock warehouses which lined its banks.

The huge central canal at the bottom of the great trench, which caught the drainage from the two upper irrigating canals, was lined with bathers of all ages who wore no clothing whatever.

The canal passed, they entered a section of the city quite similar to the one they had just left. After a drive of about half an hour in this section, they drew up before an immense and magnificent edifice, not quite so large as some of the huge commercial buildings, but much more impressive because of its superior architectural beauty.

"The Palace," said Kov Lutas. "From this point we walk."

After getting down from the vehicle, they mounted a broad flight of steps which led to the vast and ornate portico. Here they were halted and questioned by guards, who readily admitted them when shown the order of the Dixtar which Kov Lutas carried. Then, after crossing an immense busy foyer and traversing a long hallway, they came before a large circular doorway, closed by two purple curtains in which was embroidered with gold thread, the coat of arms of the Dixtar of Xancibar. Here an officer halted them and examined the order carried by Kov Lutas.

"The Dixtar is expecting you," he said. Then he beckoned to one of the guards. "Announce Kov Lutas, Jen of the Guards of Prison Number 67," he said, "and a prisoner."

CHAPTER X

A DANGEROUS ASSIGNMENT

WHEN THE CURTAIN was drawn aside, Thorne followed Kov Lutas through the doorway, and found himself in the dread presence of Irintz Tel, founder of the Kamud and Dixtar of Xancibar.

The Dixtar, his hands clasped behind him, was pacing to and fro on a plush-padded dais that fronted a luxuriously cushioned throne, which hung on four heavy golden chains depending from the ceiling. He was a small man, sparsely built and quite bald. Thin-lipped, sharp-nosed and beady-eyed, his face bore the unmistakable stamp of the zealot and reformer.

With his brows contracted in an angry frown, Irintz Tel paced up and down for some time without taking the slightest notice of Kov Lutas and his prisoner, who stood there waiting his pleasure. And Thorne observed that the two guards who stood stiffly erect at either side of the dais, wore fearful looks as if each were afraid that in this ugly mood the wrath of the Dixtar might be vented on him.

After a lapse of some minutes, Irintz Tel paused midway in his pacing and, swinging on his heel, faced Kov Lutas.

"Well?" he demanded, in a high-pitched, squeaky voice.

Kov Lutas raised both hands in salute, holding them before his face. "I shield my eyes in the glory of your presence, O mighty Dixtar of Xancibar and Commander of the Kamud," he said.

Thorne was astounded at this, for he had been told that under the Kamud all salutations of this sort had been abolished.

The Earth-man suddenly noticed that Irintz Tel was looking sharply at him, evidently expecting him to follow the example of the Jen, but a wave of rebellion at such abject homage to this pompous little rat-faced tyrant surged over him, and he kept his hands down.

"Who is this ill-mannered lout you have brought into our presence, Kov Lutas?" demanded the Dixtar.

"He is Sheb Takkor, whom I bring in accordance with the Dixtar's command," replied Kov Lutas.

"His manners are execrable," said Irintz Tel, "but they can be mended, and we hear that he is a good swordsman. It may be that we will find employment for him." He turned at this, and for a time resumed his angry pacing. Then he snapped: "We are both blessed and cursed with a beautiful daughter, as you are no doubt aware."

"I have heard of the great beauty of your excellency's daughter," replied Kov Lutas, cautiously.

"It is a fatal beauty that corrupts our most loyal followers and makes traitors of our stanchest patriots," continued Irintz Tel. "Because of it we have lost many stout fellows. And today we are again constrained to part with two more of our best swordsmen. They were her guardsmen, but they chose to let their hearts rule their heads. For such a malady, where our daughter is concerned, we have a most effective form of surgery."

"What is that, excellency?"

"In order that the heart may no longer rule the head, we separate them. A bit drastic, we will admit, but it never fails to cure. And now we come to the business at hand. We sent for you and this prisoner because we must replace the two excellent swordsmen who will shortly bid farewell to this world. Our daughter, as you know, must be well guarded.

"We will first take the case of the prisoner, here. Word came to us to-day of his defeat of Sur Det, the killer, so we decided

Thorne struck, though he knew it would spell his doom.

to personally examine into the charges against him. He is accused, we find, of impersonating the dead Rad of Takkor, of wearing a sword of the Ma Gongi, and of slaying a soldier of the Kamud, and as evidence there have come to us this Takkor family medal," lifting it from a small taboret beside the throne, "and this sword which he was alleged to have been wearing when captured. What say you to these charges, prisoner?"

"I could not impersonate the Rad of Takkor without impersonating myself," replied Thorne. "I was reported dead because my crippled gawr fell with me after I was attacked. But we fell into a small lake. After freeing myself from the safety chains and the weight of my weapons, I swam ashore. There I was attacked by a party of Ma Gongi, and after wresting the sword from one of them, beat off the others."

"We can well believe that, after the report we received of your exploit at the prison to-day. But what of this other charge? Why did you slay one of our soldiers?"

"Because he attacked me on my own doorstep," replied Thorne. "In answer to that charge I plead self-defense."

His hands behind his back, the Dixtar paced the dais for some time, chin on chest. Then he suddenly turned and looked at Thorne.

"We hereby declare you innocent and discharged of all liability on all three counts," he said brusquely. "And as a recompense for the indignities which you have suffered, we raise you to the rank of Jen and appoint you night guard to our daughter Neva."

He turned to the Jen of the Prison Guards.

"You also, my worthy Kov Lutas, we have decided to honor, in view of your exceptional skill with a sword and your record of faithful service at the prison. You, henceforth, will guard our daughter by day."

The face of Kov Lutas went as suddenly pale as if a sentence of death had been passed on him.

DESPITE Kov Lutas's apparent dismay, he managed to retain control of his features. "I am deeply grateful that our Dixtar has chosen to distinguish me by this honor," he said.

Irintz Tel beckoned Thorne to him and handed him the medal. "Take back this badge of your ancient race and wear it with honor," he said. "We regret that we cannot return your title as well, but under the present social order there are no more rads. Nor can we make you our deputy, for upon hearing of your supposed death we immediately dispatched Sel Han to Takkor to represent us, as he knows our wishes and is high in our councils."

"The Dixtar is most generous," murmured Thorne.

Irintz Tel now called to the officer at the door.

"Ho, Dir Hazef, conduct these two to the officers' quarters and see that they are suitably arrayed as palace Jens. On the way you will permit them to witness the fate which overtakes those who are unfaithful to their trust, and show them the Hall of Heads. Let a sword and dagger decked with the Takkor

serpent be brought from the armory for the one who is weaponless, as he is entitled to carry them."

The two men saluted, and as they were led away the Dixtar
stood with folded arms and chin on chest, looking after them.
Dir Hazef conducted them through a number of corridors to
a small balcony which overlooked one of the inner courts. In
the center of the court stood an officer. Dir Hazef signaled to
him, and he, in turn, signaled to some one in a near-by doorway.
A moment later there emerged from that doorway two soldiers,
driving before them two young officers with their hands bound
behind them. Following the soldiers came a tall, somber looking
fellow bearing a long, straight bladed sword and accompanied
by a boy who carried a basket.

The two prisoners were forced to kneel in the center of the
courtyard. Then the tall man stepped behind them. Once, twice,
his long blade flashed in the sunlight, and with each expert
blow a head rolled to the pavement, to be garnered by the boy
with the basket.

"Those two," said Dir Hazef, "were the guards of Neva,
daughter of the Dixtar. They had the good taste but the bad
judgment to fall in love with her and contend for her favors."
He turned, and walking to a door behind them, opened it with
a key taken from his belt. "Enter," he said.

Thorne stepped through the doorway, followed by Kov Lutas
and their conductor.

"This," said Dir Hazef, "is the Hall of Heads, a monument
to the Dixtar's justice and a warning to those who have it in
their hearts to betray him."

They were in a long, narrow room, lined with shelves on both
sides clear to the high ceiling. On the shelves stood row after
row of crystal jars. Each jar was filled with a clear liquid, and
in the liquid floated a severed human head. There were thousands of heads of young men and old; even heads of women
and children.

Thorne tore his eyes away from the ghastly exhibit with a

shudder, and turning, saw that Kov Lutas had already preceded him through the doorway. The look of horror on the handsome features of the young prison Jen told Thorne that his own feelings were duplicated by his comrade.

AFTER locking the door and leading them down another corridor, Dir Hazef conducted them through a room where a number of officers sat in swinging chairs, sipping pulcho and conversing, or playing gapun, a game of chance which consisted of rolling little engraved pellets of gold or silver at numbered holes in a board, the highest number winning all the pellets risked. Although he had never before seen Martian money, Thorne recognized at once from the use to which they were being put that these pellets must be the medium of exchange.

A number of apartments opened into this officers' club room, and into one of these Dir Hazef led them.

"I'll leave you here to bathe and change," he said. "Vorz, your orderly, will bring your new uniforms and weapons. You, Kov Lutas, are to go on duty at once, and Sheb Takkor will relieve you at the time of the evening meal."

The apartment was plainly but comfortably furnished with a swinging bed and a swinging chair for each man, a wardrobe and an arms rack. In one corner was a metal box about eight feet in height, one side of which stood open. It was lined throughout with a gray metal resembling block tin, and this lining was perforated with many holes. Beside it was a rack on which hung a number of wisps of what looked like dry moss.

As soon as Dir Hazef was gone, Kov Lutas began removing his clothing and weapons.

"I'll bathe now, if you don't mind," he said, "as I must go on duty first."

"Of course," replied Thorne. He was puzzled as to where or how the young officer was going to bathe, as he saw no sign of a tub or bathroom.

His curiosity was soon satisfied, for Kov Lutas, after kicking off his boots, stepped into the square metal box in the corner and drew the side shut. Immediately there was the unmistakable sound of rushing water, accompanied by much gurgling, blowing and gasping. A few moments later the side swung open, and the officer emerged, dripping and rubbing the water from his eyes. Then he reached for a bunch of the moss-like material and began briskly rubbing himself.

Thorne, who had meanwhile removed his clothing, now entered the box and drew the side shut. Then he looked around for a lever with which to turn on the water, but saw nothing of the sort. However, as he moved about, he accidentally trod on a round plate in the center of the metal floor. Instantly he was surrounded by a swirl of warm, scented water which came up to his chin. The water soon receded as suddenly as it had risen, and several jets opened overhead, deluging him with a fragrant creamy lather. His eyes, which he had not closed quickly enough, smarted painfully.

After about a minute of this there was a click as of some automatic mechanism, the jets ceased to spray, and the swirling water rose once more. While it rinsed off the lather this gradually grew cooler until it reached an almost icy temperature. Another click, and it drained away automatically. He opened the side, sputtering and gasping, and blindly reached for a bundle of drying material. As soon as he had the water out of his eyes he saw that an orderly had arrived with the new uniforms, and was helping Kov Lutas into his.

THORNE rubbed himself until his skin glowed warmly. Vorz, the orderly, then assisted him to don his new uniform and buckle on his weapons. His new sword and dagger hilts were fashioned like those he had found himself wearing on his first advent on Mars, but were of gold powdered with jewels instead of plain brass. And the eyes of the serpents were large rubies.

The orderly, after bustling in with a three-legged stand on which were a pot of pulcho and two cups; hurried out. Kov

Lutas filled the cups, and handing one to Thorne raised the other.

"May we die like brave soldiers," he said, tossing off his drink.

Thorne joined him, then said:

"It is a strange toast. Why do you speak of death?"

"Because it is so near," replied Kov Lutas. "To be appointed as guards to the Dixtar's daughter is equivalent to a death sentence."

"I don't see why," Thorne replied. "Certainly every man who guards her isn't going to be so foolish as to lose his head over her."

"To 'lose his head' is indeed an apt expression," said Kov Lutas. "More than a hundred have already lost their heads, even as those two we saw this afternoon. For my part, I am not entertaining any false hopes. Neva is said to be a heartless flirt, bent on conquest. Her father desires her to marry Sel Han, but she will not have him. And it is said that she flirts with every eligible male who crosses her path, just to spite them both. She is reputed to be irresistible, and her guards, of course, can't run away from her. Nor dare they affect to despise her advances, for her anger is fully as terrible as that of her father."

At this juncture an officer entered and saluted.

"Which of you is Kov Lutas?" he asked.

"I am," replied the young Jen, returning his salute.

"If you are ready you will come with me to relieve the temporary guard of the Dixtar's daughter," he said.

"I am ready," Kov Lutas told him. "Let us go."

They went out, and Thorne, after pouring himself another cup of pulcho, sat down to reflect on the situation which now confronted him. But he had scarcely settled in his swinging chair when Vorz came to the door and announced:

"Salute the Deputy Dixtar."

Thorne sprang to his feet and raised his hand smartly in salute. Then he let it fall to his side in utter astonishment at sight of the individual who had entered the room, for he recognized the flat-nosed, ruddy features of Sel Han, his arch enemy.

"Greetings, Sheb Takkor Jen," said the Deputy Dixtar with a grin. "You seem surprised at seeing me."

"And to you, greetings, Sel Han," replied Thorne coolly. "To what strange humor of the Deputy Dixtar do I owe the—er— honor of this unexpected call?"

Without replying, Sel Han walked to the taboret and helped himself to a cup of pulcho. Then he seated himself in Kov Lutas's swinging chair. For a time he sat there, sipping his drink in silence, while Thorne stood stiffly erect, watching. Suddenly he spoke, and to Thorne's surprise, used English.

"Shut the door," he said.

Thorne closed the door and returned to his chair.

SEL HAN nodded knowingly. "I thought so," he said. "Understands English, all right."

"Perhaps when you have finished talking to yourself, you will explain your business," said Thorne with frigid politeness.

"Don't get stormy with me, wise guy," said Sel Han. "I came here to make you a proposition. If you don't like it, all right. I can put you on the spot. If you are a right guy and want to ride along I can make a big shot out of you. What do you say, Harry Thorne?"

"I say you're wasting your time, Frank Boyd," replied Thorne.

"So you are in the know, eh? That's what I figured. I got wise they were going to proposition you to come here before I broke with Doc Morgan. And I got hep to who you was to-day when I heard about your little run in with old scarface, Sur Det. Pretty handy with the sword, ain't you? It's the talk of the burg. There wasn't another guy in this country except me that could have made a monkey out of that old bozo like you did. He had 'em all bluffed out.

"He was my teacher when I came here. As soon as I landed

I saw I'd need to be handy with a sword if I wanted to chisel my way along, so I picked the best teacher I could find. Being that I'm younger and quicker, and have a longer reach, I finally got so I could beat him. I went right out and started to cut my way to the top. And I ain't very far from there right now."

"Did you come here to entertain me with this modest little autobiographical sketch?" asked Thorne politely.

"No. I came here, in the first place, to find out just how much you was in the know. And in the second place, to give you a break if you are a right guy and want to shoot square with me. I can cut you in on something bigger than you got any idea of."

"Such as what?" asked Thorne, pretending to be interested.

"I'd be talking out of my turn if I told you that," said Sel Han. "First, you do the things I want you to do. Then I'll make it right with you, and in a big way."

"I don't think we can talk business, Mr. Boyd," said Thorne, rising.

"Don't be a damn fool. You are as good as on the spot right now, and can't get it through your thick head. Get this. You're takin' orders; I'm givin' 'em. Now here's all I want you to do. This dame Neva has been too up-stage with me. I don't like it. Her old man wants her to hook up with me and she won't even give me a kind word. On top of that, to spite the both of us, she flirts with every Tom, Dick and Harry she meets. She'll probably flirt with you. If you don't fall she'll send you to the mines, and if you do her old man will cut off your head. Far as I'm concerned you can fall or not as you damn please. You'll only be one out of a couple hundred or so.

"But what I'm up against is the fact that she won't even talk to me. Calls the guard and has me thrown out every time I drop in to see her. Now here's all I want you to do. I'm going to drop in to see her to-night before I fly to Takkor. She'll probably want you to throw me out. If she does, pay no attention, or tell her you can't in honor lay a hand on me, because I won that duel from you at the military school. That will let you out.

"And all I need is a few minutes to talk to that dame. I think I can sell her the idea that I'm the big moment she's been waiting for. She's probably like most other skirts—wants a big he-man to come and sweep her off her pins. And me, I'm just the guy that can do it."

At this moment the door opened and an orderly entered with Thorne's evening meal. As he arranged the dishes on the taboret he noticed Sel Han.

"May I get the Deputy Dixtar something to eat?" he asked.

"No, I'm dining with the Dixtar," replied Sel Han, rising. He swung on Thorne. "Don't forget what I told you to do," he said. "I'm not asking you; I'm telling you, and you'd better come through."

Without replying or looking up, Thorne drew his jeweled dagger and turned his attention to the food on the taboret which the orderly had set before him. A moment later he heard Sel Han stamp out of the room.

Soon after he finished his meal, an officer came in and saluted.

"It is time for you to relieve Kov Lutas in the apartments of the Dixtar's daughter," he said.

CHAPTER XI

NEVA

WHEN THORNE, ESCORTED by the palace officer, reached the apartments of Neva, the sun had set, and the luxuriously furnished rooms were lighted by the soft amber radiance of the half-hooded baridium globes which hung from the ceiling on golden chains. The size and magnificence of the suite reserved for the daughter of this apostle of simplicity and champion of the common people who would make all citizens equal, was astounding.

The chamber in which he found himself opened onto a broad terrace which led to a private garden, separated from the rest of the palace grounds by a high wall. Kov Lutas, standing in the circular doorway, smiled at their approach.

"Greetings, Sheb Takkor," he said, after exchanging salutes with the two officers. "The importunities of my empty stomach led me to suspect that it was time for your arrival. She whom we guard is resting on the terrace. The orders are to stay always within sight and call, and when she sleeps to stand guard just outside her chamber door."

Thorne took up Kov Lutas's position in the doorway.

"I'll try to carry out orders," he said. "A good dinner and a sound rest to you."

"And to you a pleasant vigil," replied Kov Lutas.

Not until both officers had gone out did Thorne steal a glance at the girl he was to guard. The reputation of this heartless beauty who lured men to their deaths had roused a deep antagonism in his breast. Yet when he saw her, half reclining on a swinging divan piled high with cushions, he was unable to suppress a gasp of surprised admiration.

Her eyes, languorous beneath the fringed curtains of their sleepy lids, were liquid pools of lapis lazuli. Her small nose was a most exquisitely chiseled bit of sculpture. Her red lips, slightly parted, revealed teeth that were matched pearls. And her hair was spun gold and sunbeams.

For some time she was motionless, gazing pensively out over the garden. If she had noticed the change of guards she gave no sign, nor did she once glance toward the doorway. Presently she arose and Thorne saw that she was as slender as Thaíne, and but slightly taller. Her slim body was encased in a single shimmering garment that covered yet revealed the seductive curves of her perfect figure.

A soft-footed slave girl appeared as if by magic from out the shadows, bearing a wrap which she draped about the shoulders of her mistress. Then she turned and silently effaced herself.

Neva crossed the terrace and descended to the garden. Watching her, Thorne stood bemused, wondering if it were possible that the scrawny, rat-faced Dixtar could be the father of so lovely a daughter.

So potent was the spell cast over his senses by this glorious creature that he lost sight of her in the shrubbery before he remembered his orders. He knew that death, swift and sure, would be the penalty for any delinquency in duty, and as he raced across the terrace and down the steps into the garden he had an unpleasant vision of a tall sad-faced man who wielded a flashing sword with machine-like precision, and of a frightened young lad who garnered gory heads in a basket.

FOR SOME time Thorne hurried blindly about in the garden, following first one winding path, then another, in the semi-darkness. Then the nearer moon, suddenly blinking above the rooftops to the west, came to his assistance. By its pale light he saw Neva not fifty feet from him, seated on the rim of a limpid pool in the center of which a fountain babbled.

Slowly he moved closer, once more enthralled by the witching spell of her beauty, and halted at a distance of about twenty feet. As he stood there lost in admiration of the lovely vision before him he was recalled to mundane considerations by a burning sensation in the region of his knees. Lowering his hand to investigate the cause, he discovered that heat rays were emanating from an ornate globe about two feet high which stood beside the path.

He had seen many such globes at various points around the garden and on the terrace. Although it had not previously occurred to him to wonder why the garden had not grown cold after nightfall, he now understood the reason. It was artificially heated.

In order to escape the discomfort caused by the proximity of the heating globe, he moved a few steps nearer the fountain. A dry twig snapped beneath his foot, and the girl looked up, a startled expression on her face.

"Have no fear," said Thorne. "I am Sheb Takkor, your new guard."

"I know," she replied. "It was the noise that startled me. You see, I am expecting some one I am not at all anxious to meet."

Though he felt quite sure he knew who that some one was, Thorne did not venture to say so. Resolutely, he tore his gaze from that lovely face—fought against the subtle witchery of those languorous blue eyes. He told himself, over and over, that he must not be dazzled by this treacherous, cold-hearted little beauty whose wiles had already brought death to so many stout swordsmen.

He tried to convince himself that her loveliness was only superficial—a mask for a haughty, selfish soul. Yet there was a look of guileless innocence about her which did not fit this hypothesis. Obviously, she was making no effort to attract him. Yet she had the reputation of being a heartless flirt.

Heavy footsteps sounded on the garden path. A shadow fell athwart the pool. Thorne glanced across to where the shadow began. Behind Neva stood a tall, broad-shouldered figure—Sel Han.

"The Dixtar's deputy salutes his fair daughter," he said.

Without replying or even turning her head, Neva called to Thorne:

"A trespasser has intruded upon my privacy, guardsman. Remove him."

The Earth-man strode forward and stood facing his enemy.

"It seems you are not wanted," he said quietly. "I trust that, under the circumstances, you will not have the bad taste to remain."

Sel Han laughed contemptuously. "Out of my way, worm," he ordered. "You dare not raise a hand against me." He sat down familiarly beside Neva. "Your guardsman is a spineless coward," he told her. "Once he faced me, sword in hand, but grew so frightened before a blow had been struck that he dropped his weapon and fainted."

THORNE ground his teeth in impotent rage. He knew that under the Martian code he must suffer in silence any abuse which this fellow, who had technically defeated him in a duel, might choose to heap on him, physical violence or an assault with a weapon excepted. He was beginning to realize why most swordsmen of this hot-blooded race preferred death to the ignominy of such a defeat. The deputy, he felt sure, would be canny enough not to lose this tremendous advantage by striking him or drawing sword or dagger, unless Thorne could find some way to provoke him to sudden anger. And he could think of no way of doing this without violating the Martian code.

But Neva, it seemed, was quicker of wit than either of them. "I would have you know, Sheb Takkor," she said, ignoring the presence of Sel Han, "that *all* the details of that unfortunate affair of yours at the training school are known to me. It was cowardly of your opponent to slash you when you were weakened from loss of blood and numbed by the virus of a desert blood-fly. And in full accord with that craven blow is his present refusal to again meet you, while he relies on the passivity which his technical victory imposes on you."

At this, the ruddy face of the deputy went sickly pale in the moonlight, and his hand shot swiftly toward his sword hilt. But he checked the movement and forced a derisive laugh.

"Would it please the Dixtar's daughter to have her guard slain before her eyes?" he blustered.

"It would please her guard," retorted Thorne, "to have the opportunity of defending himself."

"No doubt it would," grinned Sel Han. "It is not a pleasant thing to be a man defeated. To any one with courage, death would be preferable." He moved closer to Neva. "Come, beautiful," he said, "send away this cowardly guard who is powerless to help you. There is something I want to ask you."

Familiarly he passed his arm around her shoulders. And when, with blazing eyes, she would have leaped away from him, he held her tightly.

Thorne instantly whipped out his sword.

"Release her or die," he commanded, presenting his point at the deputy's breast.

The deputy let her go, and stood erect, glaring.

"Have you abandoned your honor?" he asked.

"I might ask you the same question," retorted Thorne, sheathing his sword, "but I know a man is incapable of abandoning that which he has never had."

"It seems," said Sel Han, a deadly glitter in his eyes, "that you have forgotten the code—and something else."

"I am glad you have not forgotten that you are my guardsman, Sheb Takkor Jen," interposed Neva. "And since you are acting in that capacity, and not in your own personal interests, it would seem that you are at perfect liberty to treat this trespasser as you would any other."

"I had hoped that the Dixtar's daughter would confirm me

in that belief," replied Thorne. Then he acted. The deputy was standing with his calves not an inch from the low rim of the pool. The Earth-man's fist shot up in a short arc that ended beneath Sel Han's protruding chin. Swiftly following the impact of knuckles on bone came a tremendous splash as the deputy measured his length in the chilly pool.

Thorne leaped back and waited tensely, hand on hilt. His enemy came up sputtering and cursing luridly in English, then ceased his mouthings as if suddenly deterred by the presence of the Dixtar's daughter, and stepped over the rim. Seemingly unconscious of the ludicrous picture he made standing there in his sodden garments, he bowed low before the girl.

"Permit me to congratulate the Dixtar's daughter on the singular efficiency of her guardsman," he said. "It is only exceeded by his total lack of honor."

Then he turned, and with an attempt at dignity which his condition rendered ridiculous, strode away with water sloshing in his boots and dripping from his clothing to the pathway.

Thorne's hand fell limply from his sword hilt. He was bitterly disappointed, for he had felt certain that Sel Han would come out of that enforced bath raging and eager to try conclusions with him. Here was the man who had humiliated him the first day of his advent on Mars, who had twice since attempted his life, who was a deadly menace to the people of one and possibly more worlds. And this man he had thought in his grasp at last was slipping between his fingers while he looked on, helpless to detain him.

"**THE COWARD!** The miserable, slinking coward!"

Neva was speaking, half to herself, as she gazed after the departing figure. She turned and looked up at Thorne, and again he was conscious of the tremendous power of those glorious eyes.

"He is afraid to measure swords with you," she said, "but he will find some other way to be rid of you. He is cunning, oh, so cunning, and treacherous." She laid a slim hand on the Earth-man's arm. "The deputy has considerable influence with the Dixtar, my father; but for that matter, so have I. And I will help you."

In spite of his preconceived dislike of this little beauty and his resolve never to permit himself to fall beneath the spell of her fatal charm, Thorne thrilled at her glance and touch.

"I am honored that the Dixtar's daughter should be interested in preserving my worthless life," he replied, fighting to keep his voice calm that it might not betray the emotions which her touch had aroused within him.

"He is a strange and terrible creature, this Sel Han," she went on. "Did you notice the queer gibberish he used when he came up out of the water? Some incantation, perhaps, to a strange god. No doubt he is a sorcerer."

Recalling the deputy's lurid English curses, Thorne smiled to himself as he replied:

"I doubt not that he was calling down the wrath of some deity on my head."

Neva yawned prettily.

"I am sleepy," she said. "We will go in now, for I must retire. You may walk beside me."

Slowly, side by side, stepping in perfect unison, they went up the path which led to the house. Neither spoke, and Thorne, despite his resolve, could not prevent his eyes straying from time to time toward the trim little figure beside him—a ravishing dream of loveliness from the tips of her dainty, sandaled toes to the crown of her golden head, which barely reached to the level of his shoulder.

At the steps which led up to the terrace she took his arm, and a wisp of her hair, loosed by the evening breeze, brushed his bare shoulder. Again he felt the thrill of her touch, and fought it with every ounce of will power at his command.

As they entered the doorway a slave girl hurried up to take her mistress's cloak. Another moved the lever which uncapped the baridium light globes, making the room brilliant as day.

And still another hurried in, bearing a tray on which was a tiny jeweled cup of steaming pulcho which she proffered to Neva.

"Bring another for the Jen," said the Dixtar's daughter, taking the cup.

The girl hurried out, and returned a moment later with a larger cup.

"I drink to my brave and efficient guardsman," smiled Neva.

"And I to the lovely and precious jewel which he guards," replied Thorne.

The slave girl took their empty cups, and still another drew back the curtains from a doorway. Neva stepped through, and when Thorne would have blundered in after her the girl barred his way.

"This is the mistress's sleeping room, ignorant one," she said. "You are to stand guard *outside* the door."

CHAPTER XII

AN ASSASSIN STRIKES

DURING THE EARLY watches of the night, Thorne, standing guard before Neva's chamber door, reviewed the doings of the day. Before seeing the Dixtar's daughter he had been firmly of the opinion that he loved Thaíne, the girl who had saved his life in the marshes. And he had resolved not to be overcome by the reputedly irresistible charms of Neva. But now, since he had seen her incomparable loveliness, had thrilled at her touch as no woman had ever thrilled him before, her image was ever before him, while that of Thaíne, try to summon it though he would, faded more and more dimly into the background.

But despite this subtle spell which the daughter of the Dixtar had cast over him, his loyalty to Thaíne remained as strong as ever. And he resolved that at the first opportunity he would attempt to escape from Dukor and go to her assistance, regardless of the direction in which his strangely fickle and seemingly uncontrollable affections drew him.

As he stood there, outwardly calm save for a thoughtful contracting of his brows, but inwardly perturbed by his strangely conflicting emotions, he suddenly sensed that all was not as it should be—that in the room some sinister, alien presence was quietly watching him, perhaps waiting to spring upon him in an unguarded moment.

Before retiring, one of the slave girls had pulled the levers which hooded all of the larger baridium globes, leaving only one tiny light uncovered. Its dim yellow glow, more feeble than that of a small candle, was all but lost in that large apartment, though it shed a pale golden twilight that faintly revealed the outlines of the larger objects in the room.

Over all these objects Thorne's eyes now roved, yet he could discern nothing amiss. The swinging chairs and divans, depending from the ceiling by their golden chains, were obviously unoccupied. And the shadows beneath them were not so dense as to form a hiding place for a human being. There was a tall, shelved case in which many metal cylinders were kept, containing the scrolls which on Mars answered for books. But nothing could hide there. And other than these, there were only a few large pots of flowers set here and there about the room.

Once more he settled to his former position, but this time he only pretended to be preoccupied. For some time nothing happened, yet though his face was held straight ahead, he kept his eyes turned in the direction where he thought he had seen a stealthy movement. Suddenly, he saw it again. And to his astonishment, he discovered that it was a large pot of flowers which had moved. So far as he could see this pot and its contents were not markedly different from any of the others. It was approximately the same size, about three and a half feet high and three in diameter at its center. And the two large handles projecting from its sides were of the same angular pattern as the others.

Without moving his head, he kept his eyes on this singularly mobile pot and waited tensely. Inch by inch it came toward him with almost snail-like slowness, while he watched, fascinated. As it drew closer he examined it minutely, meanwhile stealthily loosening his sword in its sheath with his left hand. Still he could make out nothing suspicious about it except its strange movements. It seemed filled almost to the brim with rich black soil, from which the flower stalks projected.

CLOSER and closer it came until but a scant five feet separated them. Then it suddenly stood erect on two spindly legs and its handles turned into two spidery arms, one of which wielded a long, slim dagger. Straight for the astonished Earth-man it sprang, its keen weapon poised for the death stroke. But in that instant he had whipped his sword from its sheath, and whirling it over his head, brought it down with all his might on the amazing pot.

The hard vitreous shoulder of the pot withstood the blow of his slender weapon with ease, but the keen blade glanced downward, shearing off the spidery arm that held the dagger. At this there was a muffled shriek of pain from inside the pot, and turning, it fled swiftly for the doorway. As he set out in pursuit, Thorne shifted his sword to his left hand, and plucking his heavy mace from his belt, hurled it straight at the center of the pot.

The weapon went true to the mark. There was a resounding crash of broken crockery, and the spindle legs collapsed, precipitating everything onto the floor. Out of the tangle of crumpled flowers there rolled a round-bodied yellow man, who writhed and shrieked on the floor for a moment while the blood spouted from the place where his arm had been. Then he suddenly stiffened and lay still, his slanting eyes staring sightlessly at the ceiling.

For some time pandemonium held sway in that quarter of the palace. Neva's frightened girls and women screamed for help, and a company of guards from the outer corridors came clanking into the room. But Neva herself, clad in a filmy wrap, came out of her sleeping room, quite unperturbed.

"What has happened, Sheb Takkor Jen?" she asked, looking calmly down at the dead man and the debris.

"That attacked me," Thorne replied, indicating the corpse, "disguised as a pot of flowers."

By this time the room was filled with soldiers and slave girls, all staring curiously at the remains Some one had unhooded the baridium globes, and the resulting bright light revealed every ghastly detail.

The yellow man's disguise had been unusually clever, and well adapted to his rotund body and spidery arms. Instead of being filled with earth, the pot had a false bottom only two inches from the top, covered with a thin layer of soil. The flower stalks were set on narrow spikes projecting upward from this bottom. There were no handles, but holes through which the scrawny arms were thrust. Painted to resemble crockery and held akimbo, they had looked exactly like handles in the dim light. And the pot, with small holes bored in it for breathing and spying, although not proof against the blow of a mace, formed an efficient body armor against sword and dagger thrusts.

"**A DIABOLICAL** attempt," said Neva, shuddering. Then to the soldiers. "Take it away."

Two men caught up the stiffening body and others cleared away the debris. A yellow slave scrubbed up the blood stains. Then, at a sign from Neva, all silently left the apartment.

She looked up into Thorne's eyes.

"You have saved me from abduction, or perhaps assassination," she said. "I am very grateful."

"Perhaps," he replied, "it is only myself I have saved. The fellow attacked me. And I have reason to believe he was the creature of Sel Han."

"What reason?"

"Because the Deputy Dixtar is said to be in league with the Ma Gongi."

Neva mused for a moment.

"There may be some truth in that," she answered, "but don't let any living soul hear you say it. My father has unlimited faith in his deputy, and has already beheaded two officers who were bold enough to accuse him of that very thing."

"I am grateful for your warning," Thorne replied, "and will be discreet."

A slave girl drew back the curtain for her, and she reentered her sleeping room.

Morning found the Earth-man exceedingly weary after a

strenuous day and night without rest. Soon after he was relieved by Kov Lutas he was sound asleep in their apartment. It seemed that he had scarcely closed his eyes when the orderly awakened him.

"Your servant is commanded to prepare you to attend the Dixtar's daughter at the state function this evening," he said. "As the preparation will take some time, I was compelled to awaken you earlier than usual."

This time Thorne, after his bath, was massaged and anointed with sweet smelling unguents and cosmetics, his day's growth of beard removed by a depilatory, and his hair carefully trimmed and brushed in the latest Martian mode. Then the orderly brought forth and helped him don a gorgeous dress uniform, resplendent with gold and jewels. The purple head-cloak, instead of being bound above the head-harness, was caught at the shoulders by two straps, the hood thrown back leaving the head bare. Carefully polishing the Takkor family medal, Vorz next hung this about his neck. Then, after flicking a speck of dust from the dagger hilt and rubbing a thumb-print from the sword pommel, he stood back, head cocked to one side, to survey his handiwork.

"Well, Vorz?" asked Thorne. "Will I do?"

"No great lord of the olden days was ever more perfectly groomed or more princely of bearing," replied the man proudly. "Now you are ready to go on duty."

CHAPTER XIII

BETRAYED

LIKE MOST OF the women Thorne had known on his own world, Neva was a long time about dressing. But when, after he had waited for more than an hour before her door, she came forth, the result was most entrancing.

A tiara of pearls and pale blue amethysts woven together in a bizarre pattern on a meshwork of golden wires, bound her sun-bright hair. Beads of the same materials formed her breast-shields and supported a clinging bodice of iridescent blue silk. This vanished in a girdle of pearls and amethysts.

Thorne stood enthralled, and she, catching the look of admiration in his eyes, smiled archly. Then she raised her arms and circled gracefully on the tips of her toes.

"Like it?" she asked.

"Immensely," he replied, "even as I adore—" He stopped suddenly, remembering that he was speaking to the Dixtar's daughter.

"Go on," she urged him, still smiling.

"Sorry. I said more than I intended," he told her. "Perhaps you will find it in your heart to overlook my presumption."

"Perhaps I shall if you will finish." Then, "Even as I adore—" she prompted him.

"—the star-strewn firmament," he replied.

She stamped a tiny foot. "Must I command you?" she asked imperiously. Her eyes flashed up into his, then suddenly softened under his direct gaze. She moved closer—laid a hand on his arm. "Where I might command," she said gently, "I will only implore."

"—the lovely jewel it adorns," he finished.

"Ah! That is what I wanted to hear you say. And now for your reward you will escort me to the reception not merely as a guardsman following in my wake, but as a gentleman and officer of the Kamud, walking at my side."

The reception of Irintz Tel, Dixtar of Xancibar, was a gorgeous affair. Held for the purpose of welcoming Lori Thool, the new ambassador from Kalsivar, largest and most powerful nation of Mars, it was a model of magnificence, for Irintz Tel, with an eye to a possible military alliance with this great power as well as a treaty which would establish favorable trade relations, was particularly anxious to impress its representative.

The function was held in the great central audience chamber of the palace, the ceiling of which towered a thousand feet above the heads of the assembled guests, its polished surface reflecting the rays of myriads of baridium globes, which made the place light as day.

Irintz Tel was standing with his illustrious guest on a dais in the center of the floor, presenting other visiting dignitaries and his chief officers, when the silvery notes of a trumpet rose above the hum of conversation. Instantly, every voice was hushed as a pompous major-domo announced:

"The Dixtar's daughter."

All eyes were turned toward the doorway as Neva entered, walking beside Thorne. And though they lighted with adoration at sight of the dainty little golden-haired beauty who was the first lady of Xancibar, not a few admiring glances were cast at the tall, handsome, sun-bronzed young officer.

Straight to the dais they went, the girl nodding to right and left to her many friends and acquaintances. As the little rat-faced Dixtar advanced to meet them, accompanied by Lori Thool, Thorne was once more struck by the incongruous dissimilarity between father and daughter.

The ambassador was tall, slender, and slightly under middle age, his hair just beginning to gray at the temples. He was quite handsome and elegant in his uniform and insignia of a great noble of Kalsivar. His cloak and cincture were of brilliant orange material, trimmed with black. Jewels sparkled, not only from the hilts of his weapons, but from every buckle, clasp and fastener where there could be the slightest excuse to wear them.

"**NEVA**," squeaked the Dixtar in his high-pitched voice, "this is Lori Thool, the noble ambassador from Kalsivar. Lori Thool, my daughter."

The ambassador saluted gracefully. "My homage to the most beautiful of the daughters of Mars," he said. "It must be that I have now met every one. Will you not join me in a game of gapun? I see they are setting up the boards."

"In a moment," she answered. "You have not quite met every one. This," turning to Thorne, "is my friend, Sheb Takkor Jen."

As he and the resplendent ambassador exchanged dignified salutes, the Earth-man exulted over the fact that she had said, "my friend."

Meanwhile, Neva had beckoned a pretty little black-haired, brown-eyed beauty to her side.

"I take it that you have met the ambassador, Trixana," she said, "but not my friend, Sheb Takkor Jen."

Thorne acknowledged with a courtly salute, and a moment later found himself walking at the side of the vivacious little brunette, following Neva and Lori Thool as they made their way toward the gaming boards. From the corner of his eye, he saw Irintz Tel standing, chin on chest and hands clasped behind him, watching them with a cynical look on his sharp features. And he was quite positive that as the Dixtar's eyes rested for a moment on him, their look was not friendly.

A moment later he saw Sel Han slip up beside Irintz Tel and, bending, whisper some secret communication. The Dixtar nodded, and again flashed a look at Thorne. As nearly as he could judge from this little pantomime, his arch enemy had been telling tales about him, and something had just occurred which seemed to substantiate them. Perhaps, he thought, the friendship of Neva might yet cost him his head.

Lori Thool and the two girls chanced much gold at the gaming boards, and Trixana won quite heavily. But Thorne only looked on. As he was standing, watching the game, he felt a touch on his arm, and turning, beheld the kindly face of the white-haired Lal Vak.

"Greetings, Sheb Takkor Jen," he said softly. Then continued: "Turn back and watch the game, while I deliver a message. We must not seem to be talking together."

Thorne looked back at the players, all of whom were engrossed in the game, and the scientist continued: "You are in great danger. Sel Han is plotting against your life, and it looks as if his scheme is about to succeed. He has denounced you to the Dixtar as being over-friendly with Neva, and her actions to-night in treating you as an equal have seemed to confirm his words. A friend has brought me news that Irintz Tel has just promised Sel Han he will turn you over to the headsman in the morning."

The Earth-man raised his hand to his mouth as if to cover a cough, and said: "What can I do about it?"

"Escape. Get away from the palace before morning."

"That I had already planned."

"How?"

"Over the garden wall."

"Splendid! It is just what we had in mind. I will have a conveyance waiting for you. Be there just after the farther moon rises and it may be that we can save you. Farewell."

When the gathering broke up, Lori Thool, after saying a lingering farewell to Neva, departed with his suite. Trixana was claimed by her father, a tall, handsome soldier in the prime of life, and Neva, left once more with Thorne, started toward the door. They had only gone a few steps when Sel Han suddenly strode up, barring their progress. He made a sweeping bow before Neva.

"May I have the honor of seeing the Dixtar's daughter safely to her apartments?" he asked.

She took Thorne's arm and replied, "The Dixtar's daughter is adequately escorted."

Sel Han continued to bar her way, smiling cynically. And the Earth-man suddenly noticed that the Dixtar himself was only a few feet away, looking on.

"Apparently you have not observed that the Dixtar's daughter wishes to pass," said Thorne, looking Sel Han squarely in the eye and toying significantly with his hilt. "Under such circumstances it should not be necessary to request any *gentleman* to stand aside."

At this, the deputy flashed a look at the Dixtar, as much as to say, "I told you so," and moved out of the way.

BACK in the apartments of Neva, as Thorne stood guard before her chamber door, his mind was a mass of conflicting emotions. She had bidden him a gracious, almost a tender, good-night which had given him a strong indication that she felt toward him as he, despite all his resolves to the contrary, felt toward her. Now, if he carried out his plans and escaped at the rising of the farther moon, she would be left unguarded. And it might be that on this very night Sel Han would be scheming to carry her off. On the other hand, if he did not escape, he felt assured that certain death at the hands of the headsman awaited him on the morrow. Then there was Thaine. By now he considered the discharge of his obligation to her purely as a duty, and not, as previously, a pleasure. For thought of separation from Neva was not pleasant to contemplate.

And so, as he stood there debating with himself, the time slipped by until he suddenly realized that the farther moon had risen and the hour had struck for his departure. He was about to steal softly away from his post when he was startled by a touch on his arm and a whispered, "Quiet."

Swiftly turning, he was astonished to see Neva standing there before the curtain clad in a filmy sleeping garment.

"Make no noise," she said, "and come with me. I heard some one on my balcony, and want you to surprise the prowler."

Softly they entered the sleeping chamber. For a moment Thorne stood there, accustoming his eyes to the dim light and taking note of his surroundings. Then he silently drew his sword and advanced toward the balcony, listening intently the while in the hope that he might locate the position of the marauder.

Reaching a window without having heard a sound, he cautiously leaned forward and peered out. So far as he could see, the balcony was deserted. He stepped out and explored. Still no sign of a prowler. Then he reentered the room, and almost collided with Neva, who had quietly followed him.

"Did you see him?" she asked.

"I saw no one," he replied. "Perhaps you were only dreaming."

"No, no! I am positive a man was there a moment ago. Not only did I hear him, but I saw his shadow just as the moon came up. I'm terribly frightened."

They were standing very close together. Her eyes, looking up into his, were wide with fear. She swayed toward him. Solicitously he threw his arms about her—felt that she was trembling. Then, with a sudden impulse that mastered him in spite of himself, he drew her to him.

Her arms stole about his neck and clung.

"Hold me tight—tight!" she whispered. "In your arms I am not afraid."

Now it was the man who trembled; but not with fear. Eagerly he crushed her to him. Their lips met, and for Thorne it was as if all things had ceased to exist except the ecstasy of that moment.

"I love you, love you, love you!" she murmured against his lips. "Say again what you said to me this evening."

"I love and adore you," he told her, his voice husky with emotion. "Yet it is madness—a sweet madness."

"Why, dear one?"

"Because to-morrow—"

Suddenly the lights flashed on, and he paused, speechless with surprise.

A DOZEN armed soldiers rushed into the room, bared blades in their hands. At their head was Sel Han, a grin of triumph on his flat features. And behind them, his small eyes flashing venomously, came Irintz Tel, Dixtar of Xancibar.

"Help! The guard! Release me, you brute!"

For a moment Thorne was in a daze. Then he suddenly realized that it was Neva who was speaking—that she was beating upon his breast with her clenched hands—hands that had caressed him but a moment before straining to break from his clasp.

Mechanically he let her go. She ran to the little wizened Dixtar, buried her face in his shoulder, and began sobbing bitterly.

Surrounded by armed foes and deserted by the woman who had just pledged her love to him, Thorne suddenly came to the full realization of his peril. Resolving to die fighting rather than be taken alive, he whipped out his sword and dagger and leaped for the door. Two warriors barred his progress.

A feint, a thrust, and one went down stabbed through the heart. He parried the thrust of the other with his dagger. Then, with the swiftness of a darting serpent, he withdrew his blade from the heart of the first enemy and sheathed it in the throat of the second.

Other warriors leaped in close, but he bounded over the bodies of his two fallen adversaries and out of the door. Straight across the terrace he dashed, then down the steps and into the labyrinth of garden paths. The swiftest of the warriors was only a few sword-lengths behind him, and the others trailed close after.

A few moments more and Thorne had reached his objective—a tall sebolis tree standing near the wall, which he had previously marked for his purpose. Pausing only to hurl his sword and dagger into the faces of his pursuers, he scrambled up the rough tree trunk, then climbed from branch to branch until he was above the level of the wall.

Walking out on the swaying branch until it sagged dangerously, he leaped. His fingers caught the edge of the wall, but it was rounded by a thousand years of weathering, and slippery with the night's accumulation of hoar frost. For a moment he clung precariously, striving to draw himself up, but in vain.

With a last despairing clutch at the curved, treacherous surface, he fell to the ground twenty feet below.

As soon as he struck, a half dozen soldiers pounced on him. Weaponless, he fought them with fists and feet until Sel Han reached over and struck him on the head with the flat of his heavy mace. Rendered limp and almost insensible by the blow, he was turned on his face while his hands were trussed securely. Then his captors, at a sharp command from the triumphant deputy, jerked him to his feet and half carried, half dragged him back to the palace.

Neva, attended by two of her slave girls, sat on a divan with a fluffy wrap around her shoulders. Irintz Tel was pacing up and down, chin on chest, hands clasped behind his back, his brow contracted in a frown and his thin lips compressed in a tight line. For some time he paced in silence, ignoring his daughter, the warriors who stood respectfully waiting for him to speak, and the prisoner who, still dazed by the blow on his head, was supported between two of his captors.

Presently a tall, sad-faced man bearing a great, two-handed sword on his shoulder, strode into the room. Behind him walked a sleepy-eyed, frightened little boy who carried a basket.

"Strike the head from this despicable traitor, Lurgo," squeaked Irintz Tel, without looking up or interrupting his pacing.

Lurgo the headsman lowered his huge weapon and stood leaning on the pommel, waiting while two warriors dragged Thorne to the center of the floor and forced him to kneel. Then he stepped back, carefully measured the distance with his practiced eye, and whirled the great blade over his head.

CHAPTER XIV

THE BARIDIUM MINES

"NO, NO! LURGO! Wait!"

It was Neva who had sprung from her couch, and now stood between the sad-faced headsman and the kneeling Thorne.

Lurgo stared sorrowfully down at her, his blade still poised in mid-air, then looked toward the Dixtar as if awaiting his further orders.

Irintz Tel ceased his pacing for the first time and looked up.

"What's this, daughter?" he asked. "Can it be that you care for this vile miscreant?"

"Care for him!" Neva stamped her foot angrily. "I hate him for the affront he has put upon me. For much less than this, you have caused minor offenders to suffer for days before death was finally granted them. Yet, this seducer, this ravisher who has dared to lay hands on your own daughter is let off with a mere stroke of the headsman's sword. Do you hold my honor so lightly as this?"

"By the wrath of Deza, you are right!" exclaimed Irintz Tel. "I have been too hasty. We must devise a punishment more suited to the crime. Let be, Lurgo."

At this, the tall headsman sadly shouldered his sword and trudged away, the sleepy-eyed boy with the basket trailing in his wake.

"Does it not seem fair, my father," said Neva after the headsman had gone, "that since the crime of this malefactor was against me, I should be the one to pronounce sentence upon him?"

"It does indeed, daughter. It does indeed," agreed Irintz Tel, tweaking his sharp nose nervously. "Suppose you name his fate."

"Why, then, I'll sentence him to labor in the baridium mines," she said. "I hear that men are long in dying there, and that they suffer much."

"But," interposed Sel Han, "there are tortures—"

"Since when," asked Neva, facing him haughtily, "has the Dixtar's deputy acquired the right to question the mandates of the Dixtar's daughter?"

"You are right, daughter, you are right," hastily interposed Irintz Tel. "You must not interfere, Sel Han. She has pronounced a most fitting sentence, and we confirm it. Away with him, warriors."

Thorne, still dazed by the blow on his head, dimly comprehended that he had been saved from the stroke of the sworder only to be condemned to a worse fate. But the deepest hurt of all was occasioned by the fact that the woman to whom he had given his love, and who had, only a few moments before, declared her love for him, had not only proved false, but had actually sentenced him to a horrible, lingering death.

As he was dragged away by the warriors, he saw the face of Irintz Tel sneering, that of Sel Han grinning malevolently, and those of the warriors stern and pitiless. But at Neva he did not look.

AFTER conducting him through numerous passageways, the soldiers led him into a small room at one end of which a hole about three feet in diameter was cut in the wall. Into this hole they thrust him feet first, attached a tag to his arm marked "Baridium Mines," and gave him a violent push. With a speed that gave him a peculiar sensation in the pit of his stomach and caused a considerable pressure on his eardrums, he shot downward in a dark, slanting tube, the inner surface of which was as smooth as glass. Presently he glided over a series of rises which slowed his progress, then out into an open trough under a long, low shed. At the end of the trough two soldiers caught him and stood him erect.

To his surprise, Thorne now saw that he was in one of the large warehouses which lined the banks of the canal over which he had passed, and reflected that he must have traveled at a tremendous velocity to reach it in so short a time. After the soldiers had examined his tag he was herded with a group of other prisoners, similarly tagged, who were huddled around a large globe-heater on the dock. Here he stood, slowly turning like the others, for while the side toward the heater was comfortably warm, the one directly away from it was subjected to the freezing temperature of the early morning air.

Presently the sun, heralded only by a brief dawn-light in this tenuous atmosphere, popped above the horizon, its blue-white shafts instantly dissipating the cold, and swiftly melting the shell of ice which covered the canal.

Moored at the dock was a low, narrow craft about two hundred feet in length. The hull was of brown metal, and the upper structure was roofed over with iridescent, amber colored crystal curved like the back of a whale.

Through one of the doors the prisoners were now driven. As he followed along with the others, Thorne noticed the strange propulsive devices used on these craft, which were shaped much like the webbed feet and legs of aquatic birds, and were fastened at intervals along the sides.

As soon as the prisoners had been herded on board, the metal door clanged shut behind them. Shortly thereafter the craft glided away from the dock, propelled smoothly and noiselessly by its artificial webbed feet.

THORNE presently tired of the sameness of the scenery and entered into a conversation with one of his fellow unfortunates—a man who had once been high in the councils of the Kamud, but who had foolishly dared to oppose Irintz Tel. Levri Thornel, for so he named himself, was a silver-haired man in the late autumn of life. Dignified, sedate, he stood out in sharp contrast to many of the hardened criminals with whom he had been thrown. He showed no rancor against the Dixtar, but took his sentence as the decree of fate.

"At most," he told Thorne, "I would have only enjoyed a few short years of life. Looking back over the years of power and pleasure which have been mine, I cannot feel that I have been cheated, even though I face a few days of torture and a painful, lingering death. But you are a young man. Until this sentence was passed you had the best of your life before you. Your case is sad, indeed, as you would have had much to live for."

For a time silence fell between them. Then Thorne asked:

"What are these baridium mines like? Have you any idea?"

"There are vast workings, which require much machinery and equipment, and the labor of many slaves. The baridium ore, after being brought up from deposits far underground, is crushed and cleaned of all impurities. Then it is distilled. The liquid which passes over in the still is mixed with phosphorus and several other chemicals, and used to fill the light globes with which you are familiar. The solid residue left in the stills is calcined until it becomes an impalpable powder, fearfully water-hungry. Then it is combined with several elements, the most important of which is metallic sodium, to make the fire-powder which instantly ignites when moistened."

Thorne was about to ask him how all this affected the health and well-being of the slaves, when the boat suddenly slowed down, then stopped beside a dock of black stone which jutted from the wall on the outer side of the canal. The metal door was thrown open, the prisoners were herded out onto the dock, and Thorne lost track of Levri Thornel.

They were marched through a high archway in the thick black wall, and thence into an immense building constructed of the same material. Here they formed in line, to be examined by an officer, who assigned them to various working groups. Thorne was pleased when he found that the dignified and

friendly Levri Thornel was assigned to this group, which numbered about twenty men.

A GUARD marched them through a long corridor, lighted by
small baridium globes, and thence into a broad courtyard which
overlooked an immense pit, several miles in diameter, the rim
of which was circled by a high black wall. As soon as they
entered this court, the prisoners encountered air laden with fine
dust and acrid fumes, which smarted their lungs and nostrils
and set them to coughing and sneezing violently.

Meanwhile, the guard urged them onward to the edge of the
pit, where he turned them over to another guard, whose face,
head and body were protected by a breathing mask, helmet and
air-tight suit.

This new guard spoke to them through a sound amplifier
which projected from the top of his helmet.

"Down the stairway," he ordered, "and step lively. I'll make
the first laggard regret his slothfulness."

The deeper they descended the more difficult breathing
became, until, when they reached the bottom of the stairway,
the fumes fairly seared their lungs, while the fine dust, settling
on the skin, caused it to itch and burn. Merely being in the
place without a protective suit was a continuous torment.

As these things came to Thorne's attention, presaging the
fate that was to be his, he thought again of Neva, the glori-
ously beautiful girl he had held in his arms, who had given him
kiss for kiss and pledged him love for love. More sharply than
the baridium fumes seared his lungs, the thought of her perfidy
seared his heart.

CHAPTER XV

AMBUSHED

THE GROUP OF slaves to which Thorne was assigned was ushered into a large building and set at the task of filling and sealing small phials of fire-powder. Here the laborers were seated at long benches, above which were suspended large hoppers of the powder. This was conveyed down to them by means of tubes with small valves at the bottom which could be opened or closed by the operator as the phials were filled.

Stoppers of red, resilient material like that which formed the suits of the guards were pressed into the bottles, then held for a moment against hot plates, the heat melting them down and sealing them hermetically.

The labor in this department was the lightest of any in the baridium pit. Yet it was the most dreaded of all, as the air was constantly filled with the searing powder which attacked skin and lungs alike, and it was impossible to work with any degree of speed without spilling small quantities on the fingers. Operators who worked slowly enough to avoid this source of torture were quickly introduced to another and a worse by their watchful guards, who prodded them with their cylinders, burning them most painfully.

With a sickening apprehension of the fate in store for him, Thorne gradually saw his own skin turning yellow from contact with the fumes and powder in the air. And despite the utmost watchfulness he was unable to avoid burning his fingers and the backs of his hands by spilling on them small quantities of powder which sifted down from the none too efficient valve.

Nevertheless, he worked diligently at his task, enduring the torture which made many of his fellows moan and even cry out from pain, with a stoicism that amazed the guards. Levri Thornel, his new-found friend, also manfully refrained from voicing his anguish, despite the fact that the stiffness of age rendered his fingers so clumsy that he burned himself severely again and again.

When night came the slaves were herded into a great communal building, the only furniture of which consisted of heating globes. Here a coarse porridge was doled out to them. They were given water to drink, but no pulcho, as this soothing, stimulating beverage would have served to ease their torture.

In this building the air was somewhat freer from dust and fumes than outside, and therefore offered some slight relief to Thorne and other newcomers whose lungs and skin had not, as yet, been badly seared. After eating their meager rations, the slaves flung themselves down on the hard floor around the heating globes, many to instantly fall asleep from utter exhaustion. There were, however, a large portion who could not sleep because of the torture of their burns, but made the night hideous with their groans and lamentations.

Thorne was about to fling himself down like the others when he saw, sprawled on the floor at his feet, a sleeping figure that somehow seemed familiar. The skin was yellow and mottled with many burns, disguising the features considerably, yet he could not mistake the broad shoulders, the huge chest, the long powerful arms and the ludicrously short legs of Yirl Du, Jen of the Takkor Free Swordsmen.

STOOPING, the Earth-man shook his faithful friend. Yirl Du's red-rimmed eyes blinked open, and for a moment he glared ferociously up at the man who had awakened him. An angry snarl died in his throat as sudden recognition came to him. He sat up abruptly, saluted, and said:

The leathery neck was arched for the kill.

"I shield my eyes, my lord. I did not dream of seeing you here, and at first I did not recognize you with that yellow cast to your skin."

"You seem to have acquired considerable color yourself, old friend," Thorne replied. "How long have you been here?"

"The seven judges sentenced me the day you were taken before the Dixtar," Yirl Du told him. "The trial was a farce. There were no witnesses, and no evidence was produced against me except an accusing letter from Sel Han which was really no evidence at all. Yet they condemned me to this pit of horrors that very day, and I have been here ever since."

Thorne made Yirl Du and the silvery-haired Levri Thornel acquainted, and for a time they conversed. Then the baridium globes which lighted the building were hooded, and they composed themselves for sleep. For some time Thorne found sleep impossible. But eventually tired nature asserted itself, and he drifted into unconsciousness.

It seemed, however, that he had scarcely fallen asleep when

a small baridium hand-torch was flashed in his face, awakening him, and a guard prodded him with his foot.

"Are you Sheb Takkor?" the fellow asked in a hoarse whisper.

"I am," Thorne replied.

"Where is he who is called Yirl Du?"

"He sleeps here beside me."

"It seems you two have a powerful friend at Dukor. At least my superior officer has ordered me to assist you hence. Awaken Yirl Du and follow me."

The guard hooded his torch and waited. Thorne shook Yirl Du awake and explained the situation to him. Then he thought of his new friend, Levri Thornel, and resolved that he, also, should have a chance. A touch awakened the old man.

"Come with me," Thorne whispered. "It may be that we can escape."

Then he called to the guard: "Ready."

The fellow opened the slide of his torch only wide enough to enable him to make his way among the sleeping slaves who sprawled on the floor. Then he started toward the nearest doorway, closely followed by Thorne, Yirl Du, and Levri Thornel. Once outside the building, the guard hooded his torch, and they made their way by the light of the nearer moon, which was dropping swiftly toward the eastern horizon. They presently came to a small guardhouse near the rim of the pit. Their conductor entered, and motioned them to follow.

THORNE marched in first, and found himself in the presence of an officer who sat on the edge of a swinging divan.

The officer looked up sharply. "What's this, Hendra Suhn?" he demanded. "You have brought three of them."

The guard seemed dumfounded. "I only awakened Sheb Takkor," he said, "and told him to bring Yirl Du."

Thorne hastened to explain. "I am Sheb Takkor," he said. "These," indicating the two men in turn, "are my friends Yirl Du and Levri Thornel. It is my desire that both accompany me."

"I was only ordered to assist two, yourself and Yirl Du," said the officer. "Levri Thornel goes back."

"Levri Thornel goes with me," insisted Thorne.

"Take him back," the officer ordered, turning to Hendra Suhn.

The guard stepped forward and grasped the old man by the arm.

"If he goes back, then I go with him," said Thorne.

"You refuse escape when it is offered you?" The officer laughed unpleasantly.

"I decline to attempt it without my friend."

"The more fool, you," growled the officer. "Yet I have my orders to assist you, and I suppose this doddering old derelict must go with you." He arose, and stepping into another room brought two bundles of warm clothing, and two of weapons. One bundle of each he handed to Thorne and the like to Yirl Du. But Thorne instantly passed his bundles to Levri Thornel.

"I won't take them," protested the old man.

"No more will I unless you are similarly outfitted," replied Thorne.

The officer glared for a moment and seemed about to speak, but he checked himself, and instead, went into the next room for more clothing and weapons, which he thrust into the hands of Thorne with ill grace.

"You win," he said angrily. "But this old wreck you persist in "taking with you will yet cause your undoing."

Swiftly the three men donned the clothing and belted sword, mace and dagger about them. In addition to these, each was provided with a bundle of javelins in a quiver that hung by a strap across one shoulder.

"As soon as the nearer moon sets," said the officer, "and before the farther rises, you will have time to make your way in the dark up the side of the pit. The rim is guarded, but one guard has orders to pass you. That guard is stationed directly above this building. When you have passed the guard, you will proceed out into the desert until you have passed five outcropping rocks. At the northern base of the sixth, which you will recognize because it leans as if it were about to fall to the ground, you will find supplies left there for you by your friends, because they would have been awkward for you to carry up the side of the pit."

"Who are these friends who have been so thoughtful?" asked Thorne.

"If I knew I would not tell you," replied the officer, "but I do not. I only know that these orders came down to me from my superiors, and that they must have had them from some one high in the councils of the Kamud."

As Thorne stood in the doorway, waiting for the nearer moon to set, he pondered much as to who his powerful friend in Dukor could be. Lal Vak, he knew, was not high in the councils of the Kamud. The scientist had never been an ardent Kamud-ist but had, like millions of others, been constrained to yield to the dictates of Irintz Tel when Miradon Vil had abdicated. However, Lal Vak was liked everywhere because of his engaging personality, and respected for his great fund of knowledge. It was not inconceivable that he should have a powerful friend who might be moved in Thorne's behalf. And so the Earth-man dismissed the matter.

So swiftly did the nearer moon move across the sky, that only a short time elapsed ere it dropped below the eastern horizon. Then the three men set out. The pit was wrapped in darkness, deep and impenetrable, save where, here and there, the faint illumination shone forth from a guard house window.

Overhead, the stars were blazing jewels of white, red, pale blue and yellow, in a sky of jet. Though their combined radiance was too feeble to light the path of the three fugitives, they were still of service, for their line of disappearance marked the rim of the pit. And one constellation which Thorne fixed in his mind served as a guide to the point, directly above the guard house they had just quitted, where they expected to find a friendly guard.

MOVING with great caution in order not to start a landslide on that steeply sloping bank, they began the ascent. It was a long, difficult climb, and they had scarcely reached the summit when the farther moon rose in the east close to the point where the nearer moon had vanished a short time before. Its light was more dim than that of the nearer and larger orb, but bright enough to reveal them to a tall guard who stood looking out over the pit. Instantly he raised a javelin and advanced threateningly.

"Who are you?" he demanded.

"Sheb Takkor and friends," Thorne replied.

The guard stared at him suspiciously. "There were to be but two," he said.

"That order was changed," Thorne told him. "Now there are three."

"I can pass but two," said the guard. "The third must go back."

"You will pass three or none," Thorne told him. "We are going on at once. Raise an alarm now, and we will kill you. Raise it later, and there is one high in the councils of the Kamud who will see that you are condemned to the powder room."

While the latter statement was pure bluff on Thorne's part, it had an immediate effect on the guard.

"I crave pardon, Sheb Takkor Jen," he said humbly. "The fact that the order was changed confused me. Pass, and may Deza guard you."

And so the three, who but shortly before had faced a horrible lingering death in the pit, now clambered over the wall, dropped to the other side, and marched out into the desert, free men.

Carefully, now, they counted the outcropping stones of which the officer had told them. They had passed the fifth, at a considerable distance from the pit, and were just coming up to the sixth when a half dozen warriors suddenly broke from a near-by clump of conifers and charged toward them, hurling a cloud of javelins.

Thorne shouted a warning to his companions, both of whom were able to dodge the barbed weapons. It was evident that their assailants, outnumbering them two to one, expected them to run, or at most, to stand and defend themselves. Realizing this, and recalling a tactical rule of a certain great general: "Always do what the enemy expects you not to do," he quickly called to his two friends to support him on the right and left, then dashed straight at the advancing warriors.

There was another exchange of javelins, in which the skilled Yirl Du transfixed an enemy, cutting the attacking party down to five.

Both sides expended their store of javelins at about the same time. Then swords and daggers were drawn and the hand-to-hand fighting began. Thorne engaged the blade of the leader of the band, and was instantly beset by another warrior on the fellow's right. Over at his left, Yirl Du fought alone, but was pitted against an excellent fencer who kept him constantly on the defensive. Levri Thornel, on his right, was attacked by the remaining two, and showed amazing skill with sword and dagger, thrusting, cutting and parrying with a calm precision that bespoke long years of practice.

FOR A TIME there was only the clash of steel on steel and an occasional grunt from one of the wounded contestants. Then Thorne thrust the leader of the band through the throat, and he went down with a gurgling cry. With his chief opponent out of the way it was but child's play for him to quickly dispose of the other. Then, seeing that the rugged Yirl Du was getting the best of his assailant, he dashed to the assistance of Levri Thornel.

The old man still stood his ground, apparently unhurt, as Thorne came in to engage one of his opponents. A clumsy fencer, the fellow quickly succumbed to the Earth-man's blade. At the same instant Levri Thornel ran his antagonist through the heart. Turning, Thorne saw Yirl Du coming toward them, cleansing his blade with a bit of fabric cut from the cloak of his fallen adversary.

"A glorious victory, my lord," he said, as he came up. "Six enemies stretched out on the sand, and we three still live."

"It was well fought," agreed Thorne. "But who could these men be? And how came they to be waiting here for us?"

"I recognized the last fellow I killed," said Yirl Du. "He was a henchman of Sel Han. The spies of the flat-nosed deputy evidently discovered the plot to release us, and he posted these assassins here for the purpose of ambushing us. He expected but two, and we were three—enough to defeat his cutthroats and upset his scheme."

"That is true," agreed Thorne. He turned to Levri Thornel. "It is you, my friend, who turned the tide. But for you, Yirl Du and I would now be stark on the sand in the place of these six assassins. Until I am able to express my appreciation more fittingly, permit me to merely thank you."

"It is I who owe you a lasting debt of gratitude," protested the old man. "But for you I would be down there in the pit, doomed to die a lingering and horrible death. As it is, I—I—" Suddenly he swayed, and pitched forward on his face.

Alarmed, Thorne sprang to his side, and, turning him over, asked:

"What is it, my friend? Are you ill?"

"Ill unto death," tire old fellow replied weakly. "I was wounded early in the-engagement and have been bleeding freely since. It is the end I would have chosen. Farewell, my two brave comrades."

Hastily, Thorne undid his cloak, exposing a wound just above the heart. For a moment he held his hand there, but felt no pulsations.

"Levri Thornel is dead," he solemnly told Yirl Du.

"He was a brave man, my lord. And now we must look for that leaning stone, and be gone. If the morning sun finds us near the baridium pit, we too are dead men."

Sadly, silently, they gathered their javelins and moved forward. Presently they came to the leaning stone.

"It was at the north base of the stone we were to look," said Thorne, "yet there is nothing here."

Yirl Du thrust a javelin into the sand. At a depth of about ten inches it encountered an obstruction. Swiftly he dropped to his knees and began scooping out the sand with his cupped hands.

CHAPTER XVI

THE DESERT MONSTER

AFTER A FEW moments of digging, Yirl Du grasped something and dragged it up out of the sand. It was a pole about eight feet in length, one end of which was inserted in a cylinder six inches in diameter and four feet long. Three pairs of straps were fastened to this cylinder and a bit of stirrup-shaped metal projected from its lower end.

At the opposite end of the pole was a cone-shaped cushion of reddish-brown resilient material.

Swiftly the Jen of the Takkor Free Swordsmen unearthed three more objects like the first, and two poles about sixteen feet long. Then he dragged out two large metal water bottles and two boxes, to all of which carry-straps were attached.

Opening one of the boxes, Thorne discovered that it contained food, fire-powder and medical supplies. Among these was a bottle of jembal gum. He heated some of this by burning a small quantity of fire-powder. Then he dressed Yirl Du's wounds and burns, after which his henchman did the like for him.

"Now, my lord," said Yirl Du, "if you will be seated I will strap on your desert legs for you."

Although Thorne had no idea what the pole and cylinder combinations were for, he began to understand when his sturdy retainer brought two of them and, after inserting his feet in the stirrups, began strapping them to his legs. When they were properly fastened in place, he next strapped a box to the Earth-

121

man's back, slung his javelins in their quiver, and hung his water bottle by a strap across his shoulder. Then he handed him one of the poles.

"Now you are ready, my lord," he said, "and I'll be on my own desert legs very shortly."

It did not take Yirl Du long to do for himself what he had done for Thorne. Then, grasping his pole with both hands, he thrust one end into the sand beside him, and drew himself up until he stood on his two long stilts. Thorne, who had not wished to reveal his ignorance of the use of "desert legs," now followed his example. With his weight on them the tops of the stilts were compressed a little way into the cylinders, which evidently contained powerful springs. The resilient, cone-shaped feet kept the stilts from sinking into the sand and added to the illusion of floating feather-like through space which the springs induced.

Yirl Du started off, walking toward the northwest. Thorne attempted to imitate his gait, but found it quite difficult, much like walking on bed-springs or an aerial artist's net. At each step his desert leg threw him forward like a springboard, so that several times he was compelled to use his long pole to keep from falling on his face.

"What ails you, my lord?" asked Yirl Du. "Have you become weakened from loss of blood?"

"I'll be all right in a little while," Thorne replied. "Just a dizziness that will pass off."

Thereafter, he set out to master the technique of walking on desert legs, with a grim determination to do so without help or instruction from his henchman. Presently he got the swing of it, whereupon Yirl Du gradually increased the pace until both of them were running. Not until then did the Earth-man discover the tremendous advantage of traveling with desert legs. At each step the stilt now sank deeply into the cylinder, then hurled him upward and forward like a catapult.

THE NIGHT was cold and frosty, and the exercise just sufficient to make him draw in great lungfuls of the sweet desert air. What a relief after the baridium pit, with its searing, acrid fumes and its deadly clouds of corrosive dust! This was freedom; exhilarating, stimulating. What if love had cheated him, mocked him, on this world and another? He still had life and health, and that siren to beckon him onward which is the true love of every real adventurer—the lure of the unknown.

As the night wore on and morning approached, the bright nearer moon once more popped above the western horizon, and hurtling forward to greet its slower, paler companion, made the sand particles and frost crystals glitter and sparkle. But long before the two moons could meet in the sky, the sun, heralded by a brief flash of silver-gray light, shot above the eastern horizon in the full blaze of its glory, and both satellites faded from view.

A few moments later, Yirl Du sighted a clump of conifers, and the two men made for it. They found a dry water-hole, but this did not daunt them with their full bottles, and the trees offered concealment and shade. Unstrapping their desert legs, they gathered firewood, brewed pulcho, and with the hot, stimulating beverage, washed down their morning meal of dried meat and hard travelers' cakes. Then, after extinguishing their fire with sand, they stretched out in the shade to sleep.

Thorne fell asleep almost immediately. Nor did he awaken until Yirl Du shook him soundly.

"The day is all but sped, my lord," he said. "I have brewed fresh pulcho and prepared our evening meal. We should eat and be ready to start as soon as the sun sets."

Refreshed by his long sleep, Thorne tackled his meal with gusto. "What of our enemies?" he asked. "It seems strange that no signs of pursuit have developed."

"But they have developed," replied Yirl Du. "I am a light sleeper, and several times during the day as I lay awake, I saw bands of warriors mounted on gawrs flying overhead. Had they paused to search our hiding place we would have been killed or captured long ere this. Fortunately they did not."

The sun set just as they finished their meal, and they packed their belongings and strapped on their desert legs by the light of the nearer moon. Then they set out once more. Yirl Du had estimated that by traveling all night and sleeping during the daytime, they would be able to reach the edge of the Takkor Marsh in three nights. Here he would know how to find Thaíne, if she were still alive and uncaptured, and they would be able to fulfill Thorne's promise to help her search for her father.

They made swift progress traveling by the light of the nearer moon, but it soon set and as on the night before there was a period of darkness during which only the stars and planets glittered overhead. This slowed them down considerably, as they were forced to proceed in the dark with extreme caution. And so, when the farther moon appeared above the eastern horizon, they welcomed it with joy, for it meant that they could set out once more at full speed.

THEY had traveled for some time by its pale light when Thorne noticed, over at his left, an object projecting above the horizon which he at first took for a tall, tufted conifer. But he suddenly became aware that it was moving; not like a tree swaying in the breeze, but actually traveling over the ground and coming with considerable speed in his direction. As the thing rapidly drew closer he was able to make out a huge head with a hooked beak, a long, scrawny neck, and a large, birdlike body supported by two legs, each of which was at least fifteen feet in length. The head of the monster, he judged, towered at least thirty feet above the ground.

He called to his companion who, with eyes only for the trail ahead, had evidently not noticed the monstrous thing that was stalking them. "Ho, Yirl Du. Do you see what is coming after us?"

His henchman looked around, then cried out in alarm. "A koree! We must hasten, or we are dead men. It is the great man-eating bird of the desert."

They accelerated their pace from a trot to a run. Soon they

had lengthened their thirty-foot steps to nearly fifty. But the koree kept coming on, and despite their utmost exertions, gaining on them.

Thorne, less skillful with the desert legs than his companion, began to fall behind, while the monster, still shortening the distance between them, soon towered only fifty feet behind. It was a hideous thing the pale moonlight revealed to Thorne as he glanced fearfully over his shoulder—a giant bird with a crest of waving plumes, and a huge curved beak that looked fully capable of cutting a man in two with a single snap.

Its long lean neck was bare of feathers and covered with a wrinkled, leathery skin. Like the neck, the body was leathery and naked. The wings, which were short and obviously useless for flight, were featherless, but covered with sharp, horny pro-tuberances which made them quite formidable weapons. The long legs were armored with large, rough scales, and the toes were equipped with sickle-shaped retractile claws. The monster ran with its ugly head projecting far forward and its wings sticking stiffly out from its leathery body, as if to prevent its intended victim from suddenly doubling back to the right or left.

In the meantime Yirl Du, noticing that the koree was likely to catch up with Thorne at any moment, dropped back beside him.

"Can you not travel faster, my lord?" he asked.

"I'm afraid I've reached my limit," Thorne panted. Trained athlete though he was, he was beginning to tire from this unac-customed exertion.

"Then we must separate," Yirl Du told him. "The bird will follow one of us. The other must then turn and follow it, hurling as many javelins into it as possible. Thus each, in turn, may distract its attention from the other until it is so badly wounded it will give up the chase. I have little hope of slaying it, as we must keep out of reach of that beak. One snap is sure death."

They separated, and the bird followed Thorne. Yirl Du instantly turned and pursued it. His first throw struck just behind the left wing, but despite his great strength and skill at hurling the javelin, he was only able to drive it through that tough skin for a little way. A second, striking below it, penetrated to a depth of about a foot. But it was enough to exasperate the monster, which turned and rushed at its persistent tormentor.

Thorne now turned and hurled a javelin. Striking at the point where the right leg joined the body it only penetrated deeply enough for the barb to hold. He tried a second cast, this time throwing with all his might. The javelin passed clear over the body of the bird and struck it in the back of the neck. Like the first, however, it only sank in up to the first barb, and therefore did not do much damage. It was enough, however, to cause the monster to turn and charge him.

Instantly the Earth-man shot out at right angles to the course he had been following. But he made the mistake of watching the bird without looking at the ground before him. As a result he ran straight into a tangle of desert sand-flowers. First one stilt, then the other, caught in the snarl of tough vines, and he plunged, face downward, into the sand about twenty feet beyond.

He managed to retain his grip on the long pole he carried, although it had been split when he fell, and now, after quickly turning on his back, attempted to raise himself onto his desert legs once more.

But he was not quick enough. Already the koree towered above him, its leathery neck arched and its huge beak distended for the kill.

CHAPTER XVII

ERINÉ

AS THE FRIGHTFUL head of the koree, with its huge, gaping beak darted down to seize him, Thorne, lying where he had fallen, gripped his walking pole with both hands. Encumbered by his desert legs, he was unable to dodge, and there was no time to seize a weapon, even had he possessed one that would have done execution against that terrible head. Instinctively, he struck at the descending horror with the pole.

The blow did the creature no more injury than if it had been struck with one of its own feathers. But it did distract the monster's attention from the man. Evidently taking the pole for a part of his anatomy, it seized it with the immense beak, and, bracing its feet like a robin drawing a worm from the ground, pulled upward.

Thorne, still clinging to the pole, was surprised to find himself standing on his desert legs once more, not three feet from the base of that leathery neck, which the bird had stretched to the utmost. Still clinging to the pole with his left hand, he whipped out his sword with his right. Then, with every ounce of strength at his command, he slashed at that taut neck. It was a powerful drawing cut, and the keen, saw-edged blade sheared through to the vertebral column.

As the blood spurted from the gaping wound, the Earth-man let go of the pole and sprang away, almost colliding with Yirl Du, who had hurled all his remaining javelins in a fruitless effort to distract the monster's attention, and was now rushing in with drawn sword. The bird dropped the pole and plunged after them. But it had only taken a few steps when it stumbled and fell. For some time it flopped about erratically, squawking weakly and scattering gallons of its life blood on the sand. Then it suddenly collapsed and lay still.

Cautiously, the two men now approached the fallen giant. Yirl Du let himself to the ground, unstrapped his desert legs and set about gathering the javelins that still had sound shafts. This done, he recovered Thorne's walking pole for him. Then he donned his desert legs once more, and they resumed their journey.

Morning found them in a bleak section of the desert that was devoid of vegetation as far as they could see in every direction. As there was no fuel available, they washed their dry rations down with plain water instead of pulcho. Then they buried their desert legs, poles, boxes and bottles in the sand, dug other holes, and covered themselves until nothing showed but their transparent masks. Thus, protected from the intense heat of the sun as well as the prying eyes of any pursuers who might chance to fly over this spot, they slept.

As soon as the sun had set they had another cold meal and were off again. In the early hours before dawn, when the combined light of both moons made everything stand out clearly around them, they reached the top of a rugged cliff which somehow looked familiar to Thorne. Then he recalled that a line of such cliffs rimmed the ancient ocean bed in which the Takkor Marsh lay.

THEY paused on the brink and looked over. About a hundred feet below them was a broad ledge. At approximately the same distance below that was still another. And seventy feet farther down was the sloping, bowlder-strewn beach.

Suddenly, to Thorne's consternation, Yirl Du deliberately stepped over the edge of the cliff. The Earth-man uttered an exclamation of horror as he saw his henchman drop straight toward the ledge a hundred feet below. He envisioned the faithful fellow lying, a bloody crumpled heap, on that stony surface. But he had forgotten that desert legs might be useful for purposes other than walking. Yirl Du alighted squarely on his, sank almost to the depth of the cylinders, and then shot forward and upward. Soaring over the rim of the ledge on which he stood, he dropped to the next, bounced onward again, and alighted on the ground below.

Thorne looked down at the ledge a hundred feet beneath him, and suddenly drew back as a vertigo attacked him. For a moment he was minded to remove his desert legs and try to clamber down the rough cliff-face. But at the sight of Yirl Du, standing on the sloping beach below, unhurt and looking up at him, evidently wondering why he delayed, he decided to risk the jump. Accordingly, he stepped over the edge of the cliff into empty air.

There was a vertical rush of wind past his face, then his stilts plunged almost to the tops of the cylinders, and he shot upward once more. As he had neglected to throw himself far enough forward he bounced twice before he got over the rim of the ledge. But when he next alighted he knew how to throw his weight to the front so he was catapulted over the rim. A moment later he joined Yirl Du, and together they scrambled down the sloping beach with gigantic steps, until they came to a zone of trees, vines and underbrush so thickly entangled that they made any further use of the desert legs impossible.

They accordingly let themselves to the ground, and removing these devices which had been so useful to them in crossing the desert, hid them in the underbrush together with the poles, and continued their advance afoot.

The rising sun found them on the bank of a little stream at the edge of the marsh. Here they brewed pulcho and ate their morning meal. Then, exhausted by the night's exertions, they flung themselves down for a short rest, lying so that the sun, shining in their faces, would awaken them by mid-morning.

Thorne awoke first, and seeing that his tired friend slumbered on despite the sunlight in his face, decided to let him rest a while longer. To his delight, he noticed that the yellow discoloration from the baridium fumes had entirely disappeared from Yirl Du's skin. He examined his own hands. They, too, had returned to their normal color. As he had no mirror in which to view his face, he went down to the stream.

He had knelt on the bank, and was just parting the rushes, when a reflection in the water before him caused him to look up. A huge black bat was pursuing what at first glance appeared to be a large butterfly. Suddenly the bat swooped, and though its prey managed to elude its teeth and talons, one of the long black pinions struck it a sharp blow. Apparently disabled or partly stunned by the blow, the smaller creature fluttered groundward, falling into the rushes not ten feet from Thorne.

IN A STEEP spiral, the bat swooped toward its fallen prey. Leaping to his feet, Thorne saw the futile fluttering of a pair of lacy, opalescent wings above the rushes, and knew that in a moment more the bat would claim its victim. Suddenly moved by a wave of pity for the fluttering, helpless thing on the ground, he jerked a javelin from his quiver and hurled it at the descending monster. It struck the black, furry neck with such force that the barbed head emerged from the other side.

Now it was the bat which fluttered helplessly. Then it tumbled into the rushes only a few feet from the creature it had struck down, floundered about for a moment, squeaking frenziedly and emitting from its defensive scent glands a pungent, nauseating odor before death put an end to its struggles.

Having satisfied himself that the ugly, odoriferous thing was really dead, Thorne stepped over for a closer look at its intended prey. But as he did so, the lacy wings suddenly rose above the rushes, and he stifled a cry of amazement when he saw that they were attached to the shoulders of a slender, perfectly formed girl about three feet in height.

Save for a girdle of filmy, pale green material drawn tight at the waist by a belt of exquisitely wrought golden mesh and ending in a short skirt, she was nude. Her silky skin was a perfect flesh tint, and covered with a fine down, delicate as peach bloom. Her golden yellow hair was bound by a fillet of woven green jade links, circling her forehead just below two delicate, feathery antennae, which swept upward and backward like a pair of dainty plumes.

Save for the wings, the antennae, and the delicate peach bloom which covered her silky skin, she might have been an unusually well formed midget of Thorne's own people. But these made it evident that she belonged to the insect, rather than the mammalian world. As he stood staring incredulously down at her, scarcely believing his eyes, and totally at a loss as to what to do or say, she suddenly faded from his view.

The Earth-man blinked and looked again. But where she had stood he now saw only the rushes which had been bent downward by the weight of her tiny body. Then, doubting the testimony of his eyes, he leaned forward and explored the spot with his hand. But it only encountered empty air.

The thought came then that this lovely, evanescent creature was only part of a dream, a hallucination, something that really had never existed at all except in his imagination. Yet a glance showed him that the bat was still lying there, black and hideous, with his javelin protruding from its neck. And his sense of smell very definitely confirmed that of sight, in this instance. Had the bat also been suffering from a hallucination when it pursued this frail being? And could a mere dream-creature flatten the rushes when it fell to the ground?

Faintly he heard the fluttering of wings overhead. He looked up and saw only the empty sky, yet the fluttering continued, beating little air currents down against his upturned face. Suddenly a little pixie voice, musical as a silver bell, broke the silence.

"I know you now, man of the Old Race," it said. "You are Sheb Takkor, the younger. You have saved the life of Eriné, daughter of the Vil of the Ulfi, and she is not ungrateful. Hold out your hand."

In obedient wonder, he extended his right hand. A glittering something dropped into his palm. He saw that it was a tiny ring fashioned from platinum and set with a sparkling green gem.

"If you should ever need the Ulfi, rub the jewel," continued the silvery voice, "and if there is an Ulf within scent of the ring-he will be yours to command."

"Very kind of you," said Thorne, "but—" He suddenly realized that the fluttering had stopped. He was talking to empty air.

YIRL DU had come down the bank and was surveying him quizzically, as if he questioned his sanity. Nor did Thorne blame him. But for that tiny, glittering circlet which he could see and feel in his palm, and the ugly, odoriferous carcass of the black bat, he would have questioned it himself. And as it was, he was none too sure.

"Your pardon, my lord," said Yirl Du. "Were you speaking to me?"

"Yes. No. I was speaking to an Ulf—that is, to an Ulf maiden." He paused to note the effect of his words on his henchman, half suspecting that the latter would suggest he had been touched by the sun. But Yirl Du did not seem greatly surprised.

"Has one of the Little People paid us a visit?" he asked.

"Not intentionally, I guess," Thorne told him. "You see, she was struck down by that bat," indicating the carcass. "I saw her fall, thinking her only a butterfly, yet I pitied the poor, stricken creature and so slew the bat with a javelin. She became invisible and presented me with this," holding out the ring.

Yirl Du exclaimed with astonishment.

"Why, that is indeed a precious thing, my lord," he said, "and such a gift as only the Vil of the Ulfi or a member of his family might present to a man."

"She named herself Eriné, daughter of the Vil," Thorne said.

Thorne was brimming over with questions about the Little People. He wanted to ask his sturdy henchman more about what they were, how and where they lived, and how it was possible for one of them to disappear before his eyes. He also wondered why Eriné, the tiny Ulf maiden, had not made use of this power to elude the bat. He resolved, however, to curb his curiosity until he could talk to Thaíne or Lal Vak. Sheb Takkor, he reasoned, would be supposed to know these things. To question Yirl Du about them would be to make him suspect either that he was not Sheb Takkor, or that he had taken leave of his senses.

Accordingly, he kept silence while they climbed the bank to get their belongings. Thorne was about to strap his box to his back when Yirl Du said:

"Wait. Let us first get our water-shoes."

"Water-shoes! I didn't see any in my box," Thorne replied.

Yirl Du opened his box and took out a cylinder of rolled, reddish brown material. The Earth-man then remembered having seen such a cylinder in his box, and raising the lid, extracted it. Unrolling it, he found it consisted of two hollow pieces of resilient material, to each of which was attached a small tube with a shut-off valve. He observed that Yirl Du had opened the valve on one of his and was inflating it by blowing through the tube, so he followed his example. Soon each had a pair of buoyant, boat-shaped water-shoes.

AFTER adjusting their weapons and other paraphernalia, they carried the shoes down to the water's edge and donned them by pushing their toes under elastic bands designed to cross the arch of the foot. This done, they stepped out onto the surface of the stream.

Yirl Du started off downstream, moving with strokes much like those of a skater. Thorne, trying to imitate him, found that water-shoeing was more difficult than it looked. At the first attempt, his legs spread so far apart he came near to sitting down in midstream. After several determined efforts he succeeded in achieving the perpendicular once more. Again and again he tried to glide forward as his henchman had done, but it always seemed that both feet were very definitely bent on traveling in different directions.

Observing his clumsy efforts, Yirl Du said:

"I fear we should have rested longer, my lord. You have grown weak from your wounds."

"No, just out of practice," Thorne told him. "I didn't use any water-shoes while I was at school, you know. I'll get back the hang of it, presently."

And at length, by persistent effort, he did get the hang of it. They started off slowly at first, but by the time the sun had reached the zenith they were making excellent speed, moving side by side in perfect unison, with long, rhythmic strokes. During this time they had traveled on a dozen winding streams, crossed six small lakes, and three times removed their water-shoes for short jaunts across the land.

At present they were gliding across the calm, mirror-like bosom of a lake much larger than any they had crossed thus far, when Thorne, chancing to notice a shadowy reflection in the placid water at his right, looked upward. To his alarm, he saw that a group of about twenty warriors, each mounted on a gawr, were gliding down toward them. And the warriors were mail-clad, round-bodied yellow men.

"Look, Yirl Du!" he cried, pointing aloft. "The Ma Gongi!"

His companion took one look.

"Straight toward that point of land, quickly!" Yirl Du exclaimed. "It is our only hope."

They had been making for the mouth of a little stream, beside which the point of land projected. Now, however, they turned almost at right angles to their course and made for the shore which was about two hundred yards distant.

But they had traveled only a few strokes toward their objective when a large net, hanging on four cables, was dropped by one of their pursuers. In an instant it had scooped up Yirl Du. Thorne saw him struggling futilely like some captured wild thing—saw him draw his dagger and vainly try to cut the metallic meshes.

Then the Earth-man heard a swish in the water behind him, and he, too, was scooped up in a huge net.

CHAPTER XVIII

THE LITTLE PEOPLE

AS SOON AS he felt the net swish under him in the water, Thorne instinctively dived forward in an effort to evade it. But it had traveled too far beneath him to make such an attempt successful. However, he was able to catch hold of the rim with both hands, and clung to this as he was borne aloft, so he did not sink into the toils as Yirl Du had done.

An instant later he was soaring fifty feet above the treetops, and though he well knew the risk he ran, decided on a desperate attempt at escape. Accordingly, he drew himself up until the edge of the net was on a level with his thighs, then turned a somersault and let go, falling feet foremost.

His feet were still thrust through the bands of his pneumatic water-shoes, and these helped, to a considerable extent, in breaking his fall as he crashed downward through the branches of a large tree. It was fortunate indeed for him that he alighted in the outer branches rather than near the trunk, thus striking no thick limbs. Straight down through the foliage he plunged, and upon striking the ground bounced upward like a rubber ball on his resilient water-shoes. After several gradually diminishing bounces, he checked himself by clutching a shrub. Then he swiftly removed the water-shoes, and, taking them under his arm, dashed away through the thick undergrowth.

So dense was the leafy tangle overhead that Thorne was unable to see his enemies, though he heard their shouts and learned that a warrior was landing to ascertain whether he had been killed or maimed by his leap, or had escaped. But this same dense canopy prevented his enemies from seeing him, and for this he was thankful.

He was grieved by the capture of his faithful retainer, and for a moment thought of returning to the spot where he had alighted and making a desperate attempt at rescuing him. Reason told him, however, that such an attempt would be worse than futile. He could not possibly help Yirl Du, and would only render his own capture or death certain. Moreover, there was his debt to Tháine, and his promise to her, as yet unfulfilled. Somehow he must contrive to escape for her sake.

It was not long before he came to a narrow stream, almost completely concealed from observers in the sky by the branches and lianas which arched and interlaced across it.

The stream, he soon found, had seemingly endless ramifications, and he followed one after another at haphazard, knowing that each new turn was an added aid in baffling pursuit. After he had traveled for several hours in this manner he grew weary, hungry and thirsty, and decided to stop for rest and refreshment. Instead of stepping directly out on the bank, he caught hold of a low-hanging liana, by means of this reached another, and swung himself up into a tree. Removing his water-shoes and slinging them over his back, he now traveled for some distance by swinging from tree to tree before alighting on the ground.

WEARILY he flung himself down on a bed of soft moss beneath the spreading branches of an immense, aromatic sebolis tree. Then, after a pull at his water flask, he opened his box and removed therefrom a ration of dried meat and a cake. These he washed down with copious draughts of cold water. His hunger and thirst allayed, he rested there on the moss for a while, then packed up and wandered on.

As he felt that he had effectively baffled his pursuers, and knew that he was hopelessly lost, he saw no great need for haste, and accommodated his speed to the weariness of his overtaxed muscles. Moreover, not knowing in which direction the hiding place of Thaíne lay, he reflected that if he chose to increase his speed he might be running directly away from her instead of toward her.

And so he wandered on through this strange Martian jungle, pausing at times to examine odd flowers or fruits, and marveling at its fantastic and often gigantic insect life, as well as its many queer beasts, birds and reptiles. Among these, he several times saw individuals large and formidable enough to make dangerous antagonists, but in each case succeeded in avoiding them without attracting their attention.

Part of the time he walked on boggy land from which the water oozed at each step, and often he splashed through shallow pools. At other times he was compelled to don his water-shoes to cross flooded areas where the trees stood in the water.

There were also considerable stretches of high, dry land, usually quite heavily wooded.

Shortly after he had entered one of these he suddenly sighted a colony of pale green caterpillars, the bodies and heads of which were protected by sharp yellow spikes. There was a great diversity of size among them, the smallest being barely an inch in length, while the largest were more than three feet long and proportionately thick. All were browsing on leaves except a few of the largest individuals, which were busy spinning cocoons. As he passed onward among the feeding larvae with their perpetually working mandibles, he noticed many finished cocoons hanging from limbs by twisted, rope-like fastenings. They were pale green in color, and of a glistening, silky texture.

Presently he came to one hanging directly above his path, its lower tip at the height of his head. Curiously, he extended his hand to feel the silky covering, and pinched it to test its thickness. But scarcely had he done so ere a mournful, wailing cry smote his ears. It sounded much like the cry of a new-born human child, and seemed to come from the cocoon he had touched.

He jerked his hand away, but the wailing continued. Then he was suddenly aware of the whirring of a host of invisible wings in the air above him. There was a sharp twang, and a tiny arrow embedded itself in the ground at his feet. A second whizzed past his ear, and a third grazed his arm.

He realized that he was being attacked by the Little People, and suddenly thought of the ring. Snatching it from the pouch in which he had placed it, he rubbed it briskly on his palm. At this the twanging of the bowstrings ceased, and where he had only heard the beating of their wings, he now saw a number of Ulf men hovering in the air.

All of them were slightly larger than Eriné. Some were well formed, with handsome, regular features. Others were thin and angular, and still others more than pleasingly plump. In short, there was as much diversity of appearance among them as there would have been in a similar sized group of humans. Like Eriné's, their silky skins were covered with a soft down, and the features of some individuals were muffled in thick, fluffy beards. Their antennae were longer than those of the Ulf girl, and projected from shiny metal headpieces, notched at the front to let them through. They wore shirts of light chain-mail which reached to their thighs, drawn in at the middle by green silk belts from which depended swords and daggers. In addition to these weapons, each man carried a small bow in his hand, and a quiver of arrows strapped to his thigh.

ONE OF the tiny warriors alighted on the ground, and advancing, saluted Thorne respectfully.

"Fleeswin, a Jen of the Ulf Archers, shields his eyes in the light of your presence, man of the Old Race and friend of Estabil, the Great One," he said. "We regret that we attacked you unknowingly, and humbly craving your pardon, place ourselves at your disposal and under your command."

"My greetings to you and your archers, Fleeswin Jen," Thorne answered, returning his salute. "Actuated by curiosity I touched this cocoon which hung in my path, not meaning to injure it."

"Our infants are easily frightened by the touch of strangers," Fleeswin said, "and it is well that this is true, as we who guard them cannot watch them all at one time. We would lose many that might otherwise be saved if they did not summon us when menaced or interfered with."

"Then I am fortunate that your marksmanship was no better," Thorne told him.

"Had you been one of the Ma Gongi, you would now be bristling with arrows," Fleeswin hastened to inform him. "But we saw you were of the Old Race, so only shot to drive you away. Though the Ma Gongi kill and eat us, it is seldom that we are attacked by a man of the Old Race. But perhaps I weary you with talk. What would you with us, Bearer of the Ring?"

"If you can help me to find Thaíne, daughter of Miradon Vil, I'll be grateful," Thorne answered. "I am the Rad of Takkor and her friend."

As soon as he had announced his title, every member of the little company saluted. Some had, by this time, alighted on the ground behind their leader. Others perched on limbs, and still others hovered lightly in the air around him.

"We are doubly honored," said Fleeswin, "that you prove to be the Lord of Takkor as well as a Bearer of the Ring. As for finding Thaíne, if she is anywhere within the Takkor Marsh, our Vil can find her for you. Permit me to conduct you to him."

After sending a warrior ahead to announce their coming, and placing another in temporary charge of the archers, Fleeswin led the way. Part of the time their path lay through thick, dark jungle, so dense that direct sunlight rarely reached the ground. But these dark stretches were pleasantly varied from time to time by open glades in which gorgeous flowers bloomed, attracting bees, butterflies, humming birds, and a host of other creatures.

Presently, above the drone of insects and the songs of birds, Thorne heard distant music. Faint at first, it gradually increased in volume as he advanced—a haunting exquisite fantasy of sound which seemed to emanate from a carillon of no less than a thousand tiny silver-tongued bells. Yet he knew, as he drew closer, that it was not bells he heard, but a chorus of Ulf voices. Soon he was able to distinguish the words of their song, and was surprised to learn that it was a paean of welcome for him.

A MOMENT later he and Fleeswin emerged into a pleasant glen, the verdure-clothed sides of which rose steeply at his right and left. The place literally swarmed with the Ulfi, both male and female, and all were singing—some hanging suspended in the air with fanning wings, some perched in the trees or upon outcropping rocks on the hillside, some standing in cave mouths, with which the place was honeycombed, and others gathered on the mossy ground.

He noticed that all were adults, and for a moment was puzzled by the absence of children. Then he suddenly remembered the horny, green-and-yellow monstrosities he had seen. Those ugly caterpillars were the Ulf children, and in their silken cocoons it must be that they metamorphosed into full grown Ulfi, their entire growth being attained while in the caterpillar stage.

Fleeswin now kept to the ground, marching with his little head proudly erect as if some great and honorable task had been delegated to him. As Thorne came abreast of the first singers, these began showering him with tiny, fragrant white blossoms. Then a group of two-score pretty Ulf maidens fluttered down with cries of welcome, and some draped Thorne with garlands while others strewed flowers before him.

Suddenly the music ceased, and Thorne, his body swathed with ropes of blossoms, found himself standing before a jovial looking, pot-bellied old Ulf with cottony white whiskers, puffy cheeks, and a merry twinkle in his eyes, who sat enthroned on the lip of a large lily.

"Greetings, Sheb Takkor Rad," cried the little old fellow on the lily throne, returning his salute. "Estabil, Vil of the Ulfi, bids you welcome to Ulf-land, and desires to publicly thank you for saving the life of his precious daughter, Eriné. If there is aught that Estabil can do for you, you have but to make known your wishes."

"I wish to find—" Thorne began.

"I'll spare you the trouble of saying more," Estabil interrupted. "You wish to find Thaíne. That we can promise to perform for you."

He leaped nimbly down from the lily throne, and continued: "Now that that is done, will you not stay to eat and drink with us? We know there are those among the Old Race who regard us with superstitious awe because of a few powers which we possess which are not familiar to them. Therefore they fabricate tales about us—say that we can transform ourselves into beasts, flowers, stones, or other objects at will—that we steal babies and bring them here as our adopted children—that if our food be eaten or our drink imbibed by a man of the Old Race he will be transformed into one of us and will never be able to leave Ulf-land. Of course a man of your enlightenment would not believe such ridiculous tales."

"Of course not," Thorne assured him, "but it is important that I find Thaíne, quickly. Under the circumstances, I should prefer to stay only long enough to drink a friendly cup with you, though if I were not pressed for time your hospitality would be most welcome. I'm sure you understand."

"We do. Indeed we do," Estabil replied. He turned and raised his hand, whereupon a little bearded Ulf struck a gong. Then there issued from the mouth of a cave in the hillside a figure Thorne instantly recognized. It was Eriné. Behind her came an Ulf maiden bearing a golden tray on which reposed three tiny platinum cups that sparkled with jewels, and a jar.

THORNE saluted as the Vil's daughter approached, and she smiled up at him.

"I hoped I might greet you at the banquet table," she said, "but since you cannot tarry with us, I bring you the cup of friendship and of farewell."

So saying, she filled the three jeweled cups from the jar, handed one to Thorne, one to her father, and retained one for herself.

Estabil raised his cup.

"Once there was a Rad of Takkor," he said, "who, wandering through his marshlands saw an Ulf maiden about to be done to death by a savage monster of the air. The Rad slew the monster and rescued the Ulf maiden, who proved to be the daughter of the Vil of the Ulfi. Every Ulf, from the Vil to his lowliest subject, will never forget. And in this cup we pledge to the Rad of Takkor our eternal friendship."

He and Eriné both raised their cups to their lips, and Thorne followed their example.

Eriné instantly replenished the cups, and Thorne saw that they were waiting for his reply. He raised his cup: "The Rad of Takkor gratefully accepts the pledge of friendship of the Ulfi," he said, "and is deeply sensible of the honor thus bestowed upon him. In return, he pledges his lasting friendship to Estabil, his lovely daughter, and his loyal subjects."

As soon as they had emptied their cups, Estabil raised his hand. Behind him the gong sounded twice, and a dozen Ulf warriors, flying six on a side, emerged from the mouth of a cave high on the hillside, bearing between them a rectangle of silken fabric about eight feet long and four wide. They alighted in front of the Vil, and saluted.

"The Rad of Takkor is ready to be conveyed to the house of Thaíne," he said. Then he turned to Thorne. "Seat yourself in the middle of the cloth, my lord," he invited, "and you will be carried swiftly and safely to your destination."

Though he was not entirely reassured as to the safety of this fragile conveyance, Thorne did as directed.

The Vil raised his hand. The gong sounded three strokes. Then the wings of the twelve Ulf warriors began whirring rapidly, and Thorne felt himself rising. All around him the Ulfi burst into song. He waved farewell. A moment later he was gliding over the tree-tops, the Ulf-song swiftly dying in the distance.

Presently they flew out over a lake, in the center of which was an island. Straight to the island they took him, and set him down in the midst of it in a small clearing.

ONE OF the Ulf warriors touched his arm and pointed.

"There is the house of Thaíne," he said.

Thorne gazed intently in the direction the little fellow indicated. Presently he was able to make out what had entirely escaped his attention before a small, irregularly shaped stone house, camouflaged with vines and creepers, and surrounded by trees. Not fifty feet away from him he saw an opening in the leafy screen which he judged must lead to the door.

"Ah, I see it now. I am beholden to you and your Vil for this favor. Please convey my thanks to him."

One of the little warriors rolled the cloth into a bundle and thrust it beneath his arm. All twelve of them saluted and swiftly faded from view.

He crossed the clearing, and entering the opening in the vines, found a large circular doorway cut in the stone. The door stood open, revealing a large room with several swinging chairs, suspended divans, and a fireplace. Three circular doorways cut in the walls led to other rooms.

"Thaíne," he called, then waited expectantly.

There was no answer.

He was about to call her a second time when he suddenly heard a low growl from one of the rooms beyond. Then, out of that room streaked a huge black-haired beast with short legs, webbed feet, a paddle-shaped tail armed with spikes, and a cavernous mouth as large as that of a crocodile. He instantly recognized it as a dalf, and knew from past experience that, armed though he was, he stood in deadly peril.

There was but one thing to do, and that quickly. Thorne seized the handle of the great door of thick planking, and swung it shut. A moment later he felt the impact of the heavy beast on the other side. He kept his hand on the latch, and it was well that he did so, for he suddenly felt that it was being pressed upward from the other side. Recalling the remarkable sagacity of these creatures, he was convinced that the beast was trying to open the door, and would have done so had he not kept his hold on the latch.

He was looking around for something with which to brace the latch, when he suddenly heard another growl, this time behind him. Turning, he beheld a second dalf, black with a ring of bright yellow fur circling its neck, swiftly bearing down upon him.

CHAPTER XIX

THAÍNE EXPERIMENTS

WHEN HE SAW the second dalf charging toward him, Thorne whipped out his sword and raised it to defend himself. But he lowered it again.

"Tezzu!" he exclaimed.

At this the demeanor of the beast suddenly changed. Instead of charging, it now bounded playfully up to him, then began skipping and leaping around him and making little purring noises deep in its throat.

And now, in the same leafy opening through which the beast had appeared, he saw a slender, girlish figure carrying a basket of fish and a trident.

"Thaíne!" he cried.

"Hahr Ree Thorne! It's really you! I'm so glad!"

Dropping basket and trident, she ran forward, flung her arms around his neck and, much to his amazement, kissed him.

"I thought you would never come," she said, her large brown eyes smiling up into his through sudden tears. "I feared they had killed you."

"They tried hard enough," he replied, "but I got away and came as soon as I could."

"I'm sure you did. Let us go inside and talk while I prepare something to eat. Why do you stand there holding the latch?"

"Because one of your dalfs is on the other side, trying to get at me."

"That's Neem. I had forgotten about him. But he won't molest you, now that I am here."

Thus reassured, Thorne opened the door. Neem, the great black dalf, waddled out to meet his mistress, but paid no attention to the Earth-man. The latter picked up the basket and trident, and they went in.

Thorne insisted upon helping Thaíne prepare the meal, and they soon had pulcho brewing, fish grilling, and fresh cakes baking.

"From your floral decorations, I judge that you have been among the Little People," said Thaíne, as she turned a beautifully browned slab of fish.

"You judge correctly," Thorne replied. "In fact, it was a dozen of their warriors who brought me here. Then they saluted and disappeared. Do you know anything about that strange power of theirs—making themselves invisible?"

"I've seen them do it many times," she told him, "yet how they do it remains a mystery. Our scientists believe they are able to surround themselves with auras of photo-electric force which cause light rays to bend around them and anything within the auras, such as their weapons and clothing. Since we see objects only by means of light rays reflected from them into our eyes, if the rays miss them or bend around them they are invisible to us."

"Sounds reasonable enough," said Thorne. "But what is this force?"

"One might as well ask, 'What is electricity, or magnetism, or gravity?' No one knows, though there are many familiar with their manifestations and many of the laws governing them. So it is with this strange power of the Ulfi. We know that when they are very weary, or weakened by wounds or illness, they are unable to generate this strange force."

"That explains why Eriné was visible when pursued by the bat. She must have been exhausted."

"The bat?"

THORNE told her how he had saved the life of the daughter of the Vil of the Ulfi, and showed her the ring.

"It is a precious gift, and one not lightly bestowed," said Thaíne. "I have one like it, and so has my father, but only because he once saved the life of the Vil of the Little People."

"You remind me," said Thorne, "that we were to go in search of your father. Have you had any word from him?"

"None," she answered. "Even the Ulfi are baffled, and they know almost everything that takes place in this marsh. If alive and conscious, he could have summoned some of them by rubbing his Ulf-ring, but it is quite certain that he has not done this or they would have notified me. I fear I shall never see him again."

Thorne saw the tears gathering in her big brown eyes, and sought to stem the tide. "We'll find your father, never fear," he said reassuringly. "And now that the food is ready, let us eat, and I will tell you of my adventures since I last saw you. I owe you an explanation for staying away so long."

And so, while they ate their simple but tasty fare and sipped their pulcho, he related the story of what had befallen him since they had parted at the margin of Takkor Lake some days before.

When he had finished, she pounced, womanlike, on that very part of the story which he most wished to forget. "This Neva," she said, "is she very beautiful?"

"Very," he replied. "I must admit it, even though she is deceitful and cruel."

"You love her?"

"Would you love a person who had tricked you—then condemned you to a horrible, lingering death?"

"That," said Thaíne, refilling his pulcho cup for him and handing it to him with a knowing little smile, "is not an answer but an evasion."

"Well then, if you must have it, I wish I had never seen her. I succumbed to her deadly charms like a hundred others who, I am told, lost their lives because of her. I thought I loved her

*Thorne's horde swept
upward to battle.*

madly. And she pretended to return my love; then betrayed me. Twice in my lifetime this thing has happened to me. The first time I was desperate. I no longer cared to live, and was prevented from taking my own life by the man who made it possible for me to journey to your planet. With this second, more trying experience, it seems that I have grown much older and wiser. I now see the futility, the absurdity of suicide as a way out. It is a cowardly act—a craven way of evading unpleasant reality rather than facing it."

He stared moodily into his pulcho cup. "But I bore you with these troubles of mine. Let us speak no more of them."

With a little exclamation of sympathy, she set down her cup and moved over to his side. Gently, caressingly, she stroked his bowed head.

"My poor Hahr Ree Thorne," she said. "You do not bore me. Your troubles are my troubles, for are we not true friends?"

He took that caressing hand, laid it against his cheek for a moment and then pressed it to his lips.

"Thaíne," he said, "you are a real friend. Before I met you there was but one link that held my faith in womankind—the memory of my dead mother. But you, little comrade, have forged another."

"I am glad," she said softly, and laid her cheek against his shoulder.

PRESENTLY she leaned forward, half turned, and gazed up into his face.

"Look at me, Hahr Ree Thorne. Is this Neva really so much more beautiful than I?"

He tried to evade her gaze, but could not. Those big brown eyes were insistent—compelling.

"What a question!" he exclaimed "It's just like a woman to think of a poser like that."

"Another evasion," she countered, "but it tells me what I wanted to find out. She is more beautiful."

He studied her smilingly. "I wouldn't say so. She is a blonde, you are a brunette. She is a great beauty of her type, and you of yours. Who can say that a sapphire is more lovely than a ruby, or a ruby more glorious than a diamond? It is a matter of opinion, and opinions differ widely. You and Neva are gems of equal luster, but different."

"Why, then, perhaps I can make you forget this Neva."

Before he was aware of what she was about, she had turned still more—was lying back across his arm. Her eyes were dark wells of enchantment. Her red lips, half parted, drew him seductively. Every maidenly curve of her lovely body was an invitation and a challenge which only a man of graven stone could have ignored. He caught his breath sharply—bent over her.

"Why don't you kiss me?" she pouted.

"You little witch!"

Fiercely he bent down—crushed those warm red lips against his own.

For a moment, she suffered his caress, unresisting. Then, with a little frightened gasp she broke from his embrace—returned to her place beside the pulcho jar. Mechanically, she filled their cups. Tears trembled on her long, dark lashes. Her lips quivered ever so slightly as she handed him his cup.

"Why, Thaine, little comrade, what's wrong?" he asked.

"I—I didn't know it would be like that," she quavered.

"You don't really love me, then?"

"I wish I really knew."

Though he was not so ungallant as to say so, Thorne knew that he, also, must have time to think. It had been a mad moment—one for which he did not hold himself entirely to blame. But now that it was past, he felt the responsibility of it. He knew that Thaine was wholly unsophisticated—that perhaps she had been motivated solely by pity for him when she had embarked on this experiment in love making for the avowed purpose of causing him to forget Neva. It had evidently fright-ened, and perhaps disappointed her. Moreover, he was not so sure that, since he had held the glorious Neva in his arms, another woman would ever have the power to attract him. By exerting her wiles, Thaine had succeeded momentarily, but now that it was over the reaction was quite different. He felt sated, and more than a little ashamed.

Reason told him that Thaine was worth a thousand Nevas. The marsh-girl was true; the Dixtar's daughter false. And he had not lied to Thaine; she really was as great a beauty of her type as was Neva of hers. It was not a question of beauty. It went deeper than that, involving subjective emotions over which he had no control—transcending all reason—flouting all logic. His attraction to Neva had been spontaneous—compelling. Thaine had drawn him by openly exerting her feminine wiles to the utmost. If Neva had done so, it had been accomplished so subtly that he was not even aware of it.

"Think, little comrade," he said. "Take your time, and when you have reached a decision, let me know. In the meantime, let us return to the old basis of friendship."

She leaned across the pulcho cups— placed her hands in his.

"I should never want to give that up, no matter what happens," she said earnestly.

At this juncture there was the noise of huge wings flapping overhead, followed by a thud. Thorne knew from the sounds that a gawr had just flown over the house and landed in the clearing. Both dalfs sprang up, growling ominously, but Thaíne silenced them.

Then, accompanied by Thorne, she ran to the door and peered through the leafy screen.

CHAPTER XX

TRAPPED

WHEN THORNE LOOKED out through the leafy screen that camouflaged the door of Thaíne's island home, he saw that a warrior in the uniform of an officer of the Kamud had dismounted in the clearing. The fellow was leading his gawr beneath the branches of a large, spreading tree, where the bird-beast would be concealed from observers flying overhead. The newcomer walked with the peculiar, rolling gait of a man whose legs are abnormally short in proportion to the rest of his body. Suddenly Thorne recognized him.

"It's Yirl Du!" he exclaimed.

Keeping cautiously beneath the trees which fringed the clearing, Yirl Du circled toward the house. A few moments later he entered the opening in the screen. To Thorne he rendered the usual salutation, but to Thaíne, the royal salute. This surprised the Earth-man until he remembered that she was the daughter of Miradon Vil, and therefore entitled to the homage due a princess.

"I have news—momentous news," said Yirl Du as he entered the hut.

"Have—have you news of my father?" Thaíne asked, anxiously.

"Ill news," he replied. "His majesty is in the clutches of Sel Han, who has imprisoned him in Castle Takkor."

"We must find a way to rescue him," exclaimed Thorne.

"Wait. I have not told you all," Yirl Du said. "Perhaps I had

best begin at the beginning. After I was netted by Sel Han's
Ma Gongi, they searched a while for you, my lord. But at last
they gave up the chase and flew with me to Castle Takkor. I
found the castle garrisoned entirely by Ma Gongi, with Sur
Det and a few of his villainous cronies in command. The scar-
faced villain had been rescued from the prison pen by Sel Han,
because the latter was shortly to have use for his expert blade
and military knowledge.

"It seems that some time ago the yellow scientists rediscovered how to generate the deadly green ray used in warfare by
their ancestors. Since then they have been building large ray
projectors, not as yet being able to manufacture small hand
projectors powerful enough for efficient use. With four of these
projectors and an army of Ma Gongi mounted on gawrs, Sel
Han yesterday flew to Dukor, overawed the army and the people
with the terrible weapons he had brought with him, and took
over the government. He captured all the high officers of the
Kamud, and it is said he intends to proclaim himself Vil of
Xancibar in a day or two. These officers, among whom are Kov
Lutas and Lal Vak, together with the Dixtar and his daughter
Neva, were sent to Castle Takkor, where they are now prison-
ers, guarded by the Ma Gongi warriors.

"Miradon Vil, who had previously been captured by Sel Han's
Ma Gongi scouts, was at first held in the secret camp where
they were making the ray projectors. But as soon as the government had been overthrown, Sel Han ordered him brought to
Castle Takkor, where he could be guarded with the other important prisoners.

"Sur Det, after boasting to me of the triumphs of his per-
fidious master, ordered me imprisoned in a room in one of the
towers, to await the arrival of Sel Han, who would then decide
what my fate should be. But, unfortunately for his plans, he had
me put in a room in which there was a hidden panel which
communicated with a secret passageway that led to the underground cellars, and thence out under the docks.

"I lost no time in making use of this means of escape, but

ran into one of Sel Han's officers who had just paddled in from a fishing trip. I caught him by the throat before he could make a sound, and hung on until he ceased to breathe. Then I donned his uniform and weapons, and boldly ascended to the dock. There, by virtue of the authority vested in my borrowed uniform, I demanded and received a gawr from one of the attendants, and flew away unmolested."

"Do you think it would be possible for you and me to return to the castle, enter by way of the secret passage, and rescue Miradon Vil?" Thorne asked.

"I fear it would not, my lord," Yirl Du answered. "His majesty is too well guarded. He is an even more important prisoner than Irintz Tel. Sel Han holds him as a hostage to prevent any uprising among the royalists, just as he holds the Dixtar to keep the loyal Kamudists from revolting."

"How many ray projectors are left at the castle?" Thorne asked.

"There are none," Yirl Du told him. "All four are in use in Dukor. Where Sel Han goes, there go the projectors, also. He will not leave them in the hands of his most trusted officers, for they are his very lifeblood. Without them he could be easily defeated by a handful of regular soldiers. And so far as I know, no others have been completed."

"Why, then, perhaps we can take the castle," mused Thorne. "You told me once that the Free Swordsmen would revolt against the rule of any but a rad of the Takkor blood."

"I'm sure they are loyal, my lord," Yirl Du said. "You have but to command, and they will fight to the last man to recover your castle for you."

"Good. I think it can be done without heavy losses. I have a plan."

THAT afternoon, shortly after Thorne had outlined his plan and given his instructions to Yirl Du, the latter flew away in the direction of Takkor City.

Some time later, when the shadows had begun to lengthen,

Thorne, who had been snatching forty winks on one of Thaíne's divans, was awakened by her hand on his brow.

"The time has come," she said.

Thorne sat up, drank the cup of freshly brewed pulcho she proffered him, and sprang to the floor.

"Now if you will be so kind as to lend me Tezzu and a boat," he said, "I'll be off."

"Why do you say 'lend,'" she asked, "when I am going with you?"

"You are to remain here. There will be fighting—bloodshed. It is too dangerous."

She drew herself up proudly.

"I am a warrior, and as good a swordsman as the man you just sent to rally your followers," she said. "I am going with you."

"But don't you see that even if we succeed in capturing the castle we won't dare to remain there?" Thorne argued. "We must scatter immediately, for as soon as he learns of our revolt, Sel Han may come and blast Castle Takkor out of existence. And I had planned to bring your father and his friends to this place of refuge. You are to remain here and make ready for our coming. If we don't come—well—you will be safe, at least."

"There is nothing here to make ready," she said, "and I, the daughter of the Vil, am going, as is my right. It you won't take me with you I shall go in a separate boat."

Seeing the impossibility of dissuading her from her resolve, Thorne set about making preparations for their journey. They then took Tezzu, the yellow-banded dalf, with them, leaving Neem, the other beast, to guard the house, and went down to the boat.

Tezzu, with the tow-rope in his huge mouth, swiftly took them across the lake and into a narrow stream where the foliage arching overhead concealed them from the sight of flying enemies. After traversing a veritable network of these tiny streams and crossing a number of small lakes, they reached the shore of Takkor Lake just before sundown.

At the command of his mistress, Tezzu dragged the boat up out of the water, upon which ice crystals were already beginning to form, and into a place of concealment, where he was left to guard it. Then the man and girl set off along the lake shore, following the same route that Thorne had followed upon his first disastrous visit to Castle Takkor, and carefully keeping out of sight among the trees.

They had not traveled far before the sun set, so they were forced to pick their way through the undergrowth by the light of the nearer moon. Shortly thereafter, Yirl Du appeared in the path before them.

"Everything is arranged," he said softly. "I have been waiting to lead you to the rendezvous."

They paused only long enough to draw up their boots and let down their head-cloaks for warmth. Then Yirl Du led them away through the glittering, frost-coated jungle. Presently they came to a large clearing where several hundred warriors, mounted on gawrs, were assembled, and more were arriving constantly from all points of the compass, singly and in small groups. There was also a group of fifty warriors who were un-mounted.

"In a little while there will be five hundred mounted warriors here, my lord," said Yirl Du. "My son, Rid Du, has assembled a thousand more afoot. They are scattered about in the city, seemingly only amusing themselves, but will rally to him at the signal, half to capture the gawrs on the wharf and the other half to rush the castle gate."

Shortly thereafter the last flying warrior arrived. Yirl Du had brought a gawr for Thorne, but had not expected Thaine, and therefore had provided no mount for her. However, one of the flying fighters gave up his gawr to her and joined the foot-soldiers, and they were ready to begin their desperate attempt.

AFTER a brief final conference with Thorne, Yirl Du led his foot-soldiers away. They were picked men, for they were going on an exceedingly dangerous mission—to follow Yirl Du through the secret passageway into the castle and then capture and throw open the gates, so the soldiers under Rid Du could rush in.

Thorne was to lead the air attack which was calculated first to draw the attention of the defenders from Yirl Du's little party, and later to assist in crushing the Ma Gongi guards.

After he had waited for the length of time agreed upon with Yirl Du, Thorne gave the signal to his men, and one by one the great bird-beasts left the ground. With the Earth-man in the lead, they formed a long line which ascended for about two thousand feet, then straightened out to fly directly for the castle. Once above his objective, Thorne led the way downward in a swift, descending spiral which, as it neared the upper parapets, flattened into a great circle that followed the outline of the walls.

An alarm had been sounded at the first approach of this flying host, and now, as they drew nearer, javelins flew up at them, hurled by the defenders on the walls. Assisted by the force of gravity, while their enemies were impeded by it, the flying warriors were able to reply to good purpose, and soon there were many dead and wounded Ma Gongi on the ramparts. But it seemed that as fast as they fell, more rushed up to take their places, until Thorne calculated that Sel Han must have garrisoned at least three thousand of his yellow fighters here.

At the first alarm, five hundred of Rid Du's warriors had swarmed down over the docks where the gawrs were kept. As they were guarded only by a few soldiers and orderlies, the bird-beasts were soon captured. In the meantime, led by Rid Du, the other half of his little company assembled before the gate and began hurling javelins up at the defenders.

Now was the time for Yirl Du to strike, and Thorne watched tensely. Presently he saw the little company emerge from one of the castle doors, quickly form a flying wedge with Yirl Du at the apex, and charge across the courtyard, cutting down or scattering the surprised Ma Gongi in their way. Just before the gate the two wings of the wedge divided, and each column ascended into one of the watch towers which guarded the gateway. A moment later the gates swung open, and in poured the Free Swordsmen from the town, with Rid Du at their head.

Now Thorne's flying warriors swooped down into the melee, abandoning their javelins for fear of injuring their comrades, and fighting at close range with sword, mace and dagger. The slaughter was appalling. At the outset, the garrison had outnumbered the attackers at least two to one, but now the balance was swiftly swinging the other way. The Ma Gongi, most of whom had been slaves and were unaccustomed to warfare, were no match for the disciplined Takkor swordsmen.

The ramparts and the courtyard were thickly strewn with their bodies as Thorne, with Yirl Du, Thaíne, and a small contingent of Takkor swordsmen, cut down the yellow warriors who guarded the entrance, charged into the castle, and began their search for the prisoners.

Yirl Du led the way to the great central tower, where he believed they would be found. Here, after a short battle with another group of guards, they gained entrance, then fought their way up the winding staircase, the yellow defenders stubbornly contesting each step of the way.

THORNE and Yirl Du were ever in the front as they climbed the stairs, and both were soon covered with wounds. When they reached the flight which led to the top story, they met with the most desperate resistance they had yet encountered. But the swiftly flashing blade of the Earth-man backed up the swords of Yirl Du and Thaíne, and the javelins of the warriors who came behind them soon cleared the stairs of living enemies, and the few who remained above to contest their way were quickly cut down.

Thorne tried the door which the last remaining Ma Gong had so gallantly defended, and found it barred on the inside. Reversing his bloody sword, he beat upon the panels with the pommel.

"Who is it?" came a cautious call from within.

"The Rad of Takkor," Thorne replied. "Open quickly."

At this, there was the sound of a sliding bolt, and the door swung open. A tall, broad-shouldered man whose shaggy hair and flowing beard gleamed golden yellow under the baridium lights stood in the doorway. Though he was without weapons, his bulging muscles, fearless gray eyes, and weather-beaten countenance proclaimed him one accustomed to manly exercises and the chase.

At sight of him, Yirl Du and the other warriors instantly raised both hands before their eyes and muttered the royal salutation, while Thaine, with an exclamation of joy, ran forward and flung her arms around his neck.

"Father!" she cried. "I'm so glad we found you safe."

Gently he took her face between his huge hands, and bending, kissed her forehead.

"Little daughter!" he murmured. "This was man's work. You should not have come."

"Did you not train me to do a man's work? And have I not done it well? Ask Sheb Takkor."

Thorne, who had instantly sensed that this regal looking personage must be Miradon Vil, had only been a shade behind the others in rendering the royal salutation. He now stood, respectfully waiting for the Vil to speak.

"It is a question I need not propound," said Miradon. "I know you have fought nobly, or you would not be here. And so have all these gallant warriors, to whom I now render the thanks of a deposed Vil who is powerless to see that they are suitably rewarded. But, come, Sheb Takkor Rad, and you, Yirl Du Jen. There are those in other apartments who will be glad to thank their gallant rescuers."

He led the way down the hall and tapped on a door. From within came a little squeaky voice, which Thorne immediately recognized as that of Irintz Tel.

"Who is there?"

"Miradon Vil with friends who have rescued us. Open."

The bolt slid back, the door swung open, and the little rat-faced Dixtar stepped out, followed by Kov Lutas and Lal Vak.

"Where's Neva?" squeaked Irintz Tel, without a word of thanks to his rescuers. "Have you found my daughter?"

"She should be in one of these apartments," replied Miradon Vil.

"Open the doors! Break them down!" ordered the Dixtar, with a wave of his hand. "Why do you all stand there, staring?"

Thorne regarded him coldly. "You forget, Irintz Tel," he said, "that this is my castle and these are my warriors. They take orders only from me."

At this, the Dixtar turned deathly pale, but Thorne, ignoring him, warmly greeted the handsome young Kov Lutas and the white-haired Lal Vak, both of whom profusely thanked him for coming to their rescue.

IN THE MEANTIME, Miradon Vil had gone on to the next door and rapped. Thorne's heart gave a great bound as he heard the voice that answered—the voice of Neva.

Irintz Tel rushed to the door and embraced his daughter as she stepped out, followed by two of her slave-girls. Kov Lutas and Lal Vak instantly crowded forward to greet her, and the latter ceremoniously introduced Miradon Vil.

Thorne held aloof, watching them, his breast seething with conflicting emotions. Despite his resolve to put Neva forever from his thoughts, he now found that sight of her had suddenly reawakened all the old longing with redoubled intensity. Here was the lovely golden head that had lain on his shoulder; the slender body that had trembled in his straining arms. Here were the soft hands that had caressed him—clung to him; the languorous eyes that had looked into his, starry with love-light; the red lips that had returned his kisses and murmured sweet endearments as they plighted their troth. He could not but wonder, now, how one so beautiful could be the offspring of the ratlike Irintz Tel. Her blond features seemed cast in a royal mold—even like those of Miradon Vil.

But cold reason bade him remember that this golden head, with cold, calculating cruelty, had betrayed him; that the lovely body contained a treacherous heart; that those little hands had clenched and turned against him in the time of his greatest need; that the eyes had scorned him; and that the lips had spoken the words which condemned him to a horrible, lingering death in the baridium mines.

Suddenly he realized that Neva had seen him—was coming toward him—holding out her arms to him. His heart throbbed wildly. His arms, his lips, his whole being hungered for her. Yet he resolutely steeled himself to break the subtle spell she had again cast over him—forced his flagging will to recall her callous betrayal of him and the hideous death to which she had unjustly condemned him.

"Sheb, beloved!" she murmured. "The time has been so long—"

"The Dixtar's daughter," he said with frigid politeness, "honors the lowly castle of the Rad of Takkor by her charming presence. The Takkor retainers will have instructions to do all in their power to make her stay a pleasant one."

With this he saluted stiffly, and ignoring her outstretched arms and startled, pleading eyes, turned and walked to where Yirl Du stood awaiting his orders.

"See that these, my honored guests, are given the best the castle affords," he said.

"Yes, my lord."

For a moment Neva stood bewildered. Then a sudden flush suffused her lovely face. Turning, she reentered her apartment, head held high and eyes flashing.

WITHOUT even glancing at the door through which she had vanished, Thorne addressed Yirl Du. "I understand that the chief officials of the Kamud, including the seven judges, are confined here," he said.

"They are in the west wing, my lord. A warrior has just brought tidings."

"Have them brought here, Jen," cut in Irintz Tel imperiously. "We would speak with them."

"They are apt to be kept in their quarters, and well guarded," continued Thorne, ignoring Irintz Tel's interruption. "Also, you are to search for Sur Det, and if he still lives, bring him to me. I would question him."

"Yes, my lord."

The Earth-man now turned to the little Dixtar, and said with studied civility: "I trust it will not be necessary to again remind you that my warriors take orders only from me."

Irintz Tel shot him a venomous glance. Then he swung on his heel and entered Neva's apartment.

Thorne looked at Miradon Vil with an apologetic smile.

"I hope that your majesty will excuse me," he said, "as I have pressing duties. Preparations must be made at once, so we can all leave the castle before morning. Sel Han may return at any moment with his ray projectors, and if he finds us here our case will be desperate, if not entirely hopeless."

The Vil returned his smile. "I understand. Can I help?"

"No, I thank your majesty."

Thorne hurried down the gory, corpse-littered stairs, and out into the courtyard. Here he set about making immediate preparations for flight, ordering that all available weapons and provisions be brought out and loaded onto the gawrs. He planned to leave the Vil and Thaine in their secret hiding place, and to find another for Irintz Tel and Neva. Then he would lead his warriors far out into the marsh and hide from Sel Plan and his fearsome new weapons until he could devise some plan for successfully combating him.

He was overseeing these preparations some time later, when Yirl Du came and asked to speak with him aside.

"My lord," he said, "I ordered that a strict search be made

for the scar-faced killer as you commanded. Sur Det cannot be found among either the dead or the living."

"Then he has escaped. We must hasten our preparations, for he has undoubtedly gone to Dukor, and will bring Sel Han and his ray projectors down upon us."

But the words had scarcely left his mouth when a guard called from one of the towers:

"A vast host of warriors mounted on gawrs is approaching. Also there are a score of the great metal gawrs."

Instantly, confusion reigned in the castle. A frightened warrior leaped on the back of a half-loaded gawr and jerked the guiding rod. The bird-beast flapped awkwardly up out of the courtyard. But it had scarcely cleared the castle walls when a strange and terrible thing happened. A green ray shot out from somewhere beyond the wall—struck the fleeing warrior and his mount. For an instant they were visible, bathed in that weird, green light. Then they seemed to suddenly shrivel and disintegrate. Where they had been there was nothing at all. The ray winked out and consternation settled over the courtyard.

Thorne, seeing the terrible efficiency of this new weapon of Sel Han's, realized that they were trapped, all of them, in the castle.

CHAPTER XXI

AN ULTIMATUM

THORNE KNEW THAT Sel Han, with his powerful ray projectors, could not only cut off any attempt at flight, but could destroy the castle and all in it whenever it suited his pleasure. Yet he resolved that he, his friends and his followers should not succumb without resisting to the utmost. He accordingly rallied his panic-stricken warriors to the defense of the walls with a few ringing commands, then mounted to the ramparts to survey the movements of the enemy.

Sel Han, it seemed, was not disposed to immediately storm the castle. All of his great metal flying machines had alighted well out of javelin range of the walls, and from the interiors of these, Ma Gong foot-soldiers were pouring. A ray projector had been mounted on the flat roof of a near-by house, and Thorne stared at it curiously. It looked much like a large telescope on a conical stand. The flying warriors were circling the castle, but the great bulk of these were alighting on the ground. Soon only a few remained in the air as scouts and observers.

Glancing out over the lake, the Earth-man saw that a second projector was mounted there on a large boat. He walked around the walls and descried a third on the roof of a building to the landward side, and still farther, a fourth, mounted on the ground to command the remaining sector of the wall.

Having completed his inspection of the disposal of the enemy troops and projectors, Thorne returned to a parapet beside the gate which opened on the dock, and before which Sel Han had massed his chief officers. Though he could not be sure in the deceptive moonlight at that distance, Thorne thought he recognized the tall, broad-shouldered figure of Sel Han himself, standing among the officers.

As he stood there on the battlement, watching every movement of the enemy, he heard a group of people coming up behind him. Turning, he beheld Miradon Vil and Irintz Tel walking side by side. Though they had always been deadly enemies it was evident that they had united to make common cause against the man who not only threatened them, but all of Mars as well.

Behind the two ex-rulers of Xancibar came Neva escorted by Lal Vak, and Thaíne escorted by Kov Lutas. All carried weapons.

"We sought you out, Sheb Takkor Rad, hoping that we might be of some assistance in the defense," said Miradon Vil.

"I fear there is little we can do save surrender or die, your majesty," Thorne replied, "though I have resolved that I, personally, will fight to the death rather than surrender to Sel Han."

"Your resolve coincides with my own," replied Miradon Vil.

"And mine! And mine!" chorused the others, with the single exception of Irintz Tel. Without a word, he strode to the wall and peered over. Then, with hands behind his back, and chin on chest, he turned and began pacing nervously back and forth on the battlement.

The ominous silence that followed was suddenly rent by the clarion notes of a trumpet. Hurrying to the wall, Thorne saw that a man had detached himself from the group around Sel Han, and walked to a point before the gate just out of range of a hurled javelin.

ONCE again the herald sounded a ringing call on his trumpet. Then, resting his instrument on his hip, he cried:

"His Imperial Majesty, Sel Han the Invincible, Vil of Xancibar, Vil of Vils, and Vildus of all Mars, commands that Sheb Takkor and his warriors instantly lay down their weapons and come forth from the castle gates unarmed. His majesty has it in his power to utterly destroy the castle and every soul within it. Witness!"

He paused dramatically, and as he paused a pencil of green light stabbed out from the projector on the housetop. It flashed to the top of one of the lesser towers, and where the ray touched, the crystal blocks and mortar shriveled and vanished, leaving a jagged hole in the battlement.

The ray winked out, and the herald continued:

"There will be no terms of surrender, other than such conditions as the Vildus of Mars shall see fit to impose."

With a farewell flourish of his trumpet, he turned and walked back to where Sel Han and his officers stood waiting.

Thorne turned to an officer who stood near by. "Get me a herald," he ordered.

The officer ran to the gate tower and immediately emerged with a youth who carried a trumpet. Thorne gave him his instructions, and mounting the wall, he blew a ringing flourish. After waiting for a moment, he announced:

"The Lord of Takkor, his warriors and his friends, defy Sel Han of the empty titles, and his bandits, who have invaded the Takkor domain. Here is Castle Takkor, and here are its defenders unafraid, for Sel Han to come and take if he can, or to destroy if he has aught to gain by wanton destruction. The Lord of Takkor further states—"

The speech of the unfortunate herald was suddenly cut off, along with his life, by a green flash from the ray projector on the housetop. Thorne had seen Sel Han raise his hand, and knew that he had signaled his operator to carry out this cowardly murder.

A roar of rage went up from the Takkor swordsmen as they saw their comrade, who by the usages and customs of warfare was entitled to immunity, blasted out of existence before their very eyes. If Sel Han had thought to frighten them by this inhuman demonstration he had a poor conception of the caliber of these men, for he only succeeded in stiffening their resolve to resist to the end.

But though this wanton snuffing out of a life had made the Takkor warriors more steadfast in their purpose, there was at least one occupant of the castle upon whom it had worked the opposite effect. Chancing to look toward Irintz Tel, Thorne noticed that he was trembling violently, his teeth were chattering audibly, and his knees were threatening to collapse.

Presently there came two more blasts from the trumpet of Sel Han's herald.

"His Imperial Majesty, the Vildus of Mars, could destroy the castle and all it contains," shouted the herald, "yet he is just and merciful. He realizes that the warriors of the Takkor Rad and the prisoners are respectively under the command and in the power of a man who is willing to sacrifice them all to satisfy his own empty vanity and make good his puny defiance of Sel Han, the Invincible.

"Wherefore, his imperial majesty gives you, each and every one, a respite from death, during which you may have time to depose this foolhardy leader and save your own lives. And to the man who will bring him the head of Sheb Takkor, the Vildus of Mars covenants to present the Raddek of Takkor with all its lands. His majesty decrees that your respite from death shall last from now until the planet has completed one turn upon its axis. If, by that time and at that very moment, you have not obeyed his edict, then will the castle and all in it be utterly destroyed."

Having said his say, the herald returned to the group of officers. Shortly thereafter, the majority of that group, led by the tall figure of Sel Han and accompanied by a guard of a hundred warriors, marched away toward the city, evidently to find sleeping accommodations.

In the meantime, small cooking fires blazed up all along the circle which surrounded the castle. The besiegers were plainly visible as they squatted around these, warming themselves and brewing pulcho.

"**LOOKS** as if things have quieted down for the present, at least," said Thorne, turning to the others. "I suggest that we all get some much needed sleep."

"One moment, Sheb Takkor," interposed Irintz Tel, who had by this time regained his wonted arrogance. "I suggest that before we retire we hold a council and decide just what we are going to do. So far, you have had your will in everything. However, there are others here beside yourself, some of us far outranking you, whose lives are in jeopardy. And it is only fair that we should all have some say in the matter."

"I quite agree to that," Thorne replied. "Thus far I have been acting under the belief that I was carrying out the wishes of the majority in defying Sel Han. If I have erred, there is yet time to rectify the mistake. Let us go into the castle."

They gathered, a few moments later, in the apartment which Thorne had chosen for himself. The Earth-man had asked Yirl Du to attend as the representative of the Free Swordsmen. The others were Neva, Thaíne, Miradon Vil, Irintz Tel, Lal Vak, and Kov Lutas.

Thorne stood at a taboret in the center of the room, filling cups with steaming pulcho, a jar of which had just been brought in by Yirl Du. These he passed to his assembled guests. Then he said to Irintz Tel:

"Since it was at your suggestion that this council was assembled, I will call upon you first to address us."

The Dixtar took a dainty sip of pulcho, then carefully held the cup before him with the clawlike fingers of both hands curled around it.

"My good friends and comrades in adversity," he began, with a smirk that was evidently intended for an engaging smile, "I, for one, see the hopelessness of our position here, and the futility of further resistance to the decree of fate. True, we can all remain here and die defending our convictions, but what will that profit us? After all, it is better to be live prisoners than dead heroes, blasted into nothingness by the awful weapons of the Ma Gongi. While we live, even though it be in durance, there is always hope of escape and happiness. But death ends all hope. I suggest that we surrender to Sel Han while he is inclined to be merciful, thus not only saving our own lives, but those of the brave Takkor swordsmen who sought to rescue us from the conqueror."

"You have all heard the suggestion of the Dixtar," said Thorne. "What is your pleasure? Will you surrender or resist?"

"Resist!" they cried unanimously, with a vehemence that startled Irintz Tel into spilling half his pulcho on the floor.

Then the Dixtar, who for ten long Martian years had never been gainsaid in anything, went suddenly pale. His brows drew together in a frown and his lips set in a tight, hard line. He seemed about to denounce them all. Then suddenly his expression changed. A crafty look came into his eyes, and again he smiled, a forced smile that sat illy on his lips.

"I fear," he said, "that you will all regret this rash decision when regret comes too late." Then he turned, clasped his hands behind his back, and with his chin sunk on his chest, strode out of the room. The others soon followed to go to their several apartments.

The Earth-man, left alone, prepared to retire. One thing kept recurring to him as he hooded the baridium globes and crept into bed. It was the fact that as Kov Lutas walked out between the two girls, he had seemed more attentive to Thaíne than to Neva. Recalling the young officer's avowal of undying love for the beautiful daughter of the Dixtar, Thorne was puzzled.

He soon fell asleep, but it seemed to him that he had not slumbered for more than a few moments when he was awakened by a sharp tug at his coverlets. He looked up sleepily. The pale light of the farther moon was streaming in through the window, and by its rays he saw a squat, broad-shouldered figure which he instantly recognized.

"Yirl Du!" he exclaimed. "What's wrong?"

"I have made a startling discovery, my lord," Yirl Du replied, "else I should not have disturbed your rest."

"I'm sure of that," said Thorne. "What is it?"

For answer, his sturdy henchman drew a scroll from beneath his cloak. After passing it to the Earth-man, he walked to the lever and unhooded the baridium globes, flooding the room with light.

"Read, my lord," he said, in grim tones.

CHAPTER XXII

IRINTZ TEL'S TREACHERY

WHEN IRINTZ TEL reached his own apartment the frown had not departed from his brow, nor the injured look of the self-righteous egoist from his countenance. As he stood with his back to the fireplace, warming his spare frame, his agile brain was working—turning over and over an idea which had occurred to him after he left the council chamber.

Despite his impressive plea for the lives of the Takkor swordsmen and the two girls, he had been actuated by but one motive when he begged his companions to surrender to Sel Han. That motive was fear. Irintz Tel was afraid to die. He had condemned many men to death—had watched thousands die, some slowly and in horrible agony, others swiftly and more mercifully beneath the headsman's sword. And he had watched them with no feeling of pity or sympathy; no emotion, in fact save that peculiar, egotistical gratification which all monomaniacs, bigots and radical reformers feel when they witness the destruction of those who dare to oppose them or their cause. Now he was face to face with death.

At one side of the room stood a writing board, equipped with scrolls of waterproof silk, writing brushes, ink, and the small wooden cylinders used by the Martians as containers for their missives. To this he now repaired, and spreading a scroll on the board, dipped brush in ink and began.

To SEL HAN, VILDUS OF MARS,
Salutation and submission:

172

With my help you can take Castle Takkor and all in it, sustaining but trifling losses. Tomorrow night, in the period of darkness between the setting of the nearer moon and the rising of the farther, quietly mass a thousand men near the lake gate. Have another group of fifty warriors bring a long stout rope, knotted for easy climbing, beneath the point where I stand when I hurl this note. I will drop a cord to draw up and make fast the rope for them. Then we will cut down the guards and throw open the gates. With a thousand of your foot-soldiers in the courtyard and your mounted warriors attacking from above, there can be but one outcome. I seek to make no terms, but align myself wholeheartedly with your cause, and now await your reply and your commands.

Irintz Tel.

He completed the note only after making many corrections, crossing out words here, inserting others there, and sometimes changing whole phrases. Accordingly, he took down another scroll, made a neat copy of the first draft, and rolling it tightly, inserted it in a wooden cylinder. With his brush, he then wrote on the outside of the cylinder:

FOR SEL HAN, VILDUS OF MARS
Retain the cord for reply.

He next went to the chest he had brought with him from the palace, containing his belongings, and drew therefrom one of his magnificent state cloaks. Ripping a corner of the lining, he loosened a thread, and began unraveling it. Soon he had a ball of stout silken cord long enough to reach from the wall to the enemy lines and back. He dropped his cloak about him, and concealing cylinder and cord beneath it, started for the door. But on the way he thought of the rough copy of the letter which he had left on the writing board. Snatching it up, he tossed it into the fireplace. Then he went out, softly closing the door after him.

Stealthily he crossed the hall and made his way down flight after flight of stairs until he reached the courtyard. Gradually he worked his way toward the tower on the west side of the lake gate. Leisurely he climbed the outer stairway which led to the parapet at the side of the tower. From this he stepped down to the wall, and standing in the shadow of the tower, he tied one end of his silken cord to the wooden cylinder. Then he swiftly unwrapped and coiled the rest of the cord, and swinging the cylinder around his head in a whizzing circle, hurled it out toward the nearest enemy campfire.

The cylinder fell short of the mark by ten feet, but the thud attracted the attention of a yellow warrior who squatted there warming his hands. He turned and stared, then seeing the cylinder, walked out, picked it up, and returned with it to the light of the fire. The warrior seemed puzzled by the long cord attached to the cylinder, but when he had read the inscription his indecision vanished. Drawing his knife, he swiftly cut the cord, tied one end of it to the hilt, and plunged the blade into the earth. Then, after a word or two with his companions around the fire, he started off for the city at a trot.

IN TAKKOR CITY, Sel Han and his officers had appropriated a half dozen residences belonging to the wealthier citizens. And in the largest and most pretentious of these slept the self-styled Vildus of Mars, surrounded by his private guards and a cordon of Ma Gong troops.

To this residence the yellow warrior who had received Irintz Tel's message now made his way. Thrice he was stopped before he could gain entrance even to the reception room, where several members of Sel Han's staff dozed. One of these, who sat with a pulcho jar beside him and a half-filled cup in his hand, stared drunkenly at him as the guard escorted him into the room. The fellow was of the Old Race, and very terrible to look at, with his huge muscles and hairy chest, and the network of livid scars that covered his ferocious countenance.

"What do you want, little fat bug?" roared the drunken officer.

The warrior gulped, and saluted humbly. "I—I have a message from the castle, for the Vildus, O mighty one," he answered.

"What's that?" The officer swayed to his feet, and lurching over to where the little warrior stood, seized the cylinder. He blinked his pulcho-blurred eyes over the brush marks for a moment, then read: "For Sel Han, Vildus of Mars." "Hum. Better let me, Sur Det, handle this for you. If any common warrior were to awaken Sel Han now, his life would answer. But Sur Det is no common warrior, and this matter seems urgent. Wait here."

He walked unsteadily to the stairway, then mounted it with much precarious swaying, crossed a hall, and was confronted by one of Sel Han's personal guards.

"The Vildus is not to be disturbed," said the guard.

"Out of my way, fool," growled Sur Det. "I have an important message for him."

Contemptuously he pushed the guard aside, opened the door and entered. Sel Han was sleeping on a swinging divan at one side of the room, but he slept lightly. He sat up abruptly as Sur Det staggered in. Then his left hand flew to the lever, unhooding the baridium globes and filling the room with light, while his right whipped out the sword that hung at the edge of the divan.

He looked at Sur Det for a moment in the unaccustomed light, then laughed unpleasantly.

"By the wrath of Deza!" he exclaimed. "You are overbold to disturb me at this hour with your drunken foolishness, killer though you be."

In the presence of his master all of Sur Det's arrogance evaporated, leaving him abjectly servile.

"A missive came from the castle, majesty," he whined. "I thought it might be important."

"Well, bring it here, idiot!"

Sur Det lumbered across the floor and extended the cylinder.

Sel Han jerked it impatiently from his hand, removed the plug, dumped out the scroll, and unrolling it, read Irintz Tel's message. As the significance of the contents slowly filtered through his sleepy brain, a cunning grin overspread his flat features.

"You have brought good news, Killer," he said, "and for that I forgive your disturbing me. Irintz Tel has turned traitor to his rescuers, and will help us gain secret entrance to the castle tomorrow night during the dark interval. The castle and all in it will be ours at the loss of only a few Ma Gong warriors—a paltry price to pay."

Sel Han dipped his brush in the ink and wrote rapidly. Then he inserted the scroll in a fresh cylinder, wrote "Irintz Tel" on the outside, and handed it to Sur Det.

"Go back with the messenger, Killer," he said. "Don't take any guards with you, for those on the walls may become suspicious. But carefully note the position of Irintz Tel on the wall, and report to me before you touch another drop of pulcho. Remember, this is important, and I will hold you accountable if you make a mistake."

"I will make no mistake, majesty," replied Sur Det as he took the cylinder and thrust it under his belt. Then he rendered Sel Han the imperial salute and departed.

CHAPTER XXIII

THE TRIUMPH OF SEL HAN

EACH PASSING MOMENT increased Irintz Tel's apprehension as he stood quaking in the shadow of the wall awaiting Sel Han's reply to his traitorous note. Presently, when he knew that the nearer moon must burst above the horizon in a moment or two more and betray him, he walked to the edge of the wall with the intention of tossing his cord over and returning to his apartment. But at this moment he saw two men coming from the direction of the city, walking toward the campfire where the dagger that held the cord was plunged in the ground. One was a round-bodied yellow man, but the other was a big, burly officer of the Old Race.

At this sight he took heart and waited with renewed hope. The yellow man squatted down in front of the dagger, shielding it from the view of possible watchers on the wall. Then the white officer plucked something from his belt and handed it to him. A moment later the yellow man rose, sheathing his dagger.

Swiftly now, Irintz Tel drew in his line. A brightness on the western horizon heralded the rising of the nearer moon, so he abandoned the neat coil he was making and worked feverishly with both hands, dropping the line in a tangled snarl at his feet. Almost at the same instant, the little wooden cylinder bobbed over the wall and the moon rose. The Dixtar thrust cylinder and line beneath his cloak and looked around to see if he had been observed. Seeing no one, he heaved a sigh of relief, and turning, made his way back to his apartment.

Once in the privacy of his own room, Irintz Tel lost no time in scanning the contents of the scroll he had been at such trouble and risk to obtain. His small, beady eyes flashed in triumph as he read the contents:

> To IRINTZ TEL,
> Salutation and greetings:
> Your plan pleases me. As soon as the sky grows dark, lower your cord with a muffled weight at the end. When you feel two tugs on the cord draw up the rope which we shall tie on the other end, and lash it to a merlon. As soon as it is secure, tug twice, and we will do the rest.
> If, through your efforts, we are able to capture the castle, I will make you Vil of Xancibar or any other vilet of equal size which you may choose, and Neva shall share with me the throne of all Mars.
>
> SEL HAN
> VILDUS OF MARS.

Vil of Xancibar! It was much more than he had dared hope for. And his daughter, wife of the ruler of all Mars! He carefully read the contents of the scroll again to fix them in his memory. Then he reinserted it in the cylinder, which he laid on the writing board, and occupied himself with untangling and winding in a ball his badly snarled cord.

He had just finished this task when a light knock sounded at the door.

Then, before he could reply, it was pushed open and a man staggered into the room, bearing a bundle of wood on his back.

"What do you want, slave?" Irintz Tel demanded.

"Only to bring wood for your excellency's fireplace," replied the newcomer. "Shall I poke up the fire for you?"

The Dixtar, now suspicious of every one with whom he came in contact, looked sharply at the man. His cloak was ragged and filthy, and he wore an unkempt black beard. To all appearances, he was one of the castle menials.

"No. Stack the wood at the side. I'll need no more fire tonight as I am about to retire."

The fellow staggered forward under his load, but as he neared the fireplace, stumbled and half turned, then fell so one of the sticks caught the writing board and overturned it. He came down in a shower of wood, ink, scrolls, cylinders and brushes in which he scrambled for a moment as if bewildered.

"You clumsy oaf!" shrilled Irintz Tel. "I'll have you beaten for this."

"The load was heavy, excellency, and I am very weary," said the man. "I'll set all right for you in a moment."

After righting the board, he fumbled about among the sticks of wood, and had soon replaced everything except the ink, which was impartially distributed over the other articles. As he picked up the cylinder in which Sel Han's note had come he stared at it for a moment, then said:

"Here is one on which your excellency's name is written. I am glad it was not broken as the contents might have been injured."

"That? Oh, that's nothing of importance." The Dixtar took it out of his hand and tossed it into the fire. "Now pile that wood and get out. You have done enough damage for one evening."

Swiftly the man did so.

IRINTZ TEL retired shortly thereafter, feeling that he had done an excellent night's work. He slept until nearly noon of the following day, had his breakfast served in bed, and went out for a stroll in the courtyard. The Rad of Takkor had put his men to work, obliterating all signs of the battle which had taken place the night before. The men were now busy scrubbing up bloodstains, tending their gawrs, and putting their equipment and weapons in order.

After a leisurely stroll about the courtyard the Dixtar

mounted to the wall. There he met Thorne, who saluted him civilly.

"It looks as if you are planning to remain here for some time, Sheb Takkor Rad," he said, "if one may judge by the way you are cleaning things up."

"Who knows?" Thorne replied. "At least it makes the place more livable, and gives the men something to do. Idle warriors in a situation of this kind do too much fretting and worrying. With work to do they have little time for worry, and are more content."

Thorne strode away to give an order to one of his officers, and Irintz Tel walked to an embrasure to have a look at Sel Han's forces. They were spread out in the same manner as on the night before, in a great semicircle that reached around the castle to the rim of the lake on both sides. The yellow warriors were lolling about, chatting, sipping pulcho, and playing gapun. Sel Han and his staff were not even in sight, though a few white officers were disposed at intervals around the circle. The crews and guards of the four ray projectors lolled as listlessly as the others.

Strolling along the wall, Irintz Tel came upon Neva talking to Miradon Vil and Lal Vak. He would have liked to tell his daughter the momentous secret locked in his bosom, but decided that it would not be wise. After all, the thing would be over in a little while, and she would learn soon enough. He passed on after exchanging a few words with them, and at the next turn of the wall saw Kov Lutas and Thaine seated together in an embrasure. The handsome young officer and the Vil's daughter seemed very much engrossed in each other, his blond head very close to her black one.

The day passed, somehow—blended into the early evening and the silvery brilliance of the nearer moon. He waited tensely, now, until the swift-moving satellite neared the eastern horizon. Then he wrapped an empty wooden cylinder from the writing board in a bit of cloth, tied the end of his cord about it, and thrusting both beneath his cloak, went out into the hallway. Softly closing his door after him, he stealthily descended the stairs.

Then he mounted to the top of the wall and posted himself in the shadow of the tower. Looking out at the position of the besiegers, he was unable to descry any special concentration of troops, and for a moment feared that Sel Han had failed him. Then he decided that the conqueror would be cunning enough to wait until darkness before massing his men.

Suddenly the moon dropped below the horizon, plunging the landscape into an impenetrable darkness which the glittering stars did not relieve. The campfires of the besiegers had been allowed to burn so low that only a few smoldering coals marked their positions without revealing the men and beasts that stood around and behind them. So far, Sel Han had managed things excellently.

THE DIXTAR strained his eyes to penetrate the inky gloom before the gate, but could see no movement—nothing. Suddenly he remembered he had a part to play, and the time had arrived. Plucking the padded cylinder and the ball of cord from his belt, he swung the weight over the wall and paid out the line until it went slack. Then he waited.

After a lapse of only a few moments he felt two sharp tugs on the cord. The signal! Slowly, noiselessly, he drew up the line. His hands came in contact with a thick rope with a running noose at the end. He slipped the noose around the merlon, and as he slid his hand down to tighten it, felt thick knots at intervals along its length. He gave the signal—two pulls. A moment later the rope grew taut and began to sway with a heavy weight.

He stepped back, now, and waited. Soon the body of a man bulked in the embrasure, cutting off the gleam of the stars beyond. There followed many more, until he had counted fifty. Then he stepped boldly into the midst of the group.

"Where is your leader?" he whispered.

"Here." A man moved up beside him.

"Who are you?"

"Sur Det, whom men call 'The Killer.'"

"Good! Your expert offices will be needed. Lead half of your men into this tower and cut down the guards. The other half I will lead across into the other tower. As soon as we have slain the guards we will throw open the gates."

Irintz Tel was bold now, with twenty-five warriors at his back and a thousand more waiting just outside the gate. Stealthily he led his little group down the stairs, across the gateway, and up the stairs on the other side. But when the time came to charge into the tower, he did not lead. Instead, he flung the door open and stepped to one side.

Swinging their curved, two-handed swords, the Ma Gongi surged into the room. Sel Han followed. To his surprise he heard no fighting—only the retreating footsteps of the guards running down the inner stairway which led to the cellars and dungeons beneath the castle.

"They are cowards, these Takkor swordsmen," he muttered, "and I had always thought them brave men." He called to the yellow warriors. "We must work fast, for those men will give the alarm and we shall have their comrades down upon us. Pull that lever, quickly!"

Two men threw their weight on the great lever which operated the gate. Irintz Tel went to the window. Looking across into the opposite tower he saw the scar-faced Sur Det busy directing his warriors, but no sign of fighting. Dimly, in the light from the tower windows, he saw the tops of the gates swinging inward. And still farther down he thought he could descry the shadowy bulk of a large body of warriors surging through, though he heard nothing hut the sliding of the gates.

Another moment and the gates gaped wide. Below him in the courtyard he could hear running and the clank of weapons. Then there was a terrific flapping of wings as Sel Han's mounted riders took off and swooped clown upon the castle.

Baridium torches flared on, revealing the walls and courtyard swarming with warriors. Sel Han, standing near one of the towers, surrounded by his staff, shouted:

"Close the gates! Let no living thing escape!"

CHAPTER XXIV

THORNE'S STRATEGY

THORNE GLANCED CURIOUSLY over the scroll handed him by Yirl Du. Then he threw back the covers and leaped out of bed.

"Where did you get this?" he demanded. "Where is Irintz Tel?"

"The traitor is in his own bed, and probably asleep by now," replied Yirl Du.

"But what of Sel Han? Did he get a message through to him, and was there a reply?"

"He did, and I have the reply, also." Yirl Du plucked a second scroll from beneath his cloak and handed it to Thorne, who swiftly perused it.

"Ah! So that's their game. They will capture the towers, throw open the gates, and take us by surprise during the dark interval."

"They will, my lord, unless we prevent Irintz Tel from drawing up their rope for them. Shall I place him under arrest?"

"No. Let him sleep. There is nothing he can do before to-morrow night, and I already have the glimmerings of a counter plan. In the meantime, tell me how you got these documents."

"It was quite simple, my lord. As you know, I am familiar with every secret passageway in this castle. When Irintz Tel left the conference I suspected him of some treachery, so I followed. Seeing him enter his apartment, I slipped into a hidden passageway which leads to a panel in the central room of his suite. There, through a small peep-hole, I spied upon him. He seemed quite agitated, and finally went to the writing board and composed this letter. He made a copy, probably because the original was full of corrections and crossed out words.

"Next, he unraveled the silken lining of one of his garments and wound the long cord he obtained therefrom into a ball. He thrust the ball of cord and the copy of this scroll under his cloak, and went out. On the way out he hurled the original letter into the fireplace. Luckily I was able to open the panel, run to the fireplace, and rescue it before it caught fire.

"I read the note, and instantly realizing its import, secretly followed Irintz Tel. I saw him tie the cylinder to the end of his silken cord and hurl it out toward the enemy camp where it was picked up by a yellow warrior. Some time later Sel Han's reply came, and Irintz Tel drew it up on the wall.

"With a false beard and tattered cloak, I disguised myself as a castle menial. Again I spied upon Irintz Tel in his room. Presently I saw him place Sel Han's answer on the writing board, and resolved to attempt to get it without arousing his suspicion. Accordingly, I went into his room with a load of wood, managed to upset the writing board, shake the scroll out of the cylinder, thrust it into my belt, and hand him the empty cylinder, which he immediately tossed into the fire."

"Obviously Irintz Tel thinks both of these documents were burned, and so imagines himself safe from discovery. That fits in splendidly with my plan."

"But aren't you going to arrest him and punish him?"

"No. I have a more subtle scheme than that. Say nothing about these notes or the Dixtar's treachery to any one. Leave all to me. To-morrow, go about your duties as if nothing is amiss. And now get yourself some rest. I'm going back to bed."

Always obedient to the Rad of Takkor, though sorely puzzled by his strange orders, his faithful retainer retired from the room, shaking his head and muttering to himself.

THORNE was up with the sun, and instantly set about his task. First he put his men to work cleaning up the place and tending

He spurted along the narrow ledge with Thaine on his shoulder.

the gawrs. Then, accompanied by Yirl Du, he explored the underground chambers of the castle. It was not long before he had mapped out a route leading through the largest doorways and archways to a point near one of the concealed entrances of the secret passageway through which Yirl Du had previously escaped, and which led underneath the docks. After investigating this passageway and the space beneath the docks, he returned to the castle cellar.

"Bring me six skilled masons," he told Yirl Du, "and have them conceal their tools on the way so there will be no suspicion of what we are about to do. I'll wait here."

Yirl Du hurried away, and presently returned with six members of the Free Swordsmen who, he said, were skilled masons, carrying tools and mortar which they had drawn from the castle stores, concealed in two large food hampers.

Thorne addressed the six men. "I want you to remove the blocks from the wall at this point," he said, "until you have made an opening large enough for a gawr to pass through. Then wait here with your tools for further orders, which will not come until to-night. Food and pulcho wilt be sent you."

Accompanied by Yirl Du, he crossed the room and stepped through the large doorway, carefully closing the door after him.

"Keep this door closed with two guards before it," he said, "and give them orders to admit nobody but you or me. Irintz Tel may take a notion to stroll through the cellars, and I don't want him to suspect what we are doing here. You, yourself, will take food to the workmen at meal-times."

After the two guards had been posted, Thorne and Yirl Du paid a visit to the tower where the officers of the Kamud were imprisoned. These, the Earth-man ordered transferred to a dungeon in the cellar. When this had been accomplished he returned to the courtyard and battlements to direct the work there, and to keep watch over the enemy.

That afternoon, after Irintz Tel had retired to his apartment, Thorne issued secret instructions to his various officers. These, in turn, transmitted instructions to the men in their charge. Every man was assigned a special duty to perform, and re-minded that failure to carry it out might mean the defeat of their plans.

Miradon Vil, Kov Lutas, Sel Han and the two girls were told nothing. Thorne did not want the Dixtar's daughter to know of the perfidy of her father until his own plans had been carried out. And though he trusted the others, he preferred that they remain in ignorance of what was to take place in order that they might the more thoroughly and naturally set at rest any suspicions of discovery which Irintz Tel might entertain.

Night came at last, with the transient brightness of the nearer moon. It was at the setting of this orb that all of Thorne's forces were to go into action, to carry out his plan. In the meantime, a secret watch was kept on Irintz Tel.

Presently Thorne, standing in the shadow of a doorway, saw the Dixtar cross the courtyard, walking unconcernedly and saluting the officers and men he encountered. Leisurely he mounted to the wall and a moment later disappeared in the shadow of the tower.

Thorne softly called to Rid Du, who stood waiting.

"Start out with the gawrs," he said, "and warn the men to be careful about making any unusual noise."

Led by a man who had been coached for the purpose until he thoroughly knew the route through the castle and cellar which had been mapped out by Thorne, the great bird-beasts, each carrying a rider, began forming in line and marching into the castle.

Thorne, meanwhile, kept a weather eye out for Irintz Tel, but the Dixtar remained hidden in the shadow of the tower, and hence out of sight of what was going on in the courtyard.

BY THE TIME the moon had set nearly two-thirds of the gawrs had entered the castle. At this moment all the warriors on the walls and in the towers began silently stealing from their posts, with the exception of the few who guarded the towers that controlled the lake gates. These had instructions to remain until the first attackers appeared, then flee down the inner stairways which led to the cellars, and join the others.

Thorne kept his post at the doorway until the last huge bird-beast had lumbered through. Then he closed and bolted the door on the inside, and ran up the steps of the central tower where, one by one, he aroused Neva, Thaíne, Miradon Vil, Sel Han and Kov Lutas.

"Come with me quickly, and make no sound," he told them. "The enemy is about to attack, and I have a plan to frustrate them. But we must be quiet."

They followed him down the stairway unquestioningly, Neva escorted by Miradon Vil, who seemed strangely solicitous of her safety; Thaíne attended by Kov Lutas, and Lal Vak walking with the Earth-man. Thorne closed and bolted every door after them as they followed the route where the gawrs had walked through the castle and descended to the basement. Here, after passing through several rooms, and bolting each door behind them, they caught up with the end of a line of warriors, among whom Thorne recognized the guards from the gate towers. This line was swiftly and silently filing through the hole opened in the wall by the masons, who, since all the gawrs had passed, had begun to fill it up under the direction of Yirl Du.

Thorne bolted the last door and told his companions to follow the warriors through the opening. Then he approached Yirl Du.

"Have you shown these men the secret passageway?" he asked.

"Yes, my lord. And I have instructed them to completely wall up the hole as soon as the last warrior has passed through, then follow by way of the passage."

"Good. Come with me, for we still have the most difficult part of our task to perform and I will need your services."

They hurried out to where the men and bird-beasts stood under the dock, amid the supporting pilings, and now heard the flapping of many wings above and around them.

"Sel Han's flying warriors are attacking the castle," said Thorne. "Now is our chance, but we must work swiftly."

In accordance with his previous orders, a hundred of Thorne's warriors had divided themselves into four groups of twenty-five men, each under the command of an officer. The members of one of these groups, all young fellows under the command of Rid Du, had stripped themselves to their loincloths and were plastering each other from head to foot with a thick coating of heavy grease, working in the dim light of a small baridium torch held by another warrior. Stacked near them was a pile of large crocks made from transparent material.

As soon as they were thoroughly greased, each man belted sword, mace and dagger about him, then took up a crock, inverted it, and lifted it over his head, so it rested upon his shoulders. They marched down to the water's edge, and Rid Du, who was in the lead, chopped a hole in the thin ice with his mace, then stepped into it and disappeared from view, still holding the crock over his head. His companions followed him, one by one, until all had dropped out of sight in the icy water.

"Do you think they'll make it?" Thorne asked anxiously. "Looks as if they might run out of air before they reach the boat."

"Don't worry, my lord," Yirl Du replied. "All are trained divers and know how to conserve the air in the crocks. Every one of them could walk out to the boat and back again without danger of suffocating. And when they break through the ice around that boat the crew of the ray projector will have short shrift, with the exception of the operator whom you ordered kept alive."

"I hope you are right," said Thorne, "and you should know if any one does. Now that they are started, it is time for us to attack the other projector crews. I'll take the one on the west, you the one on the north, and Ven Hitus the one to the east. Come!"

HE LEAPED into the saddle of a gawr held ready for him, and swiftly led the way to the west end of the dock, the great bird-beasts of his twenty-five warriors lumbering after him on the frozen ground. At the end of the dock a large ramp led up under a warehouse, open toward the lake after the manner of a lean-to. He rode out through the front of this and reconnoitered for a moment. By now there was a tremendous commotion in the castle. Baridium torches were flashing all about, and by their light he could see the warriors milling on the walls, while others mounted on gawrs circled the towers and battlements.

But what chiefly concerned him now was the ray projector which he was to capture, and which Sel Han had mounted on a house-top. He marked its position by the faint glow of the light on its instrument board. Then, with a whispered "Now!"

to his fighting men who had assembled around him, he pulled up on the guiding rod, and his bird-beast, after running a few feet, launched itself into the air.

In a few moments they were soaring above their objective, which was only about five hundred yards from the dock. Then they dived downward in a steep spiral.

The crew of the ray projector had paid no attention to the sound of gawrs flapping above their heads, evidently taking these to be the mounts of their own warriors. And so, when the great bird-beasts alighted on the roof around them, and Thorne's fighting men sprang upon them with drawn swords, they were taken completely by surprise.

Thorne made straight for the operator, who leaped up to meet him, drawing his curved, two-handed sword. But the Earth-man's skilled blade quickly sent his weapon spinning, and he clapped his hands over his eyes in token of surrender. The Takkor swordsmen made short work of the others, whose bodies they then hurled from the roof.

Setting two men to guard his prisoner, Thorne raised his baridium torch above his head and unhooded it three times in succession, the signal which he had previously agreed upon with the others. A moment later he saw it answered by three flashes from the projector on the north, and knew that Yirl Du had succeeded in capturing it. Then came a signal from the one on the east, announcing the success of Ven Hitus, and shortly thereafter another from the projector on the boat, now under the control of Rid Du.

Thorne called a warrior to his side.

"Fly back to the dock," he ordered, "and tell them they can all come out now. Send fifty men to capture the airships, but let them go on foot. I want no one in the air except the man who is to carry dry clothing to Rid Du and his warriors on the boat. And let him return to the others as soon as possible."

As soon as this messenger flapped away, Thorne turned his attention to the instrument board of the ray projector. Though it held a half dozen dials with numbers and pointers on them, evidently to tell the operator how much of this or that charge or substance the mechanism contained, he was at present concerned only with the parts intended for manipulation by the operator.

These consisted of two small cranks and a lever. One crank, he soon found by testing it, elevated or lowered the muzzle of the projector, and the other turned it to the right or left. He pointed the muzzle upward where it could do no damage, and pulled the lever. A green flash shot skyward. He swiftly shut it off, and having mastered the weapon without the operator's assistance, ordered him bound.

A moment later the farther moon rose, flooding the scene with its pale light. After making sure that his men were in charge of Sel Han's airships, and that his warrior had returned from the boat, Thorne turned his attention to the castle, where a great hubbub had arisen. Now was the time agreed upon, when the weapons of the enemy were to be turned upon themselves.

EVIDENTLY Sel Han was still unaware that his projectors had been captured—was probably searching the castle, hoping to find and slaughter its garrison and retake his prisoners. Fully a thousand of his riders still circled above the walls on their bird-beasts. Thorne aimed the projector into the thick of these and pulled the lever. Instantly the green ray flashed out, cutting a great gap in the circle of flyers. And now from the north, south and east, the other projectors went into action, their rays literally decimating the ranks of the flying warriors.

The panic stricken riders who remained quickly dived for the nearest shelter—the castle courtyard. The Earth-man instantly shut off his ray, and the others followed his example. So far, things had come about as Thorne had planned them. But there was still much to be done.

Calling two of his warriors before the instrument board, he instructed them in the use of the projector. He told them that if any of Sel Han's men should attempt to fly up from the courtyard they should be instantly annihilated. And finally he ordered them to watch for him to raise his hand, at which signal they were to blast a hole through the base of the castle wall directly in front of them, then shut off the ray.

These instructions completed, he mounted his gawr, and flinging the bound Ma Gong operator across the front of his saddle, flew to the dock where the main body of his swordsmen waited.

Dismounting, he turned his prisoner over to two guards and called an officer.

"Get me a herald," he commanded.

The officer hurried away, and reappeared in a few moments with a youth who carried a trumpet. Thorne gave him his instructions and he walked toward the gate.

As the Earth-man stood looking after him he felt a touch on his arm. Turning, he beheld Neva, who had just come up behind him.

"I cannot find my father," she said. "I've looked for him everywhere. Do you know where he is?"

He forced his voice to a calmness he did not feel, for as always, the nearness of her thrilled him immeasurably.

"I am sorry to say," he replied, "that the Dixtar saw fit to open the castle gates to the enemy. I haven't the slightest idea where he is—probably with his good friend, Sel Han."

She appeared distinctly shocked. "You don't mean—you can't mean—" she faltered.

"That he could have betrayed us? Why not? It seems to run in the family."

She went suddenly pale at this, then looked up at him with flashing eves. "Sheb Takkor Rad," she said, "some day you will regret those words. There are certain things of which you are ignorant, which I hoped you would eventually come to understand. But now—now I don't care. You are insufferable! I hate you! I never want to see you again!"

As she flung away from him the notes of the herald's trumpet sounded before the gate. Vaguely, Thorne wondered about the things she had alluded to—things of which he was ignorant. Again the trumpet sounded, and he forced himself to concentrate on the important business at hand.

"The Rad of Takkor," cried the herald, "calls upon Sel Han and his bandits to lay down their arms and march out of the castle. If they fail to comply they will be destroyed utterly, and the castle with them. As a token of surrender they will immediately throw open the gates."

Thorne waited for some time, watching the gates expectantly. They remained closed. He called to the herald.

"Continue."

Again the herald wound his trumpet.

"The Rad of Takkor is inclined to be merciful," he cried, "yet you try him sorely. Behold!"

Thorne raised his hand. A green ray flashed out from the house-top, drilled through the base of the wall, then winked off, leaving a gaping black hole. From within the castle there came the sounds of a mighty tumult—shouts, groans, curses, and the clash of weapons. Suddenly the gates swung open, and there emerged a rabble of yellow warriors, weaponless, thrusting before them two white men whose arms were bound behind them, and carrying on their shoulders the bodies of a dozen more. With the exception of those who carried the corpses and drove the prisoners, they held their hands over their eyes in token of surrender. It was obvious that the Ma Gongi, facing destruction by their own dread weapons, had mutinied to save their lives.

LEAVING his gawr in charge of a warrior, Thorne hurried forward. As he drew near the prisoners he recognized the tall, broad-shouldered figure of Sel Han, and the wizened, rat-faced Dixtar. The first corpse, borne by four yellow warriors with the head dangling limply, was that of Sur Det the Killer, who would kill no more.

"Surround the Ma Gongi,"Thorne shouted to his swordsmen. "Be on the lookout for treachery. And bring me the two white prisoners."

Under the watchful eyes of the Takkor fighting men, the horde of yellow warriors continued to pour from the castle until it was emptied of enemies. Then, at a command from the Earthman, the swordsmen closed in behind them and a small detachment entered the castle to look for stragglers.

These details attended to, Thorne turned to the two stalwart swordsmen who held his prisoners in custody, awaiting his pleasure. Sel Han was cursing luridly and straining at his bonds. Irintz Tel was quaking visibly.

"Bring the prisoners and follow me,"Thorne ordered.

He led the way to where Miradon Vil stood with Neva, Thaíne, Lal Vak and Kov Lutas.

Rendering the imperial salute to the Vil, he said:

"Your majesty, I bring you two men who have usurped the throne of your empire, one for a generation, the other for a day. They are your prisoners, to do with as you will. And since the weapons with which Sel Han set out to conquer Mars are in the custody of my swordsmen, you are once more Vil of Xancibar, with the power to clear your palace of the scum of humanity left there by these two impostors, and to enforce your edicts. As for the nest of this would-be world conqueror and his fellow conspirators, which is said to be somewhere on my estate, I promise you that it shall be found and cleaned out, also between the rising and setting of to-morrow's sun. Every prisoner here knows where it is, and I am sure that at least one of them can be persuaded to tell."

"Sheb Takkor Rad," replied Miradon Vil, his voice shaking with emotion, "I find it difficult to express—"

He got no further, for at this moment there came a sudden and unexpected interruption. Thorne's first intimation of it was the sound of a sword being whipped from its sheath. He turned in time to see Sel Han, who had managed to slip off his bonds and snatch the sword of the man who guarded him, leap across the space which separated him from the two girls, catch up Tháine, fling her over his shoulder, and dash away.

Drawing his own blade, the Earth-man was the first to spring after the fugitive. Only a short way off stood Thorne's gawr, held by a warrior. Before the unfortunate fellow, who was looking the other way at the time, became aware of what was happening, Sel Han split his head with a blow of the sword and leaped into the saddle.

Still clutching the struggling, kicking Tháine, and holding both her wrists with his left hand, he pulled up on the guiding rod with his right. The great bird-beast lumbered forward and took off, flapping noisily because of the double burden it carried, while Thorne and his companions looked on helplessly, not daring to use their javelins for fear of injuring the girl.

The gawr, obedient to the guiding rod, flew swiftly out over the lake.

CHAPTER XXV

TO THE DEATH!

BEFORE THE SOUND of Sel Han's derisive laughter died out, Thorne turned and sprinted for the nearest gawr, which happened to be the bird-beast ridden by a man who had just conveyed warm clothing and hot pulcho to Rid Du's young warriors on the boat.

"Send five hundred swordsmen after me," he told the man as he sprang into the saddle. "This may lead to an ambush." Then he lifted the guiding rod and was off.

As his bird-beast rose in the air, Thorne saw that Sel Han was already halfway across the lake, and circling toward the northeast, a direction that would carry him over the heart of the marsh and into a terrain altogether strange to the Earthman. By cutting across the arc of the circle he was able to reduce Sel Han's lead considerably, and he noted with satisfaction that the swift mount he bestrode was gaining on the doubly burdened gawr of Thaíne's abductor.

Soon he had passed the lake and was flying above the glittering, frost coated vegetation of the marsh. A glance behind him showed a horde of his riders coming across the lake. Fearing they might not have marked his course, he raised his baridium torch over his head and flashed it thrice. His signal was answered, almost immediately, by three flashes from a rider in the front ranks. Satisfied, he turned his eyes ahead once more, ever watchful for some unexpected move on the part of his resourceful enemy.

He did not doubt that Sel Han was making for his secret lair, which was believed to be somewhere in Takkor Marsh. And as he did not know just where that lair might be, he momentarily expected his enemy to reach it, arouse the Ma Gong fighters guarding the place, and send them back to kill or capture his pursuer.

But league after league of marshland unrolled beneath them, with the fugitive showing no signs of halting. And gradually, Thorne's swift bird-beast gained on the other. Presently the nearer moon rose, its bright rays accentuating the details of the scene. Now he could plainly see Sel Han still holding Thaíne swung across his back, both her slender wrists gripped in one of his huge hands, while the other held sword and guiding rod.

Higher and higher climbed the nearer moon, as if anxious to meet its slower, dimmer companion. Presently, when it seemed that the two moons were about to meet, Thorne noticed a change in the topography of the country ahead. They were nearing what had once been an island in the remote age when the marsh had been the bed of a mighty ocean. Now it was a broad, flat-topped mountain with a sloping base of sand and bowlders that led to rugged, frowning cliffs in which the waves of that forgotten epoch had eroded immense caverns whose dark, gaping mouths still opened thirstily for the foaming breakers that would drench them no more.

Sel Han's destination was obviously those frowning cliffs, but as he approached them Thorne noticed that his bird-beast began flying erratically, as if exhausted by the strain of carrying its double burden so swiftly and so far. Not more than two hundred feet behind Thaíne's abductor, now, he saw him lift frantically on the guiding rod in an obvious endeavor to get his mount to clear the summit of the cliff.

The gawr tried desperately to make it, but had reached the limit of its endurance. With its beak almost over the rim, it fell, fluttering weakly and pecking ineffectually at the sheer cliff face with its hooked bill in an effort to save itself. Fortunately there was a shelf of rock only fifty feet below, and on this the thoroughly spent creature alighted.

THORNE arrived on that shelf not five seconds later, but Sel Han had already sprung from his saddle, and with Thaíne still slung helplessly over his shoulder, was sprinting away along that narrow ledge. Whipping out his sword, the Earth-man leaped down and set out in hot pursuit.

Abruptly the ledge curved around a sharp bend in the cliff wall, and for a moment Thorne lost sight of his quarry. Then, as he rounded the bend, he saw them again. But he saw something else that aroused his apprehension. They were now in an indentation of the cliff face about an eighth of a mile deep, which had once been an inlet of the sea. And the cliff opposite him was honeycombed with baridium-lighted caverns and terraced with ledges that swarmed with Ma Gong workmen. On the top of the cliff above them a troop of mounted yellow warriors sat on guard. This, then, was the hidden nest of the conspirators. And somewhere within those lighted caverns the rest of the deadly ray projectors which were to be employed in Sel Han's conquest of Mars were being manufactured.

Though not more than five hundred feet separated Sel Han and his followers, he was unable to reach them, for the ledge ended suddenly only a short distance farther on. But if he could not cross to his men, he could call them to him, and this he did with a thunderous shout that echoed and reechoed among the barren crags.

"Ho, warriors! Your Vildus is beset! To me!"

Instantly there came a chorus of answering cries from the warriors on the opposite cliff, and the flapping of their mounts' wings as they took off. Almost at the same moment the vanguard of the Takkor swordsmen rounded the bend in the wall.

Though he had noted all these happenings, Thorne had not slackened his pace. But now, believing that his enemy could go no farther, he turned and called to his men.

"Capture those caves," he shouted, pointing across the inlet with his sword, "and everything in them."

Again he turned and dashed forward, then suddenly cried out in consternation. Sel Han and his precious burden had disappeared. At first, Thorne feared his desperate enemy had leaped over the ledge to the rocks below, carrying Thaíne with him. But a glance over the rim showed no mangled bodies lying there.

The Takkor swordsmen and the Ma Gong warriors now clashed in midair, but Thorne did not even heed them. He must find Thaíne. He ran on breathlessly until he readied the very end of the ledge. Then he saw the explanation of that mysterious disappearance—a circular doorway hewn in the solid rock at his left.

Fearing an ambush, Thorne stepped warily through that opening. He found himself in an immense cavern, lighted and ventilated by a hole in the roof through which the bright moonlight was streaming. Immediately beneath this hole a narrow wooden bridge crossed a wide chasm which split the floor of the cave from side to side. At the opposite end of the bridge was Sel Han. He had flung Thaíne to the floor, where she lay, apparently in a faint, and was hacking desperately with his sword at the two slender poles which supported the farther end of the bridge.

Seeing what he was about, Thorne sprang forward to frustrate him. But he was too late. The wood splintered and the bridge sagged, then fell into the chasm, striking the bottom a moment later with a thunderous crash.

Thorne paused on the brink of the chasm, and saw at a glance that he could go no farther. It was fully fifty feet across, and about two hundred feet deep, reaching clear to the smooth walls on both sides.

The Earth-man glared at his enemy, who laughed mockingly. Behind him, on a pedestal at the rear of the cave, was a hideous stone colossus with a sardonic grin on its repulsive features, evidently the forgotten god of some vanished race. It almost seemed as if the god had laughed.

"Now if you had a pair of wings—" bantered Sel Han, grinning maliciously.

THORNE had no intention of replying, but at this moment he noticed something which made him change his mind. Thaíne, lying on the floor behind his enemy, sat up and opened her eyes, looking about her in bewilderment. She still wore her weapons. If he could only keep the attention of her abductor for a minute or two longer—

"Sel Han, the mighty swordsman," he mocked. "The irresistible conqueror. Vildus of Mars. I am alone, yet you run away. It must be that you fear me."

"I am too great a man to engage in a common brawl with such as you," Sel Han replied. "As soon as my warriors have defeated yours, they will come and cut you into small pieces. Then—"

He paused suddenly, his acute hearing having detected a sound behind him.

Thaíne had sprung to her feet and drawn her sword.

Sel Han still clutched his own weapon.

"Put down that sword, you little fool!" he growled. "Do you think you can beat *me?*"

For answer, she extended her blade in a swift lunge that would have stretched an ordinary swordsman on the stone floor. But her abductor was no ordinary swordsman. He parried with a quick riposte which she only avoided by combining fast footwork with the lightning swiftness of her blade.

Thorne realized that Sel Han was thoroughly angry and in deadly earnest. The thrust he had aimed at Thaíne's heart was meant to *kill!* The Earth-man ground his teeth in impotent rage. If there were only some way he could cross that chasm! Thaíne, he knew, fenced well, but no better than Sur Det, whom Sel Han had defeated. She might hold him off for a while, but his greater strength, skill and length of arm would eventually win for him. And it was plain to be seen that he had no compunctions whatever against killing a girl.

Suddenly, above the clashing of the blades and panting of the contestants, Thorne heard the sound of footsteps and the clank of weapons behind. Turning, he saw Yirl Du and a dozen Takkor swordsmen.

"The traitors' nest is captured, my lord," announced Yirl Du. Then he saw what was taking place at the other end of the cavern.

"Why—why—!" he stammered.

But on the instant, Thorne had conceived a plan.

"Follow me!" he cried. "We can do no good here."

He ran out of the cave, Yirl Du and the warriors at his heels. Their gawrs were perched on the ledge.

The Earth-man leaped into a saddle and pulled up the guiding rod.

"Come with me, and bring ten men," he told Yirl Du.

Thorne guided the bird-beast up over the rim of the cliff and came down beside the hole in the roof of the cavern. Unhooking the two safety chains from the saddle, he fastened them together. Yirl Du and his ten men alighted around him a moment later.

"Bring me all your safety chains," Thorne ordered.

They brought them, and he swiftly fastened them together, end to end, until he had a chain nearly a hundred feet in length. He hooked one end of this in his belt ring.

"Now let me down that hole and swing me toward the ledge on which they are fighting," he ordered.

They seized the chain and let him down swiftly. He was directly above the appalling depth of the chasm.

Leaning down over the rim of the hole, Yirl Du set the chain in motion—a pendulum with a slender linked shaft and a human weight.

Nearer and nearer Thorne swung toward his objective, and

Sel Han, who had heard the rattle of the chain, broke away from Thaíne for a moment, to try to impale the Earth-man as he spun helplessly at the end.

But Thaíne, seeing Thorne's danger, instantly went to his rescue, attacking her abductor so furiously that he was forced to devote all his attention to her.

AT LAST Thorne's feet touched the ledge. The chain slackened, and he reached around to unhook it from his belt ring. This done, he looked up just in time to see a sight that drove him berserk with rage and grief. Two feet of Sel Han's steel were projecting from Thaíne's back.

"You asked for it, you little fool!" grated Sel Han, withdrawing his blade with a vicious jerk.

With an agonized gasp, Thaíne crumpled to the floor, her lovely face drawn with pain, the lifeblood gushing from her breast.

Thorne sprang furiously to the attack, careless now of the consequences, eager only to end the life of the man who faced him. "Thaíne is dead," he kept repeating to himself as he fought, "and her murderer stands before me. My little comrade is no more." Ever and anon as he circled his enemy, he caught sight of that lovely face on the floor, pale with the paleness of death, and he whispered to himself, "I must kill this fiend who has slain her."

Had Thorne kept his head and fenced with his usual coolness and judgment, there could have been but one outcome to the duel, and that speedily. For ordinarily Sel Han, despite his skill, was nowhere near his equal. But rage and grief are poor allies in a contest with swords. The Earth-man, fighting only with the object of quickly killing his opponent, and little caring what happened to himself, constantly risked desperate lunges which left him dangerously exposed to counter thrusts so that, though he succeeded in wounding his antagonist time after time, he received nearly as many wounds, himself.

Only when he was bleeding from no less than a score of

wounds and felt himself growing weaker from loss of blood did his common sense reassert itself. He realized that he would need every iota of strength and skill at his command to kill his adversary, and endeavored to collect his wits. Sel Han, he now saw, was in like case with himself. His wrist had grown weaker and he reeled, at times, as if intoxicated. Resolutely, purposefully, Thorne now began to fence.

Sel Han instantly noticed the change in his antagonist's swordsmanship, and in it he read his own doom. A look of fear came over his flat features. Yet he fought savagely, as a conquered beast fights.

Thorne was fencing coolly now, thrusting and parrying with ease and precision. So lightly did he hold the skill of his opponent that on hearing the clank of weapons he took time to glance across the chasm to see who had entered the cave. With a start of surprise he recognized Neva, Miradon Vil, Kov Lutas and Lal Vak. Miradon Vil, he saw, was reaching out for the end of the chain which Yirl Du was swinging toward him. But it was Neva, beside the Vil, who grasped the chain and swung across the chasm.

Thorne was so surprised that he was not quite quick enough in parrying a vicious cut for his head. Sel Han's blade parted his head-strap and bit through into his skull.

He saw a myriad dancing stars, then the blood spurted down into his eyes, half blinding him.

But for all that, he sprang to the attack, forcing his opponent back, back, until he stood on the very edge of the chasm. Again Sel Han tried that head-cut which had worked so well before. He thought it could not fail to work again, and grinned triumphantly. But this time Thorne saw it coming. He parried, then countered with a sweeping moulinet to the neck—a drawing cut that sheared off the still-grinning head. It fell at his feet, and the body toppled backward into the chasm.

Staggering drunkenly, Thorne kicked the leering head after the body. Then he lurched forward, and would have followed it into the abyss had not a pair of soft arms wound about his waist and drawn him back. He sank to the stony floor, and despite his reeling senses and blood-filled eyes, realized that his head was pillowed on a woman's breast.

Then consciousness left him.

CHAPTER XXVI

THE AWAKENING

THORNE OPENED HIS eyes slowly, blinked, then opened them again and stared in astonishment. He was looking up at a frescoed ceiling on which was depicted a Martian battle scene—a beleaguered city fighting off the attack of a vast army. Four golden chains depended from the ceiling, supporting the divan on which he lay beneath silken covers of peacock blue embroidered with a design in gold. Swiftly he glanced around, and saw that he was in a luxuriously furnished chamber of surpassing magnificence, lighted by three large circular windows through which the bright sunlight streamed, their crystal segments opened like flower petals to admit the crisp morning air.

Seated in a swinging chair nearby, a man with white hair and a benign face was poring over the contents of a large scroll.

"Lal Vak!" Thorne exclaimed.

The old scientist turned and smiled. "Ah, you know me at last," he said. He put down his scroll and walked over to the divan.

"Where am I?" Thorne asked him.

"Why, in the palace, of course." He pointed to the silken cover and the embroidered design. "These are the colors, and this the design of the royal family of Xancibar."

"But I don't understand. The last I remember, I was in that cave."

"Precisely. Neva pulled you back from the brink of the chasm. You had lost a deal of blood and fainted in her arms. Yirl Du left guards at the captured nest of the conspirators. Then we picked up five hundred more of your Takkor swordsmen at the castle and flew here. They easily cleared the palace of Sel Han's followers, and Miradon Vil was received and acclaimed by the people with great rejoicing. They were heartily sick of the atrocities of Irintz Tel and the Kamud. But all that took place six days ago. You have been delirious since. Yesterday the royal physician removed the jembal from your wounds and pronounced them healed. And last night you fell into a deep, healthful sleep which he believed would restore you. That cut on the head must have temporarily robbed you of your reason. And it came perilously near ending your life."

Thorne raised his hand, and felt the scar on his head reflectively. Again he saw the horror of that struggle in the cave—saw Thaíne with a sword through her slender body—saw her fall with the blood gushing from her breast—and remembered that she had made her sacrifice to save him.

"Poor Thaíne," he murmured.

"But Thaíne is better," said Lal Vak. "The physician says she can be up and around in a day or two."

"What! I thought her dead."

"The wound was high—just grazed the upper left lobe of the lung. Painful, but not dangerous."

Thorne threw back the covers and swung his legs over the edge of the bed. His head reeled dizzily.

"Where are you going?" asked Lal Vak.

"To Thaíne," Thorne replied."

"But you can't get up yet."

"Can't I?"

Thorne stood erect, swaying uncertainly. His legs were very weak and he felt light-headed. A jar of pulcho and several cups stood on a near-by stand. Lal Vak filled a cup and handed it to him. He drank it off at a gulp and called for another. Then he staggered to the bath box, declining the assistance of his white-haired friend. Stepping out of his sleeping garment, he entered, closed the door, and trod on the plate. A few moments later he emerged, dripping and brushing the water from his eyes. When he opened them he saw a familiar diminutive figure standing before him with two great wisps of dry moss.

"Vorz!" he exclaimed.

"The same, my lord," replied the little orderly, and proceeded to give him a brisk rub-down. "His majesty granted me leave to serve you, and I trust you will not send me away."

"Not I," Thorne replied. "If his majesty permits, I'll take you back to Takkor with me."

"Thank you, my lord."

VORZ had laid out his clothing and weapons for him, and these he now proceeded to don. There was a magnificent cloak of orange trimmed with black, the colors of nobility. Then there was the Takkor medallion to hang about his neck. And a jeweled sword and dagger with Takkor serpent hilts. As his servant buckled these about him a little slave girl hurried in with a fresh jar of steaming pulcho. Thorne fortified himself with two more cups of the stimulating beverage, then went to a mirror to survey himself in his new finery. His face was pale, as well it might be, considering the quantity of blood he had lost, but he felt his strength returning, and for this he was thankful.

"Do I look all right to go calling on a lady, Vorz?" he asked.

"Magnificent, my lord," was the reply. And Thorne thought of the last time Vorz had groomed him, the night of Irintz Tel's reception, when he and Neva had plighted their troth and she, when they were discovered, had condemned him to the baridium mines. As these scenes flooded his memory, conflicting emotions surged up within him. He pictured Neva, lovely, passionate, yielding to his embrace. And again he saw her as she sentenced him to a horrible lingering death. But now there was another picture to add which puzzled and somehow comforted him. It was the memory of Neva swinging across the chasm at the risk of her own life and drawing him back from the brink just in time to save him.

"Come," he said, taking the arm of his old friend. "Let us find the apartment of Thaíne."

They strode through the hallways in silence for a time. Then Thorne thought of Irintz Tel.

"What has become of the Dixtar?" he asked.

"I'll show you, since it lies along our way," replied Lal Vak.

Presently they came to a door which Thorne remembered. It was the entrance to the Hall of Heads. The scientist drew a large key from his belt, unlocked the door, and threw it open.

"Enter," he invited.

Thorne stepped inside and looked about him. At first he did not notice anything unusual. There were the shelves, reaching to the ceiling, with their thousands of grisly relics. Then he saw that a pedestal had been set up in the center of the hall. On the pedestal was a jar, and in it a head. A pair of small, beady eyes, glazed with the film of death, looked out at him sightlessly from a wizened, ratlike face.

"Irintz Tel!" he exclaimed. "Well, I can't say that I blame Miradon Vil."

"You wrong his majesty," said Lal Vak. "The Vil had nothing to do with this. In fact he had granted the Dixtar full pardon, and bestowed on him a magnificent estate on the Zeelan Canal. But the next day Irintz Tel disappeared. An anonymous note was received that night, suggesting that we look here. And we found this. We think it was the work of relatives of some of his victims. But no search is being conducted. The thing is done, and cannot be remedied. After all, they were certainly justified."

They quitted that place of horrors and after negotiating several more hallways came to the apartment of Thaíne. A guard saluted and admitted them to the reception room, where a slave girl bade them be seated while she went in to announce them to her mistress.

"I'll wait here for you," said Lal Vak when the girl drew back the curtain for them, "since I have already paid my respects to the young lady this morning."

THORNE went in alone. On a luxurious divan beneath fluffy blue silk coverlets lay Thaíne. Her unwonted paleness accentuated the dark depths of her big brown eyes and the lustrous black of her hair.

"Hahr Ree Thorne!" she cried a trifle faintly, and held up both arms to him. He bent, and the arms went around his neck—drew his face to hers. Their lips met.

"My little comrade," he murmured, kneeling beside the divan and looking fondly down at her. "I thought you dead. And now I'm rejoiced that you are going to get well."

"You should not be up," she said reprovingly, "for you were worse injured than I."

"My scratches have healed," he laughed, "and now I'm ready to leave—to go back to Takkor, with its limpid lakes and streams that mirror trees and sky. I don't care for cities—or palaces."

"Nor I," she told him. "This is such a big lonesome place. Already I am homesick for the marsh—for the hunting and fishing, and the blazing log fires in the evenings."

It suddenly occurred to Thorne that, since he had put Neva forever from his mind, life would be far more worth the living with Thaíne by his side—to go on hunting and fishing excursions with him, and to enliven his evenings as they sat before the fireplace with their hunting dalfs curled at their feet.

"Thaíne," he said, "do you remember that day in your father's cabin when you tried a certain experiment?"

She smiled up at him.

"How could I forget?"

"And you said you must have time to think."

"Since then I have thought—much. I was so inexperienced—so silly that I thought love was a thing which might be cultivated, little knowing that it is a flower which springs up spontaneously in the heart."

"Thaíne! You can't mean that at last—"

"Yes, Hahr Ree Thorne. At last I have found true love. It

came to me so suddenly, so unexpectedly, when I met Kov Lutas, that it left me weak and breathless."

"Kov Lutas!"

"Why, yes. We are to be wed as soon as I am well. Hadn't you heard?"

Thorne achieved a smile, but in his heart there was a feeling of emptiness—of desolation. He forced his lips to say the conventional things, to wish her joy and to proclaim Kov Lutas the luckiest man on Mars. But to himself he thought: "First Sylvia, then Neva, and now Thaíne! It is my destiny to be alone and loveless."

Rising, he said: "I must go now and prepare for my journey, little comrade. Farewell, and Deza grant you much happiness."

ONCE outside her door, however, he could dissemble no longer. Lal Vak, who rose to go out with him, instantly remarked his woebegone expression.

"Why so sad?" he asked. "I trust you found the lady well."

"Perfectly," Thorne replied. Then added: "Old friend, I'm a fool ever to have anything to do with women. From now on, I'm through, and I mean it."

"Why, what's this?" asked the scientist. "Do you fall in love with every woman you meet?"

"Well, not exactly that," replied Thorne. "But since Neva betrayed me—"

"Betrayed you! What talk is this? Betrayed you! Why she has twice saved your life! What are you talking about, boy?"

"You should know as well as I," Thorne said bitterly. "Was it not she who sent me to the baridium mines?"

Lal Vak looked at him quizzically for a moment.

"You are a greater fool than I thought, my boy," he said. "She sent you to the baridium mines to save you from the headsman—to preserve your life. And who do you think it was who aided you to escape from the mines? There were only three people in Xancibar with the power to do so. The other two were Irintz Tel and Sel Han. Do you think *they* did it?"

"Why, I thought it was you," Thorne replied.

"I had a small part," Lal Vak admitted, "but it was she who engineered everything—who pulled the strings and moved the officials in high places, so the thing could be accomplished. You should have seen her, tearful and apprehensive that next day, as she connived with Kov Lutas and me to win your freedom. And after the thing had been done, she was beside herself with worry for fear you would be captured. Every day she besought me to try to obtain news of you. You should know, also, that the tales of her heartless flirtations were utterly false, invented by Sel Han and spread by his henchmen to keep off powerful rivals. She was no more a murderous siren than our little Thaíne. That I can attest, and I have known her all her life."

Thorne was stunned by Lal Vak's revelation—and heartily ashamed of himself.

"I have done her a great wrong, old friend," he said, "and not only in my heart. I openly cut her when she held out her arms to me that night in Takkor Castle. Even if she loved me once, no love could survive such a blow as that. I have lost the only woman I ever really loved through my own lack of faith."

"She saved your life in the cave at the risk of her own," Lal Vak reminded him. "Is that the act of one who has ceased to care?"

"I don't know," groaned Thorne. "It might be. The more I see of women the less I understand them."

"At least, you should call on her and apologize."

"That I will do. Let us go to her apartment."

As they approached the door of Neva's apartment, two guards saluted smartly and stood aside for them to enter. In the reception room a slave girl met them.

"Tell your mistress Sheb Takkor is calling," Thorne told her.

The slave girl returned almost immediately.

"My mistress is not receiving callers, my lord," she said.

Thorne turned to Lal Vak. "You see, I was right," he said. "But it is no more than I deserve for my little faith. Come. Let us go back to my apartment. I must prepare for my journey."

CHAPTER XXVII

A PRINCE OF XANCIBAR

BACK IN HIS apartment with Lal Vak, Thorne notified Vorz that they were leaving. Then he went to the writing board, spread a scroll, and composed a letter. He spent much time over it, destroying three copies before at last it satisfied him. Then he rolled it, placed it in a wooden tube, and handed it to Lal Vak.

"Give this to Neva after I am gone," he said, "and I shall be grateful to you. I have apologized for my boorish conduct and thanked her for having twice saved my life—a life that has become empty and purposeless without her. But it is, as you have said, the least I can do, and unfortunately, the most I can do as well."

Lal Vale thrust the cylinder under his belt.

"I'll be glad to deliver this for you," he said. "Now I'll go out and arrange for your transportation."

Presently he returned.

"A flying machine awaits you on the roof," he said, "and his majesty is ready to receive you."

Thorne emptied his pulcho cup and arose. The scientist conducted him to a reception room where Miradon Vil, resplendent in his royal cloak of peacock blue trimmed with gold, was standing on the dais before the throne addressing a number of his nobles. But when the Rad of Takkor was announced, he dismissed them all and stepped down from the dais to receive his guest.

"My boy," he said, "I am happy to see you well, and with your memory and reason restored."

"And I," replied Thorne, "am equally happy to see your majesty restored to the throne of your ancestors; but no happier, I am sure, than every citizen, high and low, in Xancibar."

"Some time ago," said Miradon, "I rendered you the empty thanks of a deposed Vil. To-day I am in a position to show my gratitude more tangibly and practically. First, I free you and Takkor from all allegiance to Xancibar. This makes you the supreme ruler of the raddek, and the collector and dispenser of all Takkor revenues.

"Second, I have conferred with the Vils of the other great powers of Mars, and we have decided that you shall be the arbiter of our destinies. You captured the weapons and the laboratory with which Sel Han sought to conquer Mars. In unscrupulous hands they could do much harm. But we have faith in you. We want you to keep them, to protect us against any other ambitious plotters who may arise, so that we may fight our wars and settle our differences with the weapons of honor and chivalry we have always used. So, in effect, we make you the custodian of our liberty."

From a taboret which stood beside the dais, he took a golden medal, set with sparkling jewels and hung on a heavy golden chain.

"This," he said, "commemorates our resolution, and is the badge of your high office."

Inscribed on the medal Thorne read:

SHEB TAKKOR
Supreme Arbiter of Destiny
and
Custodian of Liberty
by the will of the
Associated Vilets
of Mars

The Vil snapped the chain around Thorne's neck, so the new

medal, the greatest badge of honor which the combined empires of Mars could bestow, flashed and scintillated on his chest just above the Takkor medallion.

"I am overwhelmed, your majesty," said Thorne. "The nations of Mars have placed too high a value on my poor services."

Miradon smiled and stroked his silky golden beard. "There is but one more thing, and I will give you leave to go."

HE RAISED his hand, and a flourish of trumpets sounded from the doorway. Two heralds entered, trumpets resting on hips. Behind them came six pages, carrying a gold-embroidered cloak of peacock blue like that worn by the Vil. Following the pages was another, bearing a jar of pulcho and a gem-encrusted golden cup.

The heralds separated, and stood, one at each side of the dais. The pages held the cloak spread before the Vil.

"Permit me," said Miradon, unfastening Thorne's head straps and removing his cloak of orange and black. He handed the cloak to a slave, and taking the one which the pages had brought, fastened its jeweled straps about Thorne's head. Then the last page came up with the pulcho and the cup.

Filling the cup, the Vil drank half its contents, then passed it to Thorne. "Drink," he commanded.

Thorne drained the cup and returned it to the tray.

The Vil raised both hands before his face.

"I shield my eyes to the Zovil of Xancibar," he said.

Thorne raised his hands and responded to the salutation.

"That is all," said Miradon. "And now, since you insist on leaving us so soon, Lal Vak will conduct you to the roof. I will be there to see you off in a few moments."

In the company of the scientist Thorne left the presence, and climbed the stairs toward the roof.

"Tell me something, Lal Vak," said Thorne. "What is the significance of this cloak? And what is a zovil?"

"A zovil," replied the scientist, "is a vil's son, just as a zorad is a rad's son. The cloak, and the ceremony that went with it, made you a prince of the imperial house of Xancibar."

"I seem to have gotten almost everything on this planet but the one I want the most," said Thorne morosely.

"I presume that you refer to Neva," said Lal Vak. "Well, don't consider her totally lost to you, yet. Women have been known to change their minds, you know."

Thorne caught the suspicion of a chuckle as his old friend finished this admonition, but upon glancing at him saw that his face was very grave, and decided he had been mistaken.

ON THE ROOF of the palace a great metal flying machine stood waiting. Standing around it was a group of the most exalted nobles and officials of Xancibar.

A moment later the leonine head of Miradon Vil appeared above the top of the stairway. As he stepped out on the roof the courtiers again rendered the imperial salute. He walked up to Thorne and placed his huge hands on his shoulders.

"Farewell, my son," he said, "and take good care of that which I have entrusted to you."

As he spoke it seemed to Thorne that his voice broke slightly, and there was a suspicion of tears in his eyes.

"Farewell, your majesty," Thorne replied.

The warrior went up to the forward cab with Vorz and the pilot, and closed the door after him. Thorne turned to select a seat. Then he gasped in amazement.

Seated near a window was Neva, clad in a most becoming costume of peacock blue, embroidered with gold. She smiled up at Thorne as he hurried to her side and bent over her.

"You!" he exclaimed. "I can't believe my eyes!"

"Lal Vak brought me your note," she said. "After I had read it I decided to forgive you."

"But—but, how came you here, and wearing the colors of royalty?"

"Since I am the only daughter of Miradon Vil," she said, "there is no one who has a better right to these colors."

"But what of Tháine?"

"Tháine," replied Neva, "is the daughter of Irintz Tel. Miradon Vil—my father—when he went into exile, was determined to insure my safety, and to give me the advantages which were rightfully mine. So he exchanged me for Tháine when we were babies. I am two days older than she, but an old nurse loyal to the empire managed to make the exchange without arousing suspicion. Tháine doesn't know, yet, and I only learned the truth five days ago."

Looking at her, Thorne decided that he must have been blind not to realize the resemblance between the fair-haired Vil and this girl before.

"Then—then his majesty, your father, knows you have come with me?"

"Of course. Why else should he have performed the ceremony that made you Zovil of Xancibar?"

"I'm sure I don't know."

"Because, stupid, he could only make you a prince of his house by making you my husband. There is no other way."

Full realization suddenly came to him. He caught her in his arms, sought and found her yielding lips.

"Neva, beloved!" he murmured. "Are you really my wife?"

"Unto death, Deza help you!" she replied archly.

But there was a starry light in her glorious eyes which he could not fail to understand.

ABOUT THE AUTHOR

WRITING, WITH ME, is a semi-subjective process. I mean by this that I find it necessary, at times, to wait for that temperamental and elusive entity, my Muse, to cooperate with me. Every day I try to write, and I mean *try*. But some days I produce only a few hundred words fit for nothing but filing in the wastebasket. And on the other hand I have, in a single day, produced six or seven thousand words of marketable copy.

So this, the problem of successfully wooing the Muse, is the one which I find most difficult of solution. I have a profound admiration for writers who can sit down at their desks, day after day, and, without fail, bat out two or three thousand words of good, salable material in two or three hours. Most of them will tell you this is the result of practice of continuous trying. But I've been trying for ten years, and selling stories for eight, and today my Muse is as obstinate and capricious as ever.

Although I had previously written songs, plays, and moving picture scenarios, my first inspiration for writing fiction, strange as it may seem, came from reading books on psychology. And that reading was the result of some previous incidents in my life, so perhaps I had better begin a little farther back.

When I graduated from high school, I decided that I would launch on a musical career, and gave up my plans for going to college. I became a professional songwriter. I also tried my hand at plays and moving picture scenarios, and wrote vaudeville sketches and even plots for burlesque shows. I later became a music publisher. But it was a hard life, with much night work, plugging songs in theatres, dance halls, and cafes, and I tired of it, in spite of the fascination the element of chance gave to the work.

*Otis Adelbert
Kline*

Putting out songs was like playing poker; no one could predict a hit with certainty.

I decided on a business career, and went to a business college. Shortly after this, I got a job, and at twenty-two I married. No chance, then, to go to college. But going to college had been a sort of tradition in our family. I had to work every day to keep the well-known and justly unpopular wolf from breaking down the door. But my evenings were my own. I decided to use them for the improvement of what I optimistically called my mind.

I would take one subject at a time, and study. But where should I begin? I recalled that a certain ancient philosopher had once said there are but three things in the universe—mind, force, and matter. Mind controls force, and force moves matter. It was easy to decide which of these things was the more important, so I began by studying psychology—a science which, by the way, is in its infancy—no farther advanced today than were the physical sciences a century ago.

Having read practically everything there was on the subject over a period of years, I began to have some theories about psychic phenomena, myself. I started a ponderous scientific treatise, but didn't carry it far. This medium limited my imagination too much. Then I wrote a novelette, "The Thing of a Thousand Shapes," in which some of my ideas and theories were incorporated. It was turned down by most of the leading magazines in 1922, but early in 1923 a magazine was made to order for the story—*Weird Tales*. It was accepted, and published in the first issue. This was before the word "ectoplasm" was used in connection with psychic phenomena. A German writer, whose translated work I had read, had coined the word "teleplasm," but this did not seem precisely the right term, so I coined the word "psychoplasm." I notice that it is being used today by some writers of occult stories.

I had finished writing the above novelette early in 1921, and decided to try my hand at a novel. I wanted to write an interplanetary story, and I believe the reason for this lay in the following incidents.

As soon as I was able to understand, my father, who was interested in all the sciences, and especially in astronomy, had begun pointing out to me the planets that were visible to the naked eye; had told me what was known of their masses, densities, surfaces, atmospheres, motions, and satellites; and that there was a possibility that some of them were inhabited by living beings. He taught me how to find the Big and Little Dippers, and thus locate the North Star, that I might make the heavens serve as a compass for me, by night as well as by day. He pointed out that beautiful and mysterious constellation, The Pleiades, which inspired the lines in the Book of Job: "Canst thou bind the sweet influences of Pleiades, or loose the bonds of Orion?"

He told me of the vast distances which, according to the computations of scientists, lay between our world and these twinkling celestial bodies—that the stars were suns, some smaller than our own, and others so large that if they were hollow, our entire Solar System could operate inside them without danger of the planet farthest from the sun striking the shell. He told me of the nebulae, which might be giant universes in the making, and that beyond the known limits of our own universe it was possible that there were countless others, stretching on into infinity.

My childish imagination had been fired by these things, and I had read voraciously such books on the subject of astronomy as were available in my father's well-stocked library. He supplemented and encouraged this reading by many interesting discussions, in which a favorite subject for speculation was the possibility that planets, other than our own, were inhabited.

Geology, archaeology, and ethnology were also brought into our discussions. We lived in northern Illinois, which had in some distant geological epoch been the bottom of an ocean, and took pleasure in collecting such fossil remains as were available. Dad and I could become very much excited over bits of coral, and fossil marine animals.

Then there were Darwin, Huxley, Tyndall, and others, with their interesting theories. There was the great mystery of man's advent on this earth, which religion explained in one manner and science in another. We discussed these, and a third possibility, an idea of my father's, that some of our ancient civilizations might have been originated by people who came here from other planets—the science of space-navigation forgotten by their descendants, but the tradition of their celestial advent persisting in their written and oral traditions. That such traditions did persist was beyond dispute. Whence came these traditions that were not confined to related civilizations, but were preserved by widely separated peoples?

It was with this background that I began my first novel in 1921—a tale of adventures on the planet Venus. I called it *Grandon of Terra*, but the name was later changed to *The Planet of Peril*.

The problem of how to get my hero to Venus bothered me not at all, for I had been reading about the marvelous powers of the subjective mind: of telepathy, that mysterious means of communication between minds which needs no physical media for its transmission, and which seems independent of time, space, and matter. I haven't the space to enlarge on this here, but can refer you to the thousands of cases recorded by the British Society for Psychical Research, if you are interested. There was also the many cases of so-called astral projection, recorded by the above society in a volume called Phantasms of the Living. My hero, therefore, reached Venus by the simple (try it) expedient of exchanging bodies with a young man on that planet who was his physical twin. He reported his adventures on Venus to an earthly scientist, Dr. Morgan, by telepathy.

Cloud-wrapped Venus is supposed to be in a stage similar to our own carboniferous era. I, therefore, clothed my hypothetical Venus with the flora of such an era-ferns, cycads, and thallophytes of many kinds, including algae, fungi, and lichens of strange and eerie form.

Through the fern jungles and fungoid forests stalked gigantic reptiles, imaginary creatures, but analogous to those ponderous prehistoric Saurians that roved the earth when our coal and petroleum beds were having their inception. There were Herbivora devouring the primitive plants, and fierce Carnivora that devoured the Herbivora and each other, and disputed the supremacy of man. Air and water teemed with active life and sudden dealt-life feeding on death and death snuffing out life.

There were men in various stages of evolutionary development—men without eyes, living in lightless caverns, who had degenerated to a physical and mental condition little better than that of Batrachia. There were monkey-men swinging through the branches and lianas of the fern forests, blood-sucking bat-men living in caves in a volcanic crater—a veritable planetary inferno, and gigantic termites of tremendous mental development that had enslaved a race of primitive human beings.

There were mighty empires, whose armies warred with strange and terrible weapons, and airships which flew at tremendous speed propelled by mechanisms which amplified the power of mind over matter—telekinesis.

After writing and rewriting, polishing and re-polishing, I sent the story out—a bulky script, ninety-thousand words long. At that time there but two possible American markets for that type of story, *Science and Invention* and *Argosy-All Story*, but I had not been watching the Munsey publication and did not know it used this sort of tiling. I submitted the story, first, to *Science and Invention*. It was turned down because of the paucity of mechanical science.

When *Weird Tales* came into being, I tried it on this magazine. Edwin Baird, the editor liked it, but finally, after holding it several months, rejected it because of its length. He suggested that I try *Argosy-All Story*, but I didn't do it then. I let it lie around for a long time. Every once in a while I would dig it out of the file and read it over. Each time, I found new places to polish. I was writing and selling a number of other stories in the interval-occult, weird, mystery, detective, adventure, and Western. I also collaborated with my brother, Allen S. Kline, on a novel set in the South American jungle, called *The Secret Kingdom*. This was later published in *Amazing Stories*.

One day I was talking to Baird, and he asked me what I had done with my fantastic novel. He said I was foolish not to try *Argosy-All Story*. I accordingly recopied my pencil-marked version, and sent it on. Good old Bob Davis, dean of American editors, held it so long I had some hope: that he was going to buy it. But it came back, eventually, with a long, friendly letter asking to see more of my work. I later learned that he had just bought the first of Ralph Milne Farley's famous Radio stories, the scene of which was on the planet Venus, and whose settings, therefore, were somewhat similar to mine.

After that, I spent enough money on express and postage to buy a good overcoat, sending the story around the country, and out of it.

Finally, Mr. Joseph Bray then book-buyer, and now president of A.C. McClurg & Company, told me he would publish it if I would first get it serialized in a magazine. I had turned down a couple of low-priced offers for serialization, but I started over the list again. A.H. Bittner, the new editor of *Argosy*, who has been building circulation for that magazine since he took over the editorial chair, bought the story. A month later, Mr. Bray accepted it for publication as a novel.

The Planet of Peril brought many enthusiastic fan letters to *Argosy*. I received a number of complimentary letters from people all over the country who had read it in magazine or book form. I was overwhelmed with requests for autographs, and all that sort of thing. A baby in Battle Creek, Michigan, was named after me. It was encouraging.

Last September, Grosset & Dunlap reprinted the book in the popular edition. In a bulletin to their salesmen they recently reported that, despite the fact that they had not made any special effort to push it, and that it was a first novel, it was enjoying a continuous and persistent resale—something unusual for a first novel. They suggested that their salesmen remember this item when calling on the trade. This, also, was encouraging.

Since then, *Argosy* has serialized and McClurg has published in book form two more novels—*Maza of the Moon* and *The Prince of Peril,* the latter a companion story to *The Planet of Peril.*

Right now I'm working night and day on a new novel for spring publication, in order to make a deadline date set by my publisher.

THE ARGOSY LIBRARY ™

SERIES 1 INCLUDES:

* DENT * KETCHUM * KLINE *
* MacISAAC * ROSCOE *
* ROUSSEAU *
* SELTZER *
* TUTTLE *
* WIRT *
WORTS

THE BEST FICTION
FROM THE FRANK
A. MUNSEY LINE

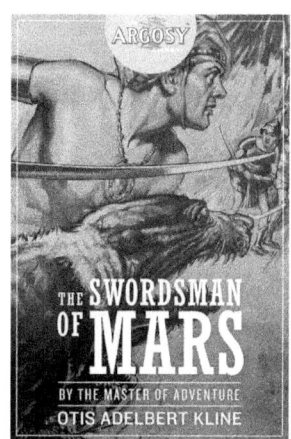

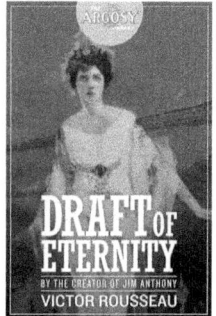

SERIES 1 • AVAILABLE SPRING 2015